THE
MARRIAGE
TEST

BOOKS BY ELLIE MONAGO

The Custody Battle

ELLIE MONAGO

THE
MARRIAGE
TEST

bookouture

Published by Bookouture in 2024

An imprint of Storyfire Ltd.
Carmelite House
50 Victoria Embankment
London EC4Y 0DZ

www.bookouture.com

ISBN: 978-1-83790-811-0
eBook ISBN: 978-1-83790-810-3

Interview between Detective Sonya Mohr of the Los Angeles Police Department and Marla Regis, the executive producer and showrunner of *Relationship Rescue*, taking place on Glass Island on November 10, 2023.

Detective: I want to thank you in advance for your cooperation. The sooner we can wrap up this investigation, the sooner you can all return to your lives.

Marla: How much longer will we be stuck here, do you think?

Detective: That'll depend on how forthcoming you, your crew, and the cast members are prepared to be.

Marla: Is it unusual for you to be sent on assignment like this?

Detective: As you know, Glass Island is a private island with no police force. Since it is a U.S. territory, U.S. laws apply. A homicide investigator was needed.

Marla: So it has been ruled a homicide?

Detective: This'll go smoother if I'm the one asking the questions, Ms. Regis. I assume you have no objection to this conversation being recorded, given your line of work?

Marla: I have nothing to hide.

Detective: So you consent to the taping? I'll need a verbal yes or no.

Marla: Yes.

Detective: Thank you. The third season of *Relationship Rescue* began shooting on this island nine days ago, is that correct?

Marla: Correct.

Detective: And the episodes air simultaneously with the filming?

Marla: Almost correct. We film all day and night and then the editors work all the following day so that the episode can air the following night. It's as close to real time as we can make it while preserving the narrative thread.

Detective: Have you been present for the entire shoot?

Marla: Yes, though I'm rarely on set. I have almost no direct interactions with the cast members. I spend the vast majority of my time in the control room.

Detective: Glass Island, as you know, is rather remote and isolated. The airport is for chartered planes only. If cast members wanted to leave before filming's complete, would it be at their own expense?

Marla: They want to be here, Detective. In our first two seasons, all eight couples not only survived but thrived. We get thousands of applicants. Season Three was an aberration.

Detective: Two of the four couples this season didn't apply, they were recruited. Why was that?

Marla: I'm looking for a very particular chemistry. Not just within the couple but across couples. We need everyone interacting in ways that make for good TV. It's no easy feat to find people who are compelling and dynamics we can storyboard.

Detective: What are storyboards?

Marla: It's a standard part of the process. We create an arc for each character and the production team works to support that arc.

Detective: Meaning, you manipulate the cast into living out the stories you've written?

Marla: Meaning, the cast and crew get very close on shoots.

Detective: Do the cast members know what's on their storyboards?

Marla: No, but the storyboards are based on the people we've gotten to know during the casting process. We vet them carefully, talking to their friends and families. We do our research so we know what—who—we're getting.

Detective: But sometimes they fool you?

Marla: Apparently. Listen, they all knew what they were signing up for. There are no innocents here, Detective. I offer the best quid pro quo in the industry: Give me good footage, I'll save your relationship. It would have worked, too, if they'd come for the right reasons.

Detective: So tell me. Whose fault is it that one of them wound up dead?

ONE

LAUREN

Day One

It's surreal, hearing the helicopter overhead and knowing that it's for Tristan and me, capturing the aerial view of our limousine as it rolls to a stop in front of the villa. There's a whole SWAT team lining the driveway, the crew in their positions with cameras and eight-foot-tall microphones and, most terrifyingly, headsets, like they have their marching orders and all I have is Tristan's hand in mine.

Across from us in the limo is a cameraman and our assigned producer, Julie. "Act natural and have fun!" she says with a big smile.

I don't want to tell Julie just how crazy her advice is because I really like her. She met us at the island airport yesterday and she's been super nice, helping orient us to the process. She uses that term a lot: *the process*. Sometimes it's *the experience* or *the journey*. It seems like they all mean the same thing but maybe by the end I'll know the difference.

I never went to college, it was straight to cosmetology

school, but I'd guess Julie is a recent graduate. She's cute, with short light brown hair and pale freckled skin. All the women on the production team are in tank tops and shorts, no time spent on their hair and makeup, no need to make an impression. I envy them.

"Be yourself," Julie says, "and everyone at home is going to love you." She's talking to me much more than to Tristan. He probably already seems like himself. But then, he's a trained actor.

I have no idea how to be me in a situation like this. I've never been to the Caribbean before, let alone a private island. At twenty-eight years old, I've barely left the state of California. Tristan says to think of this as an extravagant babymoon.

I rub the slope of my belly, a soothing habit that's developed over the past month. I can't wait for the beachball phase. Can't wait to meet my little girl. It doesn't matter that she was unplanned. Tristan and I could not be more thrilled to be her parents.

What we aren't is in love.

Well, I'm not. Not yet anyway. But this week will change that, unlocking whatever issues are preventing me from falling for the best boyfriend I've ever had, by a long shot. Julie warned me that my tagline might be something like, "I'm addicted to bad boys." She said not to worry, the viewers at home totally relate to that one.

I'm just so frustrated with myself. By some miracle I'm on the cusp of an incredible life, yet something keeps holding me back. To start with the obvious, Tristan's great looking. Swimmer's body, dark hair, eyes like smoke, olive skin, blinding teeth, cleft chin. He's kind and loving and I feel safe around him, which was definitely not true of any other guy I've ever been with.

The setting is ideal for lovers. We're parked in a circular

driveway, facing a seashell-pink luxury house (I mean, villa; I have to remember to always call it that), and beyond is an enormous blue pool and farther beyond is a white sand beach and a turquoise ocean and otherwise... nothing. There's lush rainforest on either side of the villa, and no other buildings in sight. Only paradise, like Marla promised.

Tristan and I won't be alone for long, though. When Julie gets word through her headset, we'll have to step out of the limo, go inside, and meet the other couples. The journey begins.

Tristan squeezes my hand, and I squeeze back, wishing I could look as confident as he does. His agent set all this in motion and says this'll be a boost to not only our relationship but Tristan's acting career. I don't watch much reality TV and haven't seen *Relationship Rescue*, but Tristan showed me Instagram posts from former cast members. They weren't merely happy together, they were giddy. I definitely want what they have.

I glance at Tristan in the limo beside me, wishing as always that the butterflies in my stomach were for him. I'm so scared that if I don't come off well, it could hurt him personally and professionally. What if I make myself look stupid? Make him look stupid for being with me?

I run my hand lightly over my long hair, which I've styled in artful beach-tousled waves. At least I know that's right. Hair is my stock and trade, though usually, when I don't have to go into the salon and be my own advertisement, I have it in a ponytail or a bun. It's like how the shoemaker's children go barefoot, or whatever that saying is. (My mom would know since she's fluent in cliché.)

"Five more minutes," Julie reports, "and then you'll go inside and there might be one couple already there or it could be all three. Once everyone's arrived, there'll be a champagne toast, but Lauren will be given sparkling cider." She turns to me. "Make sure you exclaim about it being the best sparkling cider ever so they can put that in the episode and you won't get blow-back for drinking while pregnant."

The mention of blowback sends a shiver up my spine. There are things that America definitely won't love about me, and if he knew, Tristan wouldn't either.

TWO

TATIANA

"Someone's here, someone's here!" I chant, my long French braids bobbing as I leap to my feet. Producers have told me they like my natural exuberance. Am I overdoing it, though?

Who gives a shit. I genuinely want to know all about my new roommates. I hope they'll be as different from Zarine and me as Zarine and I are from each other. Well, that's improbable. Still, I can't wait to get a load of them, and all their problems.

Despite the sound of the doorbell, Zarine continues to lounge on one of the couches in the great room just off the entryway, with its French doors leading to the pool and the ocean. The ceiling is high, its beams made of whitewashed wood, and the tiled floor and furniture are nearly all white, with just a few colorful accents. It's like the set has been designed to complement Zarine and she's about to be photographed for a lifestyle magazine.

She's a total fucking goddess.

I don't just think that because she's Indian, as enchanting as any Bollywood actress, but because she has the quiet confidence to stake out a spot and let the new couples come to her. Zarine's name is perfect, too, because it rhymes with *serene*. She takes that approach to everything in her life, except me. I know how to get her blood pumping.

I yank open the front door with a squeal of welcoming delight, bear-hugging the beautiful blonde in a maxi-dress, who's the teensiest bit overweight—no, wait, she's pregnant! Behind her is a V-shaped hunk of man, with broad shoulders and a tapered waist. As in previous seasons, we're all going to be attractive AF.

I just turned thirty-two but I feel old next to this girl. She should be on one of those MTV knocked-up-teen shows. The guy looks well past legal, though.

My smile widens farther. This is going to be interesting.

"I'm Tatiana," I say. The blonde looks so timid that I put my arm around her. She clutches me back, like she's in need of a life preserver.

"I'm Lauren," she says softly. Then she says it again louder, as if she's just remembered she's supposed to project her voice.

Hasn't her producer given her the spiel about how sensitive the mics are? "It's all good, Lauren," I tell her. "We're going to be a family." Her laugh is vibrato with fear.

"I'm Tristan." He angles his body to subtly communicate that there won't be any hugging. He's a one-woman man. Since I'm not into boys anymore, neither of them has anything to worry about.

"That's Zarine, over there." I indicate the couch.

"Lovely to meet you!" she calls.

"She's paraplegic," I say.

"Tati!" Zarine's tone lets on that she doesn't approve but can't help being amused by my antics in spite of herself. The producers are here for outrageousness. (*Relationship Rescue* has never trucked in political correctness.)

I've taken enough psychology classes to know I'm Zarine's id and she's my superego. I help her throw caution to the wind, and she helps ~~me rein myself in~~. We can yin and yang with the best of them.

Lauren's eyes dart around the room. Poor girl is plainly terrified. Tristan has his arm around her, holding her up.

"How far along are you?" I ask.

"Sixteen and a half weeks," Tristan answers. Oh, so he's one of those sensitive types who says "we're pregnant" but is also man enough to speak for his skittish colt. I have to hand it to central casting. He's not my bag, but he'll play well at home.

"And how old are you?" I'm looking at Lauren.

"Twenty-eight."

My mouth drops open. "What moisturizer have you been using? I need to get some of that!" As she laughs, she seems to relax slightly.

"Are we the first ones in?" Tristan says.

"I haven't seen anyone else." We've been told never to mention or look directly at the crew. "No therapists to tell us what we're doing wrong."

"Deep down, everyone knows what they're doing wrong," Tristan says.

"Are you a therapist yourself?" I ask him.

"An actor."

"Of course." I didn't mean to say it out loud. Fortunately, he seems to take it as a compliment. "I'm a therapist myself, sort of. Massage." My first white lie.

"Where are you from?" he says.

"Zarine and I live in Santa Monica."

"We're in L.A., too!" Lauren sounds pleased and amazed by this strange coincidence. Hasn't she watched the previous two seasons? Eight for eight: They all stayed together, they all resided in the City of Angels. I'd be surprised if any couple wasn't from L.A. Some people don't like to shit where they eat but Marla likes to cast where she lives.

"I'm getting hungry. Do you think I should go looking for

the kitchen?" I'm bluffing. Production told us we had to wait in the great room, where Zarine is luxuriating. But I want them to think I won't necessarily stay where I'm put.

"They'll probably serve us dinner soon, right?" Lauren looks anxious. "Eating for two, you know."

"Nothing to worry about." Tristan smiles at her. "I'll make sure you're taken care of."

"Yeah, you know how it is," I say, "they like to fatten us up before the slaughter." She doesn't laugh, which gives me an inkling. "You have watched the show, right?"

"Tristan told me all the highlights."

I try not to look incredulous. What about the lowlights? I mean, sure, ultimately the producers want our relationships to work out, Marla has a rep to protect, but they'll make us earn our happy endings.

Not to mention that doozy of a paragraph in the contract that you literally couldn't miss, even if you skimmed like I did:

I UNDERSTAND, ACKNOWLEDGE, AND AGREE THAT PRODUCERS MAY USE OR REVEAL PERSONAL INFORMATION, WHICH MAY BE EMBARRASSING, UNFLATTERING, SHOCK-ING, HUMILIATING, DISPARAGING, AND/OR DEROGATORY, MAY SUBJECT ME TO PUBLIC RIDICULE AND/OR CONDEMNATION, AND/OR MAY PORTRAY ME IN A FALSE LIGHT.

It was surrounded by pages and pages indemnifying them of any harm that may come to us, and I hadn't been too freaked out because Zarine wasn't, and being Zarine, she surely read every word. Zarine and I know what we have in each other and, really, this is a chance to show it off. *Relationship Rescue* has the most favorable edits on reality television. Sure, there will undoubtedly be torture but that's part of the show's strategy to get America to root for us. I explained that to Zarine when I convinced her to apply. I've been feeling itchy lately, like I could use an adventure.

Well, if Lauren was willing to come here based solely on Tristan's highlights, then they clearly aren't going to be the couple with trust issues.

We all spin around when we hear the door starting to open. Whoever's there doesn't think they have to knock. Someone doesn't like to ask for permission.

THREE

THE MAJOR

"Sorry!" I hadn't expected them to be clustered so close to the door that I almost rammed into them. Common sense, people. "Sorry," I say again, lower.

I have to be careful since my voice is naturally deep and commanding. Naomi wanted to ring the bell, but I told her we needed to exert control wherever we could. The production team is going to have all the advantages; we have to level the playing field whenever possible.

I'm often mistaken for military since I'm built like a tank and my sandy hair is close cropped and I have that voice. I do try to see around every corner, prepare for every eventuality, yet I've always been a pacifist, like Jesus. That's the kind of Christian I am. But those presumptions serve me well when I lead weight-loss boot camps. I can quickly establish authority. A former client who lost more than a hundred pounds affectionately nicknamed me "The Major," and it stuck. Memberships increased substantially with the rebranding: Boot Camp with The Major! But that was going on five years ago, and business has since plateaued. That's just one of the reasons Naomi and I are here.

I scan the scene quickly. Three people in the foyer are turned toward us, while the woman on the couch with lustrous dark hair is turned away.

The blonde is pretty and nervous, and I know you never ask a woman if she's expecting. The man with her seems solicitous. I have the impression he isn't sold on the other woman who has butt-length braids with tiny flowers in them. She's nearly six feet tall, wearing wide-legged pants and a skintight shirt that bares her midriff. Probably lives in Venice Beach, where they like their glitterati with a side of grime, whereas Naomi and I are in the Palisades, our ocean views unimpeded by tourists.

The woman from the couch is walking over. She's breathtaking, pure elegance in a white silk blouse and white shorts that offset her dark skin. If I were a man with wandering eyes, they'd wander all over her. But I've always been faithful. That's not the problem.

"I'm Cain," I say, "and this is my wife, Naomi."

I'm greeting them all like old friends, handshakes with the women and backslapping with the man. Tristan's his name, and he's with Lauren, who's not wearing any rings (engagement or wedding). Tatiana is the chattiest of the group, and her partner is the self-possessed beauty from the couch, Zarine. They're ringless, too.

Naomi is hugging it up in my wake. Her auburn hair is pulled back tight to emphasize her green eyes and the pale skin that's remained flawless into her forties. She's dressed classy, in a sheath dress and heels, but you can see what kind of shape she's in. Boot camps are my territory, while she does plenty of personal training. I've always been proud to be beside her. I feel a twinge of sadness at where we are now, and then I think about what the producers could do in the editing room with a look like that, so I refocus on the others.

Small talk: where we live, how we make money. That suits

me fine since Naomi and I want to mention our gym as much as possible.

"Look at those guns! Would you flex for me?" This, from Tatiana. Man, that's a mouthful. I ask if she has a nickname but no such luck.

"Cain has a nickname," Naomi says. "The Major."

Tatiana gives a hoot of approval. "The Major it is!" She seems like one of those women who has to sexualize things. I've never found that attractive, though often those kinds of women find it attractive that I don't, like I'm playing hard to get.

But Naomi isn't playing. She stares at Tatiana, unsmiling. "He's always Cain to me."

Naomi and I are approaching forty-five, while the others seem to be in their twenties, maybe early thirties. I feel the gulf in life experience. Tristan and Lauren confirm that they'll soon be parents while Tatiana and Zarine have no kids, and Tatiana quickly adds that they never will. Zarine gives Tatiana an affectionate glance and says, "You can't tie this one down." Tatiana responds with a tongue kiss. Brief, but still. Tongue, right there in front of all of us. I try not to stare, and when conversation resumes, I mention that my girls are practically grown, in their freshman year at UCLA.

"You're kidding!" Tatiana screeches. "You have eighteen-year-old twins?"

"And the tuition bills to prove it," I say.

"It is rather unbelievable." Zarine has a slightly clipped delivery that at first sounded British but now I think might be more of a generic snootiness.

"We're blessed." Naomi smiles at me, and I have to smile back, but I'm thinking, *Blessed?!? Don't tip our hand yet!* I'm almost certain one of the reasons Marla cast us is to be the sanctimonious Christians—that woman has "atheist" written all over her—but now that we're here, we're not playing her game. We've got our own agenda.

Tatiana looks Naomi over, much more overtly than she had with me. "You are definitely blessed."

"I was talking about our girls, but thanks." Naomi notices the ocean view and begins walking toward it, then looks back at the rest of us. "Should we migrate to the living room?"

"The great room," Tatiana corrects playfully, in an accent to mimic Zarine's. Zarine gives a throaty laugh. So far, the other couples seem pretty good together. I can't guess their issues and they definitely won't guess ours.

"The last couple is probably going to be here soon." Tristan's feet are still planted by the front door. He regards me in a friendly way. "Cain is a kick-ass name. Where'd it come from?"

"My parents," I answer carefully. I'm not about to mention the Bible.

"Cain slew his brother Abel," Zarine says. "Not that I can recall much else. I was raised Hindu, but I have a deep respect for the texts of world religions."

A supermodel doctor who reads the Bible in her spare time? Imagine going in for bunion surgery and meeting her.

Naomi is watching, lips pursed. "Cain was supposed to be a twin. Have you all heard about how one twin can absorb the other in utero?"

"You were a stone-cold killer before you were born!" Tatiana gives me an admiring look. A *carnivorously* admiring look. It's so over the top that I feel like she's winking at me, and not in a prurient way. She was cast to fill a certain role, too. She's playing her part.

Naomi doesn't seem to have realized it. She echoes the sexy look in my direction. I hope she's just playing for the camera, too. Because that isn't us anymore, and she better make sure to stick with our agreement. It doesn't matter what we told Marla. I run my own program.

When we signed on for this show, we entered into a different type of partnership, and there's no room for error.

FOUR

BLANCHE

A bug splatters on the limo's windshield. I consider what kind he was, having looked up all the ones we're likely to encounter in this part of the Caribbean. I'm glad that viewers at home can't smell me, as I've practically pickled myself in DEET. I'm projecting the right image, though, after a goldening at the salon and a trip to Rodeo Drive. (Think *Real Housewives of Beverly Hills* rather than *Real Housewives of Orange County*. Some cleavage, not the whole crevasse.) It hurt to spend all that money, but I really had no choice.

The driver turns on the windshield wipers, yet the bug is out of reach. I ponder whether the dearly departed planned it that way, if it amused him to be as big a nuisance to humans in death as in life.

In novel situations, I'm prone to novel thoughts. I know better than to share them with anyone. No one wants the prom king and queen to contain hidden depths.

The limo pulls into the circular drive. The villa, as they'll call it ad nauseum, is familiar from the show's credit sequence. The exterior is pink Mediterranean and I've memorized the interior—simple, well-appointed, all about showcasing that view —from the two seasons that I've been mainlining since my good friend Elle first suggested I participate. One of *her* good friends, Marla, is the executive producer and swore that the alumni couples are, in fact, happy and it isn't just social media bullshit.

Until now, Elle's been the only person to know that Joshua and I have hit a rough patch. People generally assume we're perfect for each other, Barbie and Ken, which is a comparison I've never liked. Marla must have picked that up because in her hard sell, she changed it to prom king and queen.

My royal wardrobe is per Marla's advice: designer clothes, and always jewelry, even by the pool. This isn't the time for the Lululemon athleisure that I wear to chase our kids around at home in the BHPO (Beverly Hills Post Office, a neighborhood that shares the 90210 zip code but features slightly lower property values and a lower level of prestige than its namesake). Joshua and I have been coached to leave off the *Post Office*.

I ache just thinking of the kids. Lily is three and Kyle is six, in kindergarten now, but still, when I tried to explain where we were going, I got choked up. What could be so important that Mommy and Daddy won't be there every morning when they wake up? Well, Daddy wasn't there anyway but Mommy has been a fixture every day of their lives. Joshua has wanted to vacation without them before, and I've always said no.

Seeing the tell-tale look on my face, Joshua says, "They're going to have a great time with my parents. It'll be Disneyland every day. No rules, all the junk food they want. They won't even miss us."

They won't miss you. But I remind myself that Joshua works long hours to take care of us: first to start his business, then to scale upward, and recently, to try to save what he's built.

"You're right, it'll be fine," I say. "Your parents will document pretty much every minute, and Marla guaranteed us two video chats a day."

"We need this"—he moves closer—"just for us." He puts his hand on my knee, and I get a little jolt. It's a bodily memory of last night. Our best sex has always been makeup sex. It's a pity that we fight so rarely.

At home, we generally keep a safe distance. I get another jolt forecasting what it'll be like to spend more than a week straight together. But we'll be on our best behavior since we're surrounded by cameras, production, and the other participants. We might have to fight just to be alone.

All the couples arrived yesterday but last night, each duo was kept in separate nondescript rooms in a viewless compound surrounded by trailers. That's where the crew will be staying throughout the shoot. I had to keep telling Joshua to lower his voice because I didn't know who our neighbors were, and I didn't want them to get the wrong idea about us. He'd been uncharacteristically agitated, insisting that we needed to turn around and go home immediately, before filming began. I wasn't about to indulge his cold feet, not after all the planning and expense. I intend to make the most of our time here. I've never been one for regrets.

Joshua and I agreed to operate from one simple rule: Don't be an asshole. The producers can't show what you don't do.

Right now, he's caressing my hand, his finger tracing the large diamond of my engagement ring, and the cameraman in the seat opposite us shifts, probably zooming in. The producer next to him—I've forgotten her name—gives us the signal.

We disembark into the tropical swelter, knowing that in seconds, we'll be inside the next air-conditioned container. If the previous seasons are any indication, we'll seldom be outside.

That works for me. I don't feel any compulsion to be filmed in my bikini. I'm still a size two and a very natural-looking 32D but since having my kids, I don't spend hours at the gym anymore. Then there are the scars. And don't get me started on the bugs, just waiting to eat me alive.

We approach the door, hand in hand, and Joshua knocks. It's opened instantly by what looks like a bohemian dominatrix with long, dark, complicated braids and huge green eyes. Gorgeous, of course. It's an honor to be chosen, when you think about it: You're good-looking enough and your relationship is the precisely calibrated amount of fucked up to be granted admittance. They wouldn't have let us in if they didn't think we were fixable in a week's time. Marla has made it clear she wants to maintain her batting average.

The cast members swarm us, their greetings effusive. Tatiana, who opened the door, clearly feels a need to be the center of attention. Meanwhile, The Major is smiling like a kindly father figure, though I'm not buying the act quite yet, not with an egomaniacal nickname like that. His wife seems nice and sane, maybe too nice and sane. Naomi, I think? But Zarine... there's no forgetting her. The bombshell foot surgeon, where do they find these people? Lauren has a kewpie doll face and an emerging bump; she's hanging on everyone's every word.

Then there's Tristan. My my my.

"Your name is really Blanche?" Tatiana asks me.

"Who'd pretend?" I say.

"You take the prize for the person who looks least like her name. I don't just mean in this house; I mean like in the history of ever."

Tatiana is in her thirties, just a tiny bit younger than me, only she has the speech patterns of someone significantly younger. Professional provocateurs often do. She isn't going to rattle me, if that's her intent. "My mother loved *A Streetcar Named Desire*."

"Couldn't she have named you Stella, then? It didn't have to be Blanche."

"Tati," Zarine intercedes.

I address Tatiana, standing my ground but making sure

there's a friendly smile on my face. "If you've seen the play, then you know it has to be Blanche."

Tatiana doesn't answer, just strides from the room, with Zarine following. Then she's back with a bottle of champagne while Zarine gracefully manages a tray of champagne flutes.

"The instructions were for us to do the toast once everyone arrived." Zarine speaks like music. She and Tatiana have a visible sexual chemistry but otherwise seem incongruous.

As glasses are distributed, Lauren nearly whispers, "They said there would be sparkling cider? I want to be festive, but you know..."

"I'll handle it," Tristan says, walking deeper into the house. I hope this is just opening-night jitters and Lauren will settle in. I find needy women tedious, though Marla must be banking on America finding her appealingly vulnerable, especially when you factor in the pregnancy. That's probably why they're here, to get support as they transition into their new role as parents. Yawn.

I conceal my irritation, giving Lauren a warm pat. She smiles at me gratefully.

Tristan is back with the sparkling cider. He seems like a total catch, which is what people used to say about Joshua.

Joshua. I've practically forgotten he's here as I've been ingratiating myself with the group. But then, he's been doing the same. Look at him over there, talking to Tatiana like he finds her fascinating. I'm glad to see him smoothing out the slight edge to my repartee with her. Joshua and I are both socially adept people, and neither of us need saving.

Tatiana pops the cork with giggly fanfare. Once the glasses are half-filled (eight people, one bottle—oh, right, seven), it seems only fitting that The Major does the honors. He's the oldest, and he has that basso profundo voice. "To becoming what we once were, what we could be, and more." While it's a bit convoluted, he has the gravitas to pull it off. "To us."

I'll clink with the best of them but deep down, we all know it's every man and woman for themselves.

I can't resist casting another quick glance at Tristan.

My my my.

Interview between Detective Sonya Mohr and producer Julie Lindstrom, taking place on Glass Island.

Detective: Would you like tissues?

Julie: No, thank you.

Detective: Were you close to the victim?

Julie: I just wish none of it had happened. Honestly, I wish I'd never taken the job.

Detective: You were the producer closest to Lauren and Tristan, is that correct?

Julie: I was assigned to them. I had other duties, too, but I was their number one. For the vast majority of the shoot, I didn't have to interact with the rest of the cast. I was never even introduced to some of them. I was supposed to be all about Lauren and Tristan. And I thought it was going to be so easy. A plum assignment.

Detective: Why's that?

Julie: Because I wasn't supposed to have to do much lying or manipulating. I was just going to show them the ropes and boost Lauren's confidence. Keep them their lovable selves. Tristan and Lauren were expected to be the fan favorites.

Detective: Why's that?

Julie: There's something fragile about Lauren, like she doesn't have as many layers of skin as the rest of us. Tristan's your garden-variety hunk.

Detective: Did you personally want Tristan and Lauren to end up together?

Julie: I'm a romantic. I wanted all the couples to end up together. It's part of why I was excited about this job. It wasn't supposed to be mean-spirited reality TV.

Detective: I'm going to have you take me through each day of filming. Let's start with the first night's dinner when the cast was all together. My understanding is that a lot more goes on than can make it to air because of running time.

Julie: Well, yeah, each hour-long episode is really only forty-two minutes because of commercials and there's a lot of ground to cover. But it's not just about the length. The viewer sees what Marla wants them to see. She has a specific narrative vision.

Detective: What was the feeling in the room that first night?

Julie: The cast was on edge because unlike the previous seasons, the therapists hadn't made an appearance yet. They were all told to wear cocktail attire but then the food was just laid out on the table and the alcohol was on the bar. Production called it the ghost dinner.

Detective: I've watched the episode. What didn't I see?

Julie: The room was so hot that the cameraman used a white cloth napkin as a bandanna so he wouldn't spatter sweat on the lens. The cast kept leaving to powder their noses, literally.

Detective: The air conditioning didn't work in the villa?

Julie: It did. Marla must have decided to shut it off. Turn up the heat on them, literally.

I've come to think that reality shows are like that Stanley Milgram experiment, the one where he had people administer electric shocks to see how far they'd go. You can really find out what people are made of. In our case, I'm not just talking about the cast but the crew, too. How long would we producers keep on zapping because Marla told us to?

Detective: What you're saying is that the cast was already psychologically uncomfortable because the therapists hadn't shown up yet, but they were also being made physically uncomfortable?

Julie: Exactly. Lauren came to ask me if it was safe for the baby, and I told her yes. I mean, there were medics nearby and I figured there was no way the producers would endanger her kid. I was so naïve then.

Detective: What else did you notice?

Julie: Tristan didn't sweat at all, not one bead. Tatiana thought the situation was a riot, she kept talking about jungle armpits, and Zarine was doing her patient, indulgent smile. You could tell The Major didn't like Tatiana's comedy routine but he was trying to look easygoing. I can't really remember anything about Naomi.

Detective: What about alcohol?

Julie: They barely drank. That was one of the problems with not having a waitstaff or a bartender. There was no one to refill the glasses, so it became conspicuous, mixing your own drink. They ended up finishing two bottles of wine for six people, which is like an unheard-of level of temperance.

Detective: Six people?

Julie: Lauren didn't drink, and Tristan didn't drink. I guess in solidarity with her? And given everything that came later in the shoot, Joshua must have been sneaking shots.

Detective: What about tensions?

Julie: There didn't seem to be any. The power of repression, I guess. Or denial.

Detective: What about cross-couple attractions?

Julie: My suspicion is that The Major had a thing for Zarine because he never looked at her, and Naomi compensated by being extra-nice to her. I'd say that Tatiana took some notice of The Major, but maybe it was only to stoke Zarine's jealousy and keep things spicy because their sex that night was triple-X rated. Mostly, people do things under the blankets because they know we've got the night-vision camera but with Tatiana, we needed to still, you know, blur things.

Detective: And the others?

Julie: Tristan only had eyes for Lauren, and she barely looked up from her plate. Sometimes she'd glance at the camera, which was a big no-no.

Detective: How did Blanche and Joshua behave?

Julie: Blanche seemed like she was hosting a dinner party. She kept the conversation flowing, made sure it was boring and conventional: jobs, kids, who vacationed where, some name-dropping. At that point, Joshua was still following her lead.

It wasn't long before everyone stopped playing nice.

FIVE

LAUREN

Day Two

I don't know what time it is since Julie took our cell phones away for safekeeping, and there are no clocks in the room. I want to open the curtains and see the ocean, reassure myself that I really am in paradise, but Tristan is still asleep.

In the enormous bathroom mirror, I'm horrified by my appearance. I came to the island with two massive pimples and now there are three. Terrific, even more to conceal.

Last night at dinner, I was trying so hard not to embarrass Tristan that I barely spoke, and now I'm worried that America will think he's in love with a mute. I wish I could have been like Blanche, immune to the heat, comfortable in my skin. Hers, of course, is perfect. She and Joshua are so well-matched and socially at ease that I really have no idea why they're here. Actually, all the couples seem great together, which is terrifying. Are Tristan and I going to be the sore thumb or the squeaky wheel or some other hack expression from my mom? Anyway, Blanche's stories about Kyle and Lily were so funny. She makes parenting sound effortless. At least my daughter will know her father, so I'll automatically give her more than I've had.

When I emerge from the bathroom, Tristan is stretching in bed. He starts out smiling and then switches to a concerned frown as he takes me in. "Morning sickness?"

"Not yet." I knock on a nightstand that I presume to be real wood.

"Is everything okay?"

"Definitely!" I force a smile. "I'm just looking forward to getting started. You know, with the process."

"It's okay to be nervous."

"Are you?" I ask. "Nervous?"

"Just glad we're here." He reaches out to touch my belly. "That we're all here."

I feel my body relax a little. That's the effect he has on me, and that someday, he'll have on her. On our little girl.

So why can't I just love him? Why can't he have *that* effect?

I beeline for the bathroom, shutting the door and positioning myself over the bowl. Normally, my ruse isn't this elaborate, but I have the camera to think about. My shoulders begin to heave, and the sobs are silent. Once I've calmed down, I flush the toilet. "All better!" I call to Tristan.

It's a well-practiced routine. He thinks I puke every day, sometimes morning and night. While (true) morning sickness would likely have ended by this point in the pregnancy, mine can go for as long as it's needed.

I take a long shower and then apply my makeup. I can hear him in the bedroom talking to someone. Julie, probably.

I pull on a cute sundress—new and from H & M, like everything I'll be wearing this week—and blow-dry my hair while Tristan showers. I always like when we get ready together. It feels so domestic, and it's even better in this bathroom, which is more than double the size of ours at home. We moved in together after finding out about the pregnancy. We haven't even been together a year.

Tristan has a towel around his waist and no microphone, and mine is in the other room. He's just started to blow-dry his hair, so that's providing white noise. I might not get another chance for quite a while, so I move closer. "Am I doing okay?"

He turns off the dryer. "You don't have to do anything to be okay. I love you."

I kiss him, which is my usual answer, since I don't want to lie, not about that. He's told me that the first time I say it back will be the greatest moment of his life, the beginning of everything.

Please, let this process work.

When we emerge from the bathroom, I see Julie's in our room, dropping off our phones. "You've got twenty minutes with the outside world, and then it's downstairs for breakfast!" she announces cheerfully. Then she reiterates the rules yet again: Texts and calls are being monitored and no friend or family member is allowed to tell us anything about what's aired in the episodes or how we're being perceived/received by America; we're forbidden to furnish any details from our time here that could fall under the category of "spoilers"; we're not permitted on the internet, not even for so much as a single Google search or to check the news; and under no circumstances can we engage in social media. All of this is under threat of stiff financial penalties and for truly egregious violations, participants can be ejected from the show. "It's just so you remain in the therapeutic bubble," Julie concludes. I don't really get what that means but it's not a problem. I've never been that social anyway.

Tristan pounces on his cell, eager to talk to his three sisters. He practically raised them, and they adore him. Me, I'm a whole lot slower. I have casual friends at the salon, no one close.

No brothers or sisters. My mom and I get along all right but a chat once a week is plenty.

Tristan is on the balcony, showing the panorama to his sisters. I hear the commingled laughter (he must have all three of them on at once).

I can see how amazing he is. All I need is to feel it.

It's not like we don't have sex, or that it's bad, but there's something missing that I can never put my finger on. He's so hot and yet, I boil for other, lesser men. I never fantasize about him. There are orgasms but not one has been volcanic. Could this process really change something that elemental?

"Time's up!" Julie says from the doorway.

Tristan and I go downstairs to the dining room, where the others are already assembled around the table, drinking mimosas and eating frittata. The crew and producers are there but it's another self-serve buffet. The vibe is subdued. We must all be thinking it: When will the head shrinking begin?

The Major is complaining that he wasn't able to reach the twins for a video chat. "It would help if we were given a daily schedule," he grumbles, and Zarine agrees.

Naomi tries to bring me out of my shell with pregnancy talk. "Have you thought about natural childbirth?" she asks. I shake my head. "Not that I'm selling it! I was epidural all the way. My justification was that I could have handled pushing one out of the chute, but two?"

"She made the right choice," The Major says. "I did it natural, and it was *rough*!"

We all laugh, mostly to release the communal tension. Blanche launches into a story about her labor and delivery, only to be interrupted by an intercom announcement. "Freshen up and report to the great room in ten minutes!"

"Ten minutes," Joshua repeats solemnly, "until shit gets real."

My hands tremble as I set down my fork. This could be it, the beginning of everything. Or the end.

SIX

TATIANA

Report to the great room, like we're in military school. Is this how they spoke to the other casts? Were the previous participants left in the lurch for the first sixteen hours, an eternity when you're in televised purgatory? Fuckers.

It's not like I'm worried. I'm just grumpy from sleep deprivation. Zarine and I used to have this bad habit of telling each other everything, so she knows that men who look like Joshua—like walking Ken dolls—are my weakness. Not anymore, now I'm all about the puss, about her puss, and last night, after dinner, I had to prove it. For, like, hours. I might have given myself TMJ.

Somewhere in there, I made the tactical error of saying that if there was a gun to my head and I had to pick a man in this house, it wouldn't even be Joshua. The Major is the real tower of power. All those dad jokes but that is not a dad bod. Now she's acting like I want two-thirds of the male cast. This morning, I couldn't look left toward Joshua or right toward The Major. It was torturous, a brunch vise. Normally at home, I can make the necessary adjustments to avoid these types of situations; I can try to head off potential jealousy at the pass. But the reality of reality TV is starting to sink in.

I have to remind myself that Zarine and I are naturals. We don't know how to be boring, unlike these other couples. Really, I'm mystified by this season's casting choices. Lauren's scared of her own shadow, Blanche and Joshua were factory produced, and The Major and Naomi—well, Marla might have something with those two. I'm pretty sure they're hiding something major. (The puns just write themselves. I can't wait to see what the trolls come up with.)

Zarine emerges from the bathroom, looking airbrushed. No one nails the no-makeup look like she does. I wish I had time to go down on her again, aching jaw or not.

We walk down the stairs to the great room, and there they finally are, Sam and Dave, in the flesh. Not *that* Sam and Dave, had been their joke in the very first episode, which had caused everyone at home to Google that Sam and Dave, who turned out to be an R & B duo from the 1960s, leading to speculation about how old *this* Sam and Dave really were. The joke never made it to the second season.

This Sam and Dave are wife and husband, both licensed therapists. Sam is well-put together, attractive in a formidable way, and IMDb puts her age at forty-nine. Her bob is dark and severe, her olive skin immaculate. She isn't naturally beautiful, isn't naturally anything. You can tell she's worked for it all and there's no shame in that fact.

Dave has a peculiar charisma of his own. He's bald on top and a little shaggy on the sides, and his eyebrows are thick, black thunderclouds. They're remarkably expressive, conveying everything that Sam won't, given her persona, or maybe can't, due to fillers. He has a pot belly. He's short. And in short, he doesn't care about any of that, which gives him tremendous presence.

The great room has been reconfigured. Now there are four

loveseats, one for each couple. The last to arrive is Joshua and
Blanche, holding hands as always.

I've been telling Zarine the truth: Joshua has no appeal for
me. He's all new-car smell. I feel like everyone at home is going
to want to see the doctors crack Joshua and Blanche's veneer,
like porcelain wedding figures on top of a crumbling cake.

If the show's not all sweetness and light this time around,
then there's a chance I could be seen as a gold-digger. I told the
cast that I was a massage therapist but the producers know that
I did the training and never set up an office. Without Zarine, I'd
have to move back in with my father and try to remember
whether he's on his fourth wife or his fifth.

"Welcome," Sam says, taking us all in without a smile. She's
swathed in a red satin pantsuit with tapered legs and five-inch
stilettos. On a *Caribbean island*. As always, she's riding the edge
of camp and class, and for a second, I'm a little bit starstruck.
Last night during that interminable dinner, I was afraid I'd
made a mistake and this wasn't going to turn out to be any fun,
but that pantsuit gives me hope.

"Always a pleasure to meet the new class," Dave says,
smiling for both of them.

"We've got big plans for you all." As Sam's gaze sweeps the
room, she's decidedly less ridiculous. To the viewer at home, it
looks like theatrics, but in person, her ice-blue eyes are
genuinely piercing.

The unstaffed dinner at Bikram yoga temperatures. The
long wait to meet the therapists. The unusual casting choices (I
mean, who's going to root for Blanche and Joshua?). And a
slightly unhinged quality to Sam, like she's a pit bull who's just
been taken off leash.

Something is different this season. I can feel it.

I flash back to the contract. Has it always been written like
that, or was it updated so that the producers and the therapists
would be able to do absolutely anything to us with zero liability?

Then there's this setting. We really are at their mercy. No phones, no Uber, no hotels or restaurants, nowhere to go. I haven't even seen a dock. The only way off the island is by private plane.

I'd been my usual whimsical, impulsive self in applying for the show, half-expecting Zarine would put the brakes on. Instead, after we'd binge-watched the first two seasons, she agreed that it would just be, as she called it, "a bit of fun." Sure, she can be jealous on occasion and I—well, I've got my things— but since she didn't seem worried, I wasn't going to worry either. We'd go have a frolic, offer sexy comic relief, and come home with a "Remember that time we..." Even our casting process had seemed lighthearted, with Marla joking that I'm the right amount of underweight for television. Exactly what she was looking for.

I'm not laughing now.

SEVEN

THE MAJOR

We started out in the sunshine but then they led us underground, into the dungeon.

This isn't your mother's group therapy room, that's for sure. It's definitely not the one that was used in the first two seasons. My best guess is that this space is normally a massive wine cellar and it's been cleared out for the shoot. The walls are concrete gray, matching the floor. It looks like a holding cell, like there ought to be a drain in the center. With ten chairs in a circle, it's a scene from the world's grimmest AA meeting. Why are we here? The only answer seems to be: Because production wants it this way. Marla wants it this way.

For an executive producer, she'd seemed awfully involved in the casting process, conducting many of the interviews herself. I recognize a fellow control freak when I'm looking right into her bloodshot eyes. She's probably about my age, brown hair striped with gray, too proud to wear makeup or have work done, wanting to stand out in L.A. by embracing her age. She radiates intelligence through funky glasses and monochromatic, loose-fitting clothes in expensive fabrics. When she didn't want to answer a question, she told Naomi and me to "trust the

process." But I persisted, determined to make an informed decision. It had felt contentious at times and in the end, I was
surprised to be cast. I thought she might have wanted to work
with someone more bovine. But then, Naomi and I aren't the
kind of people you see on reality TV every day, so maybe Marla
hadn't wanted to pass us up.

After she offered us a spot, we took a week to say yes. I did a
cost-benefit analysis, and there was soul-searching and much
discussion, and then Naomi and I made our choice. It's like I've
always told my daughters: You can do whatever you want so
long as you're willing to deal with the consequences. That's
what personal responsibility means.

"So," Sam says, after going around the room with that hairy
eyeball of hers, "why do you all think you're here?"

I figure I might as well field this softball. "We're here to
work on our marriages. Our relationships," I correct.

"What needs work in your relationship—I mean, *marriage*?"
Dave parrots.

"Naomi and I have been together a long time. We're empty
nesters now. We could use a tune-up."

"Huh," Dave says, "long way to fly for a lube job."

Tatiana snickers. I'm not about to get hot under the collar.
He's just trying to establish his dominance when we all know
his wife has much bigger balls.

"I heard your lube jobs are world-class." I grin around the
circle.

Dave laughs the loudest. He also turns his attention elsewhere. I know he'll be back, but this early, it's about low-
hanging fruit.

"Joshua," he says, "why are you here?"

"I work too much, and I don't communicate enough."
Joshua looks over at Blanche. "I need to be a better listener. I
need to show my wife how important she is to me."

"And Blanche is blameless?" Sam raises an eyebrow. "We'll

just work our magic on you so she can sit back and feast on your admiration?"

"I don't know what you're asking." Might be true. Joshua doesn't seem like the sharpest tool in the shed.

"Sometimes I pay too much attention to the kids and not enough to Joshua," Blanche interjects.

Sam addresses the group. "If you intend to make any progress this week, you need to realize something fundamental. Everything is about dynamics. Action and reaction. Reinforcing feedback loops. You do this, your partner does this, and you're off and running in circles, the same circles every time. Together, we're going to blaze a new trail. Make your lives way less predictable."

"Predictability isn't the problem for Zarine and me," Tatiana boasts.

"Don't flatter yourself. You spend every day putting on a show for Zarine like you're a dolphin at Sea World. It's getting old. Then there's Zarine's jealousy, and all that reassurance sex. I could set my watch by it. Your volatility's as dull as Blanche and Joshua."

Blanche opens her mouth as if to protest, then closes it. Joshua seems immune to the insult. Zarine's face flushes, while Tatiana glares at Sam like a petulant teenager.

But Sam has moved on to Naomi and me. "You two live in your own judgmental safe zone, but it's gotten too small. You've merged into one person. No wonder you don't have sex anymore. It would be masturbation."

Neither Naomi nor I flinch. We understand boot camp tactics. Break 'em down to build 'em up. Besides, none of this might even make it to the actual episode. It depends whether anyone in this room gives them better material.

Sam is on to the next, and at that point, you can feel the shift in the room. We all know who's left, the person who seems least able to handle tough love. I'd want to catch the bullet myself but based on what I've seen so far, Tristan already has that covered.

"Why do you think you're here, Lauren?" Sam asks with sudden gentleness.

Lauren bursts into tears. Tristan scoots closer and says, "You don't have to say anything if you don't want to."

"It's okay. I can do this. I want to." She takes a shuddering breath. "It's not a feedback loop, it's not Tristan. It's me. I'm the problem."

"How so?" Dave asks.

"Tristan is the best man I've ever known, and I just... I can't seem to get there fast enough. Something's broken inside me."

"There's no rush," Tristan responds. "I'm not going anywhere."

"See?" Sam turns to the rest of us. "That's the cycle. Lauren castigates herself for not loving such an obviously loving man. Such a smothering man."

"He's not smothering," Lauren objects. "He looks after me."

"He overpowers you," Sam says. "Tells you what to think and what to feel. Answers questions before you can. Or stops you from answering them in case you'll say something he's not ready to hear."

"He's overriding you," Dave says to Lauren. "Aren't your feelings valid?"

This is a sweet young couple in a two-headed shark's mouth. There's no way I can stay quiet. "Did you even meet them before today? Because you haven't met me or Naomi."

Sam swivels her head toward me, eyes glittering like a serpent's. "The Major to the rescue. Such an interesting nickname."

"He doesn't like to see people bullied," Naomi says. I bet no one else in the room can tell that she's nervous, hoping I won't go too far.

"Bullied?" Dave looks bewildered. "We were pointing out a

dynamic that Lauren and Tristan might not have been aware of, an impasse that's keeping them from the love they want."

Lauren gives a shaky smile. "I'm fine." Then to me, "Thanks."

"Look at that," Dave says. "Not even twenty-four hours and you've turned The Major into the dad you never had." So that's how it's going to be. He and Sam haven't met any of us, but they've seen our data. All those invasive questionnaires, all the interviews with Marla and the other producers. They're fore-warned and forearmed, thinking they have our diagnoses—and prognoses—at the ready.

Suckers.

"Bad-boy and daddy issues," Sam says. "That's Lauren. But what about you, Tristan? Because you were drawn to each other for a reason." She looks around. "Just like all of you. In every case, your pathologies fit together like a lock and a key."

EIGHT

BLANCHE

"You smoke?" Tristan and I both ask at once. He's holding his unlit cigarette while mine's been smoldering for a while.

"Only on vacation," I say. "I'd never do it near my kids. I don't remember telling the producers but there was a pack of my brand of choice in the room."

"Thoughtful of them. I had to bring my own." He pulls a Bic from his pocket. "I smoke a few a day to blow off steam, literally. But I'm like you. When the baby's born, that habit's dead."

I stub my cigarette out and stand up. I'd chosen this pool lounger because it's the farthest from the exterior cameras, so the footage would be of poor quality and therefore, my vice will be less likely to air. "Best seat in the house," I tell him, gesturing.

He sits on the neighboring lounger and smiles up at me. "I wouldn't mind company."

Back home, I'm always hanging out with moms, or on the increasingly rare occasions Joshua's not working, we socialize with other families. I'm suddenly aware of how unusual it is for me to be alone with a man.

Well, I've got no itinerary, nothing to do until we're all

ordered to report to the next location. Fraternizing with my fellow castmates has been encouraged. It's an extension of group therapy, according to my producer.

I sit back down. Tristan hands me a cigarette from his pack (turns out we smoke the same brand) and leans forward with the flame. Nice to have a handsome man lighting me up.

The true surprise of the trip so far is how relaxing it's been. The lack of control. The lack of a set schedule. My kids aren't spoiled but the demands feel constant. They're quite clear on the fact that they're the center of my universe, and after the childhood I had, I want them secure in that knowledge. But it means I spend almost all my waking hours anticipating and meeting their needs. Right now, Joshua's parents are the ones on call; I'm off duty.

The island has been good for Joshua and me already. During the therapy session, we both refused to take the therapists' bait. For once, it felt like we were really a team instead of leading our separate lives. I'm not about to give Sam and her troglodyte husband the satisfaction of spilling my guts like a piñata she's broken open, and neither is Joshua. The viewers at home will respect that.

This is a much-needed vacation, and I plan to enjoy it. I take a deep drag on my (second!) cigarette as I look out at the vista. From this vantage point, all I see is white sand and ocean before me, and rainforest to the left and right. It's stunning and a little bit forbidding, like we're the last bastion of civilization.

"It's the most beautiful place I've ever been." Tristan sounds wistful.

"Wishing you were here under different circumstances?"

"No." That phenomenal jaw of his takes on a determined set. "I'm exactly where I need to be, and this is going to work out just how it was meant to."

"So you're a hopeless romantic." Emphasis on the *hopeless*. From what I've seen, his baby momma and his relationship is a mess. Marla's outdone herself. And to think, I initially assumed Tristan and Lauren were just going to be window dressing. "Well, I hope you're right."

He meets my eyes. "You can't know anything for sure, not when it comes to other people. But I trust Sam, Dave, and Marla."

Can he really be that dim? I thought that was just an act his girlfriend was putting on.

"Their reputations are on the line," he adds. "They've got big egos and they don't want to fail."

"You trust them because your interests are aligned with theirs."

He nods. So, he's not dim at all. I'd checked out a lot during the morning's therapy session because other people's issues don't grab me. But I'd tuned in to Tristan.

"Do you trust Lauren?" I ask.

"She's here even though she doesn't like the spotlight. She did it for me. That's love, even if she's not saying it yet."

I feel for him, watching the shot clock tick down until the birth of their baby. "I was the first one to say 'I love you' to Joshua. I had to wait weeks to hear it back."

He watches me with wide, curious eyes. Are they slate gray?

"I remember how exhausting it was. I kept trying to do everything right, like this was the thirty-day return period and he might take me back to the store. Submitting yourself for someone else's approval is the worst."

The other cast members are focused on Lauren, trampled flower that she is. It peeves me, actually. What about Tristan, who spends all his time on tenterhooks, trying to be pleasing?

"Lauren's not trying to judge me," he says. "She's a good person."

"I'm sure she's wonderful." When she's not weeping. It was tedious, watching her cry her makeup off, exposing a rather monstrous cyst beneath, while she talked about her absent father and the string of losers to whom she'd previously pledged her love.

"I brought her here, so I'm going to take care of her. That's my job."

I suspect it's the same job he's working off the island. Lauren's no dummy, she knows exactly what she's doing.

"So why did Joshua say it back?" Tristan asks. "What made him fall?"

"You know, I'm not really sure. He made it an event, though. He surprised me with a trip to Vegas and got this incredible suite. He said it while we were swimming around in the Jacuzzi tub, surrounded by bubbles. We were laughing, a bubble went up his nose, and he started coughing, and in between coughs, it just came out."

Tristan smiles. "His life flashed before his eyes."

"In those days, he spent a lot of money on trips and swank restaurants and lavish gifts but what really sold me on him was his family. He has incredible parents who are still passionately in love forty years in. His older brother already had kids when Joshua and I met, and the feeling when they were all together was like nothing I'd experienced before. I wanted to be part of it, and I wanted my future kids to be part of it."

I hadn't expected to say all that but something about Tristan and those gray eyes of his had unwittingly drawn me out. I could easily resist Sam and Dave but Tristan's another story.

"So what happened?" he says. "Where did it go wrong?"

I'm still miked, regardless of how far away the cameras are. So I say, "You'll find out soon enough. Once you have kids, there's not much time or energy left over. Joshua and I need to put each other first again."

"If you already know the answer, then why come here?"

"Knowing and doing are different, I guess." But enough

about me. "Could I give you a suggestion as an older, wiser woman?"

"Come on. You're not much older."

Glad he noticed. "When it comes to Lauren, doting hasn't worked. Maybe it's time to try something else."

His face hardens instantly. "It's not a strategy. I love her. I'm going to take care of her, no matter what."

"I've been married a long time, and I can tell you, love always involves strategy."

He shakes his head, pushing my words away. I slap at my arm, thinking I felt a mosquito landing. Despite the DEET and as much as I'd like to stay, I'm not sure I can last out here much longer.

"You can be good to her without catering to her every need and whim. Make her a little less sure of you."

He appears to consider. "Thanks for telling me what you really think."

After that, the conversation changes. I forget we're on camera—well, distantly—as I talk about my kids and my very recent discovery that I can ache for them like phantom limbs and yet not entirely miss them.

"I get it, that sense of responsibility," he says. "I have three younger sisters. I wanted to go away to college but I worried what would happen to them, so I kept living at home until I was sure they'd be okay. I know I can make sacrifices. I've got that part down."

"Why couldn't you leave?"

"My father's a mean drunk and my mother was so busy covering up for him that she could barely take care of one kid, let alone four." He gives me a crooked smile. "No complaints, though. It gave me the chance to develop certain skills. I'm the fastest gunslinger in the West at diaper changes."

I laugh. "Oh, yeah? You challenging me to a diaper-off?"

"And a colic-off, too. Crying babies fucking love me. But I'm good with older kids, too. I know how to make everything into a game, for me and for them. Use your imagination and make it exciting so nobody has to think about what's really happening. We were out dodging land mines or digging tunnels or hiding from monsters, the make-believe kind, until the coast was clear and it was safe to go home. That way, they didn't have to lose their childhoods."

He doesn't look sad; he's animated, as if he's remembering moments with his sisters, the fun they had. It's like he's still playing a game with himself in order to forget the worst of it. I've played those kinds of games, too. I can see how much love there is inside him, and I can only imagine how lucky his little girl is going to be.

I sink back into my chair. The thing people don't immediately realize about me is just how resilient I am. Don't let the hair, nails, and jewelry fool you. I'm a survivor.

I can withstand the elements—like the mosquitoes, like Lauren—for as long as I need to.

Continuing interview between Detective Sonya Mohr and producer Julie Lindstrom, taking place on Glass Island.

Detective: Let's talk about the text.

Julie: I go back to that moment all the time. If I'd just deleted that text, maybe the rest never would have happened. Like, maybe it's the butterfly effect, and that text was the wings flapping, and it changed all the events that followed. Am I making sense?

Detective: You feel guilty.

Julie: I am guilty. I was in charge of Lauren's and Tristan's phones. We had everyone's password, and on the second night, the text came in. "Wanna fuck?" plus a dick pic. I couldn't believe it. I mean, this was Lauren, our angel.

Detective: What happened next?

Julie: I agonized over it. I didn't want to blow up Lauren and Tristan, for their sakes and because they're having a baby. And selfishly, I was afraid that my assignment might get a lot harder and a lot more underhanded.

Some of the producers love that kind of thing. They love tricking people into giving up good footage. They love the frankenbiting. But that's not me.

Detective: *Frankenbiting?*

Julie: Editors take a word here and a word there and splice them together into a new sentence. You can make people say anything you want, and it's legal because the contracts the participants sign allow everything.

Detective: So what did you do with the text?

Julie: I showed Marla. I hoped that she'd tell me we could ignore it and stick with the storyboards. No such luck, she tells me to write back as Lauren.

I pushed back, so she said to call him as myself. I was supposed to fish for information we might use for the lie detector test. I hoped I'd find out that the last time she'd been with Alexei was before Tristan was even in the picture. But instead... well, you saw.

Detective: You told Marla what you learned?

Julie: Now I know I shouldn't have. She decided it was too good to pass up. We had to entirely rework the exercises and the storyboards. Six weeks of work undone overnight.

Detective: Sounds intense.

Julie: I hate to admit it, but it was kind of fun, too. We were high on Red Bulls and on ourselves, thinking, "This is how great TV gets made." None of us talked about who'd get hurt. Sometimes we could forget, you know? Forget they were actual people. I know how terrible that sounds.

Detective: Similar to how it is for viewers watching them on TV.

Julie: That's behind their backs. Me, I was in their faces. Maybe if I'd made other choices, everyone would still be alive today.

NINE

LAUREN

Day Three

"Good morning." The voice from the other balcony is meant to be low so it won't disturb anyone sleeping inside, but since it's The Major's, it's still loud enough to startle. I jump and he apologizes.

"I didn't think anyone else would be awake yet." I double-check that I've shut the balcony doors behind me.

"If the sun's up, so am I."

I move closer to the edge of the balcony, that is, the edge closest to The Major. He does the same. From our corners, if we'd reached way out, fully extending our arms, we could have touched.

"I'm not miked, in case you're wondering," he says, "and I don't see any cameras or wires out here."

Good to know, maybe Tristan and I could steal a few private moments. "Is Naomi still sleeping?"

"She's working out. Can you keep a secret?" I definitely can. "I hate exercising."

I laugh. "You own a gym!"

"I wanted to be a motivational speaker and Naomi convinced me that this was a good substitute. She's got a gift for creative compromises. I'm the Tony Robbins of fitness boot camps. She does the personal training."

"I just assumed..."

"What?"

"That you must like it. Because you're so big." I feel myself blush. "I don't mean it like that."

"I know. You're not Tatiana." Now we both laugh. "Tatiana's okay, though. She's just doing what she's told."

"Sam and Dave said she's always performing for Zarine."

"But they also said Zarine gets off on it, right? What I took away from that marathon therapy session was that we're all playing parts in our relationships, whether the cameras are rolling or not."

I really want to tell The Major my own secret since I was tossing and turning about it all last night. But if I did, he wouldn't be looking at me all fondly like he is now. He's an upstanding guy, that much is obvious. What you see is what you get.

"How are you playing a part?" I ask.

His brow furrows. "I'm acting like I know what the hell's going on when really, I have no idea."

"You mean on this island?"

"I mean in the world. There's always been plenty of ugly but people have become so free with it. They celebrate it. They don't just disagree, they denigrate. They annihilate. You don't know where to find the truth anymore."

"The truth about...?"

It's like he hasn't even heard me. "You can burrow so deep in a rabbit hole that you might never find your way out. Sometimes I feel like I'm always bracing myself for the next bad thing even though the bad's already here. There's no stopping it."

Is he saying that the bad has followed us here? Or that it's inside us?

I'm getting an eerie feeling, listening to him. But I remind myself that he started this by saying he has no idea what's going on. It's likely that nothing is.

"Sorry." He gives me a sheepish smile. "I'm probably just looking for a new audience since Naomi's tired of listening to me."

"Can I ask you something?" His vulnerability this morning combined with how protective he'd been toward me yesterday means I can trust him more than any of the others. Except for Tristan, of course.

"Sure."

"I was up all last night thinking about something Sam and Dave said. Remember when they talked about how we get together with people who are equally damaged, you know, like the lock and the key? Well, I know my issues, but I can't name Tristan's. They must be there, right? So why can't I see them?"

"Maybe he hasn't let you in all the way yet. Or maybe Sam and Dave are full of crap."

Sam and Dave seem pretty smart to me, and they've obviously helped a ton of people. It could be that Tristan doesn't have enough issues to unlock me.

I hear a loud knock from deep inside the room, and then Julie's voice: "Rise and shine!"

"I guess that's my cue," I say.

The Major smiles. "It's been real nice talking to you, Lauren. I hope we can do it again."

"I hope so, too."

Back inside, Tristan is still in bed, trying to rouse himself. When I let Julie in, I see she's holding a breakfast tray. She seems borderline frantic. Someone keeps talking to her through her headset and it's like she's answering them in code. I have the sense that something isn't going quite according to plan. Julie's too distracted to make eye contact.

"Eat quickly," she says, without her usual perk, and when she leaves the room, Tristan and I dig into the eggs, bacon, and toast. Afterward, we get ready just as quickly. I've barely finished brushing my teeth and applying my lipstick when there's another knock on the door.

This time, it's Sam and Dave. She's in a silver jumpsuit that makes her look like an erotic astronaut while Dave is in shorts and a T-shirt. He intones, "Lauren, come with us."

It's like getting summoned to the principal's office, and I turn to Tristan, frightened. He gives me a brief hug, much less than I'm used to from him. What's going on here?

"Could you tell me what this is about?" I stall.

"It's an exercise," Sam says curtly.

"Come with us," Dave says again, with so much authority that I feel like I have no choice but to follow him and Sam downstairs. They lead me into a barren, white-walled room. A woman is already there, sitting at a table with a laptop computer in front of her and what appears to be medical equipment. There's a chair opposite her. Sam points to it, and I sit.

"It's lie detector day already?" I thought Tristan said that was always toward the end of the week. I really should have watched the show.

The woman doesn't answer. I pivot toward Sam and Dave, who are still standing, and I'm still feeling like a small child who's in some kind of unnamed trouble.

Sam indicates the large television on the wall. "You'll be shown a series of images. Barbara will be charting your reactions. First, she'll attach electrodes to your head to monitor your brain waves, as well as monitoring your respiration and blood pressure."

I have the impulse to walk out but this is the first exercise. I can't let Tristan down. So I get hooked up, Sam and Dave leave the room, and the images begin.

First is a series of family photos. Birthday parties, kids running through sprinklers on a sunny day, etc. The one that makes my eyes water looks the least staged. They're all gathered around the dinner table, the mom serving food, the dad in mid-sentence, the two kids laughing. It's pleasantly banal, utterly normal, and entirely foreign to me.

Next are pictures of couples, the kind of publicity photos you'd see in an ad for a casino resort: golfing, out at a nightclub, rose petals on the bed. Those are replaced by couples fighting, and a woman holding on to a man's arm, begging him not to go. A pregnant woman alone, weeping. I feel myself go very, very cold.

Then it's pure relief, because on the screen is Tristan. There are candids from his social media as well as professional headshots from his acting portfolio. A few of Tristan and me from his Instagram, plus stills from our time here so far. There's a grainy image of us in bed, Tristan sleeping, me staring up at the ceiling. I don't have to look at the laptop to know my pulse has quickened. What's really going on here?

It's followed by more pictures of darkened bedrooms, with indistinct forms moving under covers, the suggestion of sex. But that can't be Tristan and me, not on the island. Who is that? I can finally make out Blanche and Joshua. She's on top, from the back, and it's dark so I can't see anything explicit, but what they're doing is unmistakable.

Tatiana and Zarine are fire. Even in a still, even in the dark, they're kinetic.

So what if some of the other couples have already had sex. No big deal. And it's okay if that turns me on a little. That's perfectly—

Oh my God. No. It can't be.

Alexei is standing in front of a mirror, showing off his abs and his erection. His face isn't in the picture but that's his body. He's sent me plenty of pictures where he posed like that, and they've always had the desired effect. Until now.

It seems like that picture is on the screen three times as long as the others, like it's all been building to this crescendo. My heart is racing, yes, but it's not that type of arousal. I hope the machine can tell the difference.

I think of how little Tristan said as we were wolfing down breakfast, and the brevity of his hug just before my perp walk. Could he have known this was coming? Had he found those pictures on my phone and given them to production?

No, I've always been careful to delete them. Besides, Tristan would never have brought me all the way here as a setup. He loves me too much. This will be his humiliation as well.

The show is over.

I take off the equipment, fighting for calm. I need to focus on what I know for sure. There were interviews during preproduction where I told them about ex-boyfriends, including Alexei. They'd asked to see pictures. Not of his dick, obviously, but they saw his physical build. Maybe they'd found someone who looked like Alexei from the chest down. It could be an exercise about attraction. They probably didn't even know about the cheating. No one would suspect me.

I stumble out into the hall, mind whirring, and Julie's there. She's been picking her cuticles and I can see they're bloody. I recall her lack of eye contact earlier.

"I'm sorry," she says quietly. "There was nothing I could do."

I've never watched *Relationship Rescue*, but I watched a few seasons of *Survivor*. I know what it means when no one will look at you before tribal council. It means you're about to get your torch snuffed.

TEN

TATIANA

I grab Zarine's hand and pull her up the stairs to our bedroom. I'm sure production isn't going to stop us. Whatever they have planned for the afternoon can wait. Last season was criticized for too little sex, or at least, too little intimation of sex (not enough writhing bodies on night cam). Zarine and I are the antidote. I'm ready to give the people what they want. Give Zarine what she wants, for as long as she wants it.

Afterward, she's full of energy while I'm about to doze off. It's always like that, we're opposites in every way. It's a paradoxical form of closeness, always being a little bit (or a lot) unknowable to one another. Sam and Dave could not be more wrong: Zarine and I are nothing like Blanche and Joshua.

The postcoital is even better than usual, nuzzling each other and giggling. Then Zarine takes aim at the other couples. I glance at the nightstand toward our microphones. Our ultrasensitive microphones.

"You think The Major has affairs?" she asks in my ear. "Because you can tell he's not into Naomi anymore."

"He's not the type," I whisper back. "He's straight as an

arrow." My antenna is up. It's never good when Zarine talks about attractive men while we're naked.

"I bet Blanche and Joshua have the most vanilla sex. I bet she falls asleep during. Or more likely, he does. Does a cock stay hard if its owner's slumbering?"

I laugh uneasily. She's never been with a man, and I'm not about to start sharing what I know of cocks and their owners. "Crazy to think they've actually fucked since they've been here."

She rears her head back. "How would you know that?"

Shit. I'd assumed that Zarine had the same deck of images as me. "From the exercise."

"You saw pictures of Blanche and Joshua having sex?" Zarine says loudly.

"I didn't ask for it, believe me."

She reaches out from under the sheets for her clothes. Emotional as she is, she's still modest enough to pull on her clothes under the covers as if we're in summer camp and she doesn't want anyone to see her budding breasts. That's why I'm obsessed with her. Even when she's out of control, she's still in it.

"I don't want anyone but you," I say. She's standing now, glowering down at me. "You know that. Please, come back to bed."

She takes a step away, eyes brimming with tears. "Those photos were chosen for you for a reason. You've been telling me I'm way off but obviously, the experts disagree. Who were you thinking about when we were together just now?"

I'm out of bed, moving toward her, knowing my naked body is in full view of the camera. Well, they can look but they can't listen. We're out of earshot of the mics (I hope). I say in Zarine's ear, "Those photos *were* chosen for a reason. To make us fight."

This season's different. But Zarine and I are the same.

ELEVEN

THE MAJOR

I'm not afraid of the results. Any red-blooded male would have responded to those images just like I did. Naomi will understand that. Besides, we're in a different situation than these other couples. In a way, we can be the most honest. We've got nothing left to lose.

It's entirely possible that what Sam and Dave (and Marla, always Marla) wanted was for me to refuse to participate, to out myself by saying the exercise offended my sensibilities. And it was offensive, no doubt about that, having to watch the sex acts of my fellow cast members while my bodily functions were measured, but I wasn't going to play into the producers' hands by being holier than thou.

Naomi and I sit on our loveseat companionably, while Joshua and Blanche are doing that death grip handhold of theirs and Tatiana and Zarine look fresh from some afternoon delight.

What worries me is Lauren. She's cried off her makeup again, revealing more angry red pimples, and she and Tristan are sitting farther apart today than yesterday. I don't know if she —or they—can survive another four days of this.

Sam and Dave take the floor. Time for them to make maximum drama out of a bunch of foolishness.

"Today," Sam says, "you were all given a uniquely curated set of images. They were designed to root out your subconscious desires, the ones that propel so many of your actions, and they're all the more powerful because you're entirely unaware of them."

I'm hoping to catch Naomi's eye, so I'll know that she finds this as ridiculous as I do, but she's fixed on the "experts."

"Let's start with Tristan and Lauren," Dave says. "Tristan, based on your results, you're physically attracted to Lauren, and you responded positively to images of supportive love and a devoted family." Dave shifts his attention to Lauren. "Lauren, your results were much more mixed and, frankly, troubling. You did respond positively to images of family, but not of connected couplehood. Your arousal levels were significantly higher when you were shown images of a man who didn't fit Tristan's physical profile."

All the color leaches from her face, and I'm afraid she might faint dead away.

I shouldn't be here, listening to this. None of us should. There's a reason therapy is supposed to be confidential. How come I hadn't realized just how sick it was when I watched the previous two seasons?

Naomi seems riveted.

Sam continues talking to Lauren. "Your results are suggestive of a person who is deeply ambivalent about romantic commitment, who is not monogamously inclined while still wanting a happy family. It's an almost schizophrenic presentation, this disconnect between what you want most and what you're capable of sustaining."

It's a scathing indictment delivered with clinical precision. Sam and Dave turn to the next loveseat, to Joshua and Blanche. Meanwhile, Lauren is shattered, a limp doll against the cushions. Like I said, I've always been a pacifist, but in that moment, I could tear Dave apart with my bare hands. At least Tristan has found his compassion, moving closer and speaking in her ear. She nods, and he takes her hand. Later, though, I imagine he'll get to thinking about what he's heard. Do Sam and Dave want to destroy their relationship? It sure looks like it.

"...Joshua seemed to have a particularly aversive reaction toward women with scars," Sam drones. In other words, I haven't missed much.

"What women?" Blanche cuts in. For once, she looks less than entirely composed. Not much less, but still.

"It was no one we know," Joshua tells her.

"Let's talk about you, Blanche," Sam says. "Your results were straightforward, for the most part, though you did exhibit higher levels of attraction to younger men than to your peers. You showed a preference for darker skin and hair." Hmm, like Tristan?

If Joshua is surprised or bothered, he isn't letting on.

Sam and Dave go into a spiel about the masks we all wear, and I start to zone out again. I come back, though, when she mentions my name.

"Cain, we found what we expected. You showed a low level of arousal regarding Naomi, a much higher level of arousal for white women, and a strong negative response to lesbian images."

What the...?

I feel Naomi staring at me. *Don't give them that to work with. We said no dramatic reaction shots.* They can take those and put them anywhere they want.

"Some of the masks we wear are because we don't know our deepest hearts," Dave says. "We don't even know they are masks. But sometimes we knowingly conceal ourselves." He looks around. "This whole process is predicated on honesty, and some of you have committed to it more than others. Cain and Naomi, you've given us no choice."

"Religion is a big part of your lives and identities back home," Sam says, "and your church has prohibitions against homosexuality, doesn't it?" She actually seems uncomfortable, like these are lines she hasn't scripted and would prefer not to deliver.

"We don't subscribe to every bit of church doctrine," Naomi says. "We're free thinkers. We make up our own minds."

"The results don't lie." Dave turns to me. "You didn't simply find the lesbian image less than stirring. You found it repugnant."

Tatiana shoots me a glare. Zarine doesn't deign to look in my direction. Zarine, who's perhaps the most beautiful woman I've ever seen. That's how I know that the results are either inaccurate, falsified, or flat out lies.

"None of this is true," I say.

"You're against gay relationships and gay marriage," Dave says. "You're against sex before marriage and having children outside of wedlock. You have strong views on adultery as well. Essentially, you think the majority of the other participants are going to hell."

Through the haze of my fury, I'm trying to formulate my response. That's when Sam lasers in on Naomi. "You showed high levels of arousal to the lesbian images that Cain rejected."

I know my wife. If they've forged my results, then they could easily have forged hers. Marla's fingerprints are all over this.

I look around. There's no denying it now. This year's cast is not like that of the previous two seasons. Lauren's constant crying, Tatiana and Zarine's hypersexuality, Blanche and Joshua's Blanche-and-Joshua-ness. And then there's Naomi and me, cast to be the right-wing foils.

Did Marla bring us all here to rescue our relationships or to destroy them? Are the viewers at home supposed to root for our success, or our demise?

This is a microcosm of the larger world we're living in. No one wants nice anymore. It's not about salvation or redemption or reconciliation. Truth is irrelevant. Now, it's about the bloody battle. Carnage, entrails, and viscera.

So for Season Three, Marla decided to flip the script.

God help us all.

TWELVE

BLANCHE

"There's an elephant in this room," The Major says.

There are a few elephants, actually, but I assume he's talking about the fact that he hates lesbians while his wife wants to switch teams. I put my fork down. I love dinner theater.

It's another serverless buffet, though there's a bartender mixing stiff drinks. The Major and Naomi are standing at the head of the table. If you didn't know better, you'd think he was about to give a holiday toast. "Naomi and I are Christians, that part's true. But like Jesus said, only people without sin should cast stones. We are not those people." He looks around at us, lingering an extra beat on Tatiana and Zarine. "We respect all of you and your life choices."

"Your subconscious sure doesn't," Tatiana says.

"Were the test results accurate about your subconscious?" Naomi counters. "Because you may be a flirt, but I don't believe you're interested in any men. I can see with my own eyes how much you love Zarine."

Well, that shut Tatiana up. Score one for Naomi.

"Sam and Dave talked about how they were seeing things

we didn't even know we felt. Doesn't that seem like a license to make things up?" Naomi continues. "They're acting like they know us better than we know ourselves. I'm forty-three years old. You think I wouldn't know if I wanted to sleep with women by now?"

"Don't knock it till you try it." I can't tell if Tatiana means it to be funny or aggressive.

"Did anyone else think their results were fishy?" The Major asks.

"Yes," Lauren says immediately while Tristan stares down at his plate.

I'm looking forward to our next cigarette break so I can ask how he's really feeling. Today he learned that the mother of his child isn't wife material. Better to find out before you put a ring on it.

"The results seemed fishy to me, too," Joshua says. It's the first time I'm hearing it. I'm not sure if it's what he thinks or an attempt to bond with the group. Joshua has a need to be liked by people who don't know him very well.

I notice in my peripheral vision that Tatiana is kneading the back of Zarine's neck. Zarine closes her eyes. Are they going to get off right here at the table?

"I can tell you're good people," Lauren says to The Major and Naomi, "and no exercise is going to change my mind. I don't think you're trying to judge or hurt or lie to any of us. Can we say the same for this show?"

It's a mic-drop moment. The Major's face is suffused with gratitude. Tristan whispers in her ear, but she shakes her head, shaking him off. "You all know I'm right," she says, "and I'm starving." She begins eating ravenously. Before this, I'd only seen her peck at her food.

In spite of myself, I'm intrigued.

When no one else offers an opinion, The Major says, "Well, thank you all for hearing us out."

For a while, the only sound is the scraping of cutlery against plates. I'm getting tired of acting like a conversational traffic controller at every meal. Someone else needs to step up.

The bartender has no wine, only the hard stuff, so with the exception of Lauren, we all have mixed drinks or straight whiskey. We down them quickly and they're replaced just as fast. The mood lightens considerably.

"What do you all think about a midnight swim?" Tatiana says.

Tristan laughs. "What is it, nine-thirty?"

"There's no way to tell. Anyone seen a clock in this place?" I gesture toward the walls.

"You know what this reminds me of?" Tatiana leans in conspiratorially. "The Agatha Christie novels I used to love. You know, everyone trapped together on a deserted island, disappearing one by one."

"So which of us will be the first to go?" The Major cocks an eyebrow in mock fiendishness.

"Lauren," I answer immediately. She seems a dash hurt. "Because you're the star."

"The star?" Now she looks confused. But she can't fool me into thinking she's some dumb blonde; I know wily when I see it.

"Who do you think's getting the most screen time?" I say. "All those tearful close-ups?"

"I think Blanche would be first to go," Tatiana says. "She looks like Laura Palmer in *Twin Peaks*."

"Wait, are we talking Agatha Christie or David Lynch? Pick your poison!" Joshua laughs too loudly. He's way drunk, I realize. Wait, so am I.

"I'd get it first," The Major says.

Naomi shoots him a look like he should keep quiet. Those two may not be closed-minded bigots like Sam and Dave were saying, but they're definitely hiding something.

Another lemon drop appears in front of me, and I suck it down greedily. Vacation has no calories.

"I don't think it's a mystery." Lauren's big eyes are solemn. "I think it's a thriller where someone is pulling all of our strings. The scary part is none of us *can* disappear. We can't go anywhere. We're stuck here being their lab rats."

"No one's pulling my strings," Tristan says.

"No one you can see." I've never heard Lauren contradict him before. It's like she has some liquid courage in her, though she's the only one of us who isn't imbibing.

"Any of you laid eyes on Marla since we arrived on the island?" The Major asks.

Dead silence. Do these people really think that just invoking her name could invite her wrath? Ridiculous. She's an executive producer, not the devil herself.

"I like Marla." Zarine glares at The Major, and I can see she hasn't forgiven him for today's exercise. "Perhaps your real turnoff is powerful women."

Naomi shakes her head. "He's got no problem there."

"But he doesn't want to have sex with you, now does he?" Zarine fires back.

We all freeze at the low blow. This wasn't supposed to be *that* kind of reality show. The drink-tossing, table-throwing kind.

"Are we really going to pretend we're all friends here?" Zarine gives each of us a challenging stare. "Are we really just a bunch of *actors*?" Tristan shifts in his chair but says nothing. Zarine stands up and looks at Tatiana. "I've had enough for one night. Are you coming?"

Tatiana keeps her eyes on her plate. "I feel like the party's just getting started."

Zarine lingers for a fraught thirty seconds. Then when she's gone, Tatiana asks the rest of us, "So how many of you have seen us?" I'm perplexed. "Today I saw some of you having sex, so I assume that some of you saw Zarine and me. Were Zarine and I the lesbian images The Major found so repellant?"

"Repugnant," I supply.

"I didn't," The Major protests. "I swear to you, I didn't."

"You didn't see us, or you didn't find us repugnant?"

"I saw you," he admits, embarrassed, "but it wasn't repugnant. Far from it." Naomi gives him the side-eye. "Hey, you thought it was sexy, too!"

She looks aghast. "My results were faked!"

"For Pete's sake," I say, "lots of straight women are turned on by lesbian porn. Or maybe you're bisexual, who gives a shit. Let's stay on topic. Tatiana, I didn't see you."

Lauren and Joshua say that they did. I glare at Joshua. Why didn't he tell me sooner?

"But it was tasteful," Joshua says to Tatiana.

"Probably as tasteful as the images I saw of Blanche riding you," Tatiana says.

What.

The.

Fuck?

Joshua and I haven't had sex in the villa, so I'd assumed we were safe during the exercise. Those images must have been from the night we arrived on the island. The fight. The makeup sex. The producers made us believe that filming hadn't started yet. They lied to us. Worst of all, they'd heard everything.

"Who else saw us?" I demand.

Tristan and Lauren raise their hands timidly. We didn't make the cut for Naomi and The Major.

"This is a violation!" I look to Joshua. We were misled. And spied on. "It was out of bounds. We were specifically told that they weren't filming us that first night and then they did it anyway. And used the footage." Why isn't he angry?

"Nothing is out of bounds," he says. "That contract gives

them carte blanche to do whatever they want. So let's not be assholes about it."

Is he trying to say "I told you so" about the fact that he wanted to leave and I insisted we stay, or is he reminding me of our asshole rule so I won't get myself in trouble right now? Normally I can read him like a book but he's currently inscrutable.

My best guess? He is angry. But not at Marla. At me.

"This is how it works," he says. "They put us through the wringer so we can leave happy."

"That's how it usually works," The Major says. "But doesn't it seem...?" He's posing the question to all of us.

Tatiana is the first to respond. "This season is different. I've felt it from the beginning, and I'm very intuitive."

"I don't know exactly what's come before, but I know that none of this is okay," Lauren says. "If they're faking the exercise, what else would they fake? We have to stay strong. We can't let them turn us against each other."

"Hear hear." The Major tosses back his scotch on the rocks.

I stare at Lauren, trying to figure out when she could have watched *Erin Brockovich*.

"The producers must want to top themselves this season," Tatiana says. "They don't care what happens to us."

"You do realize they can hear us?" Tristan asks. "That we're being filmed right now?"

It's amazing how quickly the crew can blend into the wallpaper in a dimmed room after four cocktails. Maybe five.

"They won't air this," Naomi says with authority. "It would make them look bad."

"Or make us look paranoid," Tristan counters.

"What if we go on strike?" Tatiana has to look around for support, since Zarine deserted her. "You know, for better working conditions."

"We just got here," Tristan says. "What if they boot us all

and bring in a whole new cast? They'd probably sue us for wasting their time, and they'd win. I don't have that kind of money."

"They don't want that kind of publicity," The Major says, though he doesn't sound completely sure.

"What would our demands even be?" Tristan continues. "That we get prior approval on exercises? That we can dictate the therapy sessions? It'd never work."

"Let's not just dismiss it out of hand," Naomi says. "Not after what they pulled today. Who knows what they've got in store for us tomorrow?"

"We've all had a lot to drink, it's been a long day, we're under stress." Joshua sounds reasonable but he's starting to slur. "Let's leave it be and have some fun."

Tatiana shakes her head, disgusted. "You really are a Ken doll, aren't you? No balls at all."

It annoys me that he looks so wounded. Who cares what Tatiana thinks?

"Whatever we do," she says, "we need to do it together." She lifts her glass. "To safety in numbers."

We all drink. And because we're marooned on a desert island with our very own bartender, we drink some more.

Then, somehow, we're laughing at nothing and everything. The night feels infinite, no one is sure how long production will let this go on. Maybe they're as curious as we are about where it'll all end up. Maybe no one's really driving this bus.

Lauren is attempting to work her magic on me, telling me how much she loves my style, asking where I buy my clothes and which salon does my hair. I'm onto her, though. She tries to make men feel big and strong; she tries to make women feel beautiful and admired. Her one-down routine drives me crazy because it's working so well with the others. Hell, it's the life's blood of her relationship with Tristan. For all I know, the viewers at home have already fallen for it, seeing as the episodes have already started airing.

I turn away and stumble into a diatribe by The Major. He's saying that the world has gone to pot, that civility has taken its last bow, that kindness has become a rare commodity, that blind obedience to a false authority might end us all.

"What, you think we're going to be smote or something?" Joshua asks, then laughs loudly. The Major doesn't.

Naomi puts a restraining hand on his arm. "This probably isn't the right time." Or the right audience. Joshua is the last person to think about his soul.

You can see The Major wants to keep talking but is loath to defy her. It seems to be true, what she said earlier about him not having a problem with powerful women, but it might also be true that he doesn't want to touch her anymore. Are those two related?

Another round of drinks, and we're feeling no pain. But I do feel a hand on my knee.

Joshua's, though I like to imagine that it belongs to someone else. Since Joshua's talking to Lauren, I'm able to focus on Tristan. I can't stop staring into his eyes, which appear onyx in the low light.

"How are you holding up?" I ask.

"My whole life, people have said I should go to therapy and I've avoided it and now I see why."

"Why?"

"What do you mean, why?" We're too inebriated for a decent conversation, this is becoming a who's-on-first routine, but I suddenly realize I've been waiting all night for this moment.

"Why did people tell you to go to therapy?" I clarify.

"Because of what I've been through with my family. But there are other ways to handle things besides talking about them."

"I hear you. People assumed I should go because of what happened to my father, and because of how my mother is." Wait, have I told Tristan anything yet about my parents? I can't remember. "But that's them, not me. I'm fine."

"Yeah, you are."

The hand pulses on my knee. Meanwhile, Joshua seems quite engaged in conversation with Lauren. What could those two be talking about so intently?

It doesn't matter. I've got Tristan all to myself.

"My biggest fear is that no matter how hard I try, my kids will wind up hating me," I say.

"That'll never happen. No one could hate you. I just hope that someday I get to see you with your kids."

It's possibly the most romantic thing anyone has ever said to me, only it's followed by the unwelcome interruption of Joshua's breath in my ear. "Let's go upstairs."

I push his hand off my knee. "I'm not tired."

Lauren's eyes are on me. I can tell that whatever she's seen between Tristan and me hasn't been to her liking. That means my connection to Tristan is visible; it's not only in my head. I start to smile, though I'm unlikely to remember much of this in the morning. It might be better that way. There's no point in getting ideas.

"We should all go upstairs," Naomi nearly purrs to The Major.

"I'm good where I am," he says stiffly. But it's the wrong kind of stiff.

"Come on." Naomi walks her fingers up his arm. "We've barely had a minute to ourselves all day."

"You don't have to prove anything to me. I know you're not gay." I think he meant to speak softly but with that voice of his, we all hear.

Naomi jumps back as if she's been struck. Then she stalks out of the room.

"Sorry," The Major says. "That's not normally how we act."

"Who's 'we'?" Tatiana is ready to pounce. "Was that Christian of you, rejecting your wife in front of a room full of people, in front of millions of people?"

"Don't do this," he says. "Don't give them what they want. The lesbian versus the Christian."

"Don't tell her what to do," Joshua says. I gape at him. Joshua's courteous, not chivalrous. He doesn't stand up to people who could wreck his pretty face. "I go to church twice a year, if that, and I still know better than to look down on people."

"Who am I looking down on?" The Major seems more bewildered than angry.

Joshua's on his feet now like he's spoiling for a fight. What has gotten into him? Countless martinis, that's what. "I hate hypocrites."

The Major's up, too. They're chest to chest.

I look around for a producer to intercede. It's only camera and sound guys in the room who can't risk interfering with the shot. Normally, producers are hovering at the periphery but I haven't seen one for an awfully long time.

Are they all watching from the control room? Or have they gone to bed and left us to our own devices?

"Let's all chill out," I manage.

The Major and Joshua are bumping into each other like neither wants to back down, but maybe they don't want to go further, either.

"This is fucking hot," I hear Tatiana saying to no one in particular. Two men fighting over her. Or are they? What are they even fighting about, really?

I should be saying something, or doing something, but I'm just too dizzy.

Fortunately, Tristan is on his feet now, too. "We're sticking together, remember? Safety in numbers?"

After a pause, The Major steps backward and thrusts his hand out. Another pause, and Joshua shakes it. I'm mostly relieved. I mean, it's not like I wanted Joshua to get his ass kicked or anything.

"As long as we stick together, we're going to be okay," Lauren says.

I roll my eyes, hoping that she'll be the first to disappear.

Continuing interview between Detective Sonya Mohr and producer Julie Lindstrom, taking place on Glass Island.

Detective: Marla told me about trying to get a certain cast chemistry, that it's an art and a science.

Julie: It sure is, if the science is eugenics.

Detective: Meaning?

Julie: Three seasons, twelve couples, and the first and only stab at diversity is an incredibly hot foot surgeon with multiple Ivy League degrees who's also a member of our first gay couple.

Detective: Were you there the night of the "drunken dinner," as you called it, to see how the cast chemistry played out?

Julie: They cut me at ten and the more senior producers took over. But I experienced the aftermath. The drunken dinner was when it started. The us versus them mentality. I mean, they—the cast—were the *us*, and people who worked on the show were *them*.

Detective: Is that unusual?

Julie: This is my first reality show but from what I understand, cast members typically bond with production right away and it lasts throughout the shoot. They're in an unfamiliar and stressful environment where they feel dependent and the producers act like friends. They might also think being liked by production can prevent an unkind edit.

The truth is, the producer is a slave to the storyboard. I learned the hard way that our job is to get the footage by any means necessary.

Detective: So what changed after the drunken dinner, specifically?

Julie: No one trusted their producers anymore, except for Lauren with me, and I wish she hadn't. Brandon was having a hard time getting anything he could use in the confessional.

Detective: The confessional was where the private interviews took place?

Julie: Yes, that's where the cast members are supposed to comment on everything that's happening. Sometimes they'd spill their secrets; sometimes they'd spill other people's. But that came to a grinding halt.

Detective: Why did they ever do it to begin with? They know they're on camera, and that contract offers zero protection.

Julie: Maybe it's Stockholm syndrome. You have to remember that they have cameras on them twenty-four/seven so it gets normalized very quickly. Some are used to oversharing on social media anyway. It just starts to seem inevitable that they'll let their guards down, especially when their producers keep flattering them.

Plus, Brandon's really good at working the confessional—he's got a lot of tricks for eliciting compliance, basically—only after the drunken dinner, he said it was like dealing with hostile witnesses.

Detective: So the cast did try to go on strike?

Julie: They did. But then they came face to face with Marla.

THIRTEEN
LAUREN

Day Four

"I have a surprise for you!" Julie's excitement sounds forced. We're in the hall and once she opens the door to my room, I'm introduced to my glam squad, two women who've been flown to the island just for me: an esthetician to help with my acne and a professional makeup artist.

If Marla still wants me to look good, that means she's still invested in how I'm being perceived. Which could mean that she doesn't know about Alexei and that picture wasn't him, it was a fluke. Or she knows but it's never going to air.

Maybe going on strike isn't the best decision for me. I was the one pushing hardest last night, but I need to keep my options open. Blanche seems to think I'm the favored child, and she could be right.

I lie down on the portable massage table as the esthetician goes to work. I can tell she's a seasoned professional because she senses and respects that I'm in no mood for small talk. That was a key skill for me to master when I became a stylist, reading clients' cues and knowing when to chatter away and when to shut up. I'm not the best at cutting hair but I make some of the highest tips. It occurs to me that reality television might be a service industry. The question is, who am I serving?

While my face is steamed and my pores vacuumed, I think back to last night. Seeing Blanche flirt with Tristan, I'd felt this surge of desire. Not need, because I often feel like I need him, but instead, I wanted him so much that when we finally got upstairs to bed, I was the one to initiate sex, which practically never happens. He'd been in no condition, with all the drinking. But still, if I felt that kind of desire once, then I can feel it again. This process is working after all. I just have to make sure that he never finds out about Alexei.

I don't like thinking this way, I'm not some catty bitch, but there might be another threat on the island. Blanche wanted nothing to do with me last night; she was all about Tristan. And if it hadn't been for Joshua's reaction, I might have been able to convince myself that their flirting was no big deal. But there was Joshua, watching, and Blanche had been too absorbed in her conversation with Tristan to notice. Tristan had been pretty absorbed, too.

Joshua's look of hurt and anger was the realest thing I've seen from him so far. He seemed to be thinking out loud when he said about Blanche, "She makes the rules. But she can always break them when it suits her." I asked what he meant, and he backtracked: "I do love her, you know."

"I can tell." Only in that moment, though. Before, I'd wondered. About both of them.

He got visibly sadder, like he was shrinking before my eyes. "The thing is, she's right almost all the time. If I just listened to her..." Then he shook his head and smiled and put his game face back on. "If any of us were perfect, none of us would be here, right?"

That's what he does in therapy all the time, strings words together meaninglessly, wraps things up rather than unpacking them. I feel like he's scared of going deeper. Or maybe he's scared of Blanche. She does seem formidable, and she's determined to project a certain image.

Yet that last line had managed to strike a chord with me, how imperfect we all are. I thought once again about what Sam and Dave said about a couple's pathologies being a lock and a key. Maybe some couples fit together when they shouldn't. When they'd be better off picking someone else's lock.

Once the extractions are done, the makeup artist gets to work. It's not quick but the results are worth it. When I examine myself in the mirror, I can't find the puffy, acne-riddled girl from yesterday. Instead, I see a woman Tristan won't be able to resist.

Julie comes back in and does a double take so exaggerated that I have to laugh. "You look incredible! How do you feel?"

"A lot better."

"We should get you down to breakfast."

I follow her out and then on an impulse, I pull my microphone off, leaving it in the corner nearest my room, and lead her down the hall. I don't know if it's safe to talk to the therapists but Julie cares about me. Otherwise, she wouldn't have been so torn up after the exercise.

"I need to know," I say, desperation coating every syllable. "That dick pic, was it a coincidence?"

"I—I'm not sure what you mean." Julie's stammer tells me otherwise.

"The dick pic," I repeat. "Is it going to come back and bite me later this week?"

Julie looks down, clearly conflicted. She must know that was Alexei. That means Marla does, too, and is going to decide whether to expose me. It's still possible that she won't because isn't the whole premise of the show that Tristan and I—that all the couples—will end up together?

I should have come clean to Tristan before we came here. No, I should never have done it at all.

I'd handed over my phone to Julie so carelessly. Handed over my life to Marla. And now that I'm more into Tristan than ever before, I'm the closest I've ever been to losing him.

I feel myself welling up and I will myself not to cry. I can't afford to ruin this makeup.

Even after knowing about Alexei, I see that Julie's still in my corner. If I don't tell someone the truth, I'm going to burst.

"Tristan and I had only been together a little while before I got pregnant, and the whole time, I kept thinking it was going to fall apart. When he told me he loved me, I thought, 'That's because you don't really know me, because you haven't figured out that I'm not worth anything.' I mean, no other guy thought I was. How could they all be wrong?"

"They *were* wrong." Julie sounds surprisingly fierce.

"I've been afraid to love Tristan because if he started to treat me like the other guys, it would kill me, okay? But this journey or process or whatever is working. My walls or whatever are coming down. So there are things that he can't know, not yet. Not ever. Do you get what I'm saying?"

"Maybe you'd feel better if you told him. Then you'd know your relationship is strong enough to survive anything."

"Tell him here? On camera? He doesn't deserve that kind of public exposure. I do, but he doesn't."

"You deserve a lot more than you think."

I wipe at my eyes. "I'm ready to try for more."

Julie grabs me in a hug. "There are two possibilities," she whispers in my ear. "You've been sabotaging yourself. Or Tristan's not the one."

I think back to how Blanche looked when she was talking to Tristan last night. How I felt watching them. The whole country is probably already in love with him, and his acting career is going to shoot into the stratosphere. His agent said so.

"Who wouldn't be into Tristan? Only someone with major issues."

"I can't tell you what's coming next, but you have to listen to your gut. Trust yourself. Love yourself."

She lets go of me and the conversation is over. I thank her, put on my microphone, and go down to breakfast, where everyone else is just finishing up. Tatiana and Zarine are noticeably absent and the others seem subdued. Tristan gives me a look of appreciation that feels obligatory (though it's possible that I'm just feeling raw from the recent sexual rejection). Blanche goes on at length about how beautiful I am, sounding sincere. Could I have imagined last night's cold shoulder? Beneath her effusion, she looks washed out and exhausted and obviously hasn't been given her own makeup artist.

She's right, I'm the star. Marla wouldn't shoot down her star, would she?

The ten-minute warning blares on the intercom. I'm relieved that there's so little time to talk, and I decide that scrambled eggs will be easiest to eat quickly without disturbing my makeup. Tatiana shows up with wet hair. She munches on a donut and goes on about the joys of swimming naked, with no mention of Zarine.

"I wish I could skinny dip in broad daylight," Blanche says, which is weird since she has an awesome body. Maybe she's fishing for compliments.

Joshua squeezes her hand. Even during meals, they often hold hands, which is also weird. Like, they cut their food and then clasp again. It might not be some great love that holds them together but there could be other adhesives that are just as strong.

I try to catch The Major's eye. He's a natural leader, and other than Tristan, he's the person I feel closest to. I'd gone onto the balcony this morning in hopes of another chat but no such luck. I'm a little worried that everyone either blacked out or blocked out last night, that the talk about Marla's dishonesty might not have been as memorable for them. Since I don't know for sure what she's planning to do about Alexei, I need reasonable doubt—and the other cast members—on my side.

"Report to the group therapy room!"

This seems foreboding. I'd been hoping for the sunlit great room rather than the gray chamber of horrors. But I file downstairs with the others. At the very last second, Zarine slips in, not looking at anyone, though Tatiana seems desperate to catch her eye. Had Tatiana's morning skinny dip been a bid for attention, with the vain hope that Zarine would watch from the balcony?

Once inside, it becomes evident that no one has forgotten last night. No matter what Sam and Dave ask, they're met with either silence or vague answers that give away nothing, à la Joshua.

But Sam and Dave seem unfazed. Of course they are; they must have been briefed. They can always be five steps ahead of us, it's their island. Theirs, and Marla's.

"We're going to need to break through this resistance," Dave says. On cue, a screen descends from the ceiling.

It's footage from the previous night. There's the fight between The Major and Joshua, with Tatiana saying it's hot, and there are Tristan and Blanche deep in conversation, with a close-up of a hand on her leg under the table.

"I'm not allowed to touch my wife?" Joshua says with an unusual edge to his voice.

"You're absolutely allowed to touch your wife," Dave says. "We encourage it. Only you didn't."

"Sure I did."

"Look at the seating. That's not the side you were on, was it?" The camera zooms in. "See, no wedding ring."

"That's because it's my right hand!"

"I know my husband's hand," Blanche says. "I know his touch."

My heart sinks. Dave pounces. "Lauren, do you recognize that hand?"

"I must have thought it was Lauren's knee," Tristan says. He looks at me imploringly. "I'd had how many drinks by that point?"

"He wouldn't do that." Regardless of the pit in my stomach, I need to speak up. "He's the most loyal man alive. Someone must have doctored the footage. Just like they doctored the results from the exercise yesterday."

"That is an outrageous accusation." Sam tries to bore holes in me with her alien eyes. I feel myself quaking inside.

"Not as outrageous as turning us into porn stars without our consent," Blanche says.

The enemy of my enemy is my friend. As my mother used to say.

"We have the right to use unorthodox methods to break through your denial," Sam says. Like an expert markswoman, she aims her rifle scope at Naomi. "I noticed you were working out with Joshua this morning in just your sports bra and shorts. You couldn't get attention from your husband last night, so you had to seek it elsewhere?"

"You don't know me," Naomi says, "if you'd think something like that."

"Cain rejected you in front of everyone last night. Then he and Joshua played whose-dick-is-bigger over Tatiana," Dave summarizes, before casting his eyes over to Zarine. "You missed a lot last night."

"I didn't miss a thing," Zarine says stonily.

Tatiana hasn't moved a muscle in I don't know how long, and her face has gone pale. Now she's in Sam's scope. "You obviously enjoyed the fireworks last night between Cain and Joshua."

"It wasn't the way you're making it look," Tatiana says, just above a whisper.

"We seem to have a lot of lying cameras in this house." Dave's tone is mild.

"You had the bartender there on purpose," Tatiana sputters. "You wanted us to be overserved."

"You're saying you're not responsible for what you do when you're drunk?" Sam asks. "Some would argue that with lowered inhibitions, you show your truest self."

Tatiana swallows. "Zarine and I need to talk in private."

"I'm quite curious," Zarine says. "Since it's not how it looked, why don't you go ahead and tell me how it really was?"

"I can't do this." Tatiana stands up, on the verge of tears. "I'm hungover, I'm confused—"

"I would have thought you'd be refreshed and restored after your morning swim," Zarine says. "Was that for my benefit, or for theirs?" She indicates Joshua and The Major.

Tatiana runs out. We all look to Zarine, assuming she'll follow. She sits back in her chair, recrossing her legs.

"Who's going to bring her back?" Sam asks the rest of us. "This is a pivotal moment. We can get to the core of her issues. Are you here to help each other or not?"

Joshua gets to his feet. For a second, Blanche's disgust shows through before she papers over it. I know exactly how she feels. So much for strength in numbers. This is definitely not the crew you want in your foxhole.

"Thank you, Joshua." Sam smiles. "It's good to see someone is fully committed to the process."

FOURTEEN

TATIANA

My stomach lurches when I hear the knock at the door. I'm not ready to face Zarine. I can't keep explaining myself.

Sometimes it feels like there's no way to win. I'm supposed to be wild and free and fun—her entertainment, Sam and Dave would say—until I cross some line in her mind. But I'm not the kind of girl who runs out of rooms crying. What is this house doing to me? To us?

"Come in," I say, steeling myself.

It's not Zarine. It's Joshua, of all people. So not my type, regardless of gender, but there's no convincing Zarine of that.

It's like I'm seeing the condition of the room for the first time, seeing the wreckage, through someone else's eyes. The curtains are drawn, glasses tipped over, clothes everywhere, and hair extensions on the floor like cat tails.

"Sorry, I wasn't expecting company." I excavate two chairs and place them far away from each other.

He remains standing. "I'm supposed to bring you back to therapy."

"Oh, really? And how are you supposed to do that? Caveman-style?" I sit down. "Well, I'm not going anywhere."

If I were him, I'd want a break, too. Last night it had been pretty obvious Blanche was salivating after Tristan but the idea that Tristan might be attracted back... well, that's a plot twist I hadn't seen coming.

Joshua doesn't so much sit as perch, which is pretty comical since he's over six feet tall and absurdly handsome. There's a goofy charm to it, like when I was a little girl and my dad would have pretend tea parties with me, this big guy with his pinkie out.

Wow, I haven't thought of that memory in ages. He could be sweet, my father, when he wasn't so busy getting married.

I twine my fingers in my hair. Well, what Joshua now knows isn't really my hair. "Did Zarine say anything after I left?"

He averts his eyes. "I'm sure she wants you to come back."

"Not enough to get me herself, though?"

"She must really love you."

"How would you know?"

"My room is on the other side of yours. We share a wall." As in, he hadn't just seen the images; he must have heard (and perhaps visualized) a lot more. "You two can't live without each other. And not in a pay-the-bills-raise-the-kids way."

"Zarine pays all the bills. I can't even justify it with kids."

"Aren't you a massage therapist?"

"I trained to be one, I'm not really anything." I hear how pathetic it sounds and wish I could take it back but it's already out there, recorded for posterity. "It's not for lack of trying. I've taken all different classes and courses and certifications. I was almost a paramedic. Almost a landscape artist. Almost an animal trainer. Almost a taxidermist." His eyebrows shoot up. "Just checking to see if you were paying attention."

"So what happens in between the training and the doing?"

"I say that I'm bored, that I can't imagine committing a whole life to just that one thing, but it's probably more that I get scared. I start to doubt myself. Every time, it's worse. I'm older, and I've set the bar too high. Made the stakes too high. Like, why this, and none of the others? I'm just going to fail anyway." I look away. "Sorry for babbling."

There was some strategy in going on that long, being so dull and introspective. It doesn't fit my character. Marla will never use it.

Joshua, though, seems transfixed. "So you haven't failed then; you've never tried. Does Zarine encourage you?"

"She's totally supportive. She says I don't need to work."

His eyes are warm on my face. "Does she say, 'You can do it'? Or 'It's okay if you fail, just keep going'? Or 'I believe in you'?"

"You have to understand how she grew up. Her parents moved from New Delhi to L.A. so she could have opportunities. Failure was not an option. She fulfilled their every expectation, Ivy League all the way." I laugh bitterly. "Every expectation except one. By now, she was supposed to have married a man. Or at the very least, be with a more accomplished woman."

"Sounds like Zarine doesn't want you to accomplish anything. She wants you barefoot and pregnant, minus the pregnant."

Upset as I am with Zarine, I can't believe that. "You don't know her."

"She doesn't want to be known. She's barely spoken to any of us. All I'm saying is, you should have someone in your corner to tell you you're amazing, you can do anything."

He seems like he means it, and I'm embarrassed to admit I like hearing it. "You don't know me either."

"I think I do." His gaze is so intent that I almost fall for it. "I get what it's like to be with someone and feel like you can never measure up. You want to prove them wrong but you feel so bad that you can't stop proving them right. It's this fucking hamster wheel and you can't get off."

"Did you come to the island to get off?" I ask.

I realize a second too late how suggestive that sounds, though for once, it was purely accidental. He does this little smile, which manages to be impish and a touch forlorn and not at all perverted. "In college, I had to read this story by Samuel Beckett and it had this great quote you might recognize: 'Try again. Fail again. Fail better.'" Huh. Where have I heard that before? "I came here to fail better."

"That's... really depressing."

He laughs. "It sounded better in my head."

"Want to sit here for a while and not talk? I could use some companionable silence."

He stands up and crosses the room, drawing back the curtains and opening the balcony doors. "Light and air," he says with a smile.

We spend a few glorious minutes staring out to sea, minutes where nothing is being asked of me, where I don't have to worry about Zarine or the producers' intentions. Then Joshua comes and squats beside me. He covers his microphone with his hand and whispers in my ear, "I know it's been a long time, but you really don't recognize me?"

I study his face at close range, my heart beating faster.

That's when Brandon comes in. "We need you both downstairs."

He might have been outside the door, awaiting Marla's signal. If she doesn't want the conversation to continue, it could be because she wants a big reveal later. Maybe Joshua wasn't supposed to tip me off. The fact is, I don't recognize him, but I have a bad feeling about where I might have made his acquaintance.

Is it a coincidence that we've both been cast, or a trap?

"Come on, guys. Please," Brandon pleads. They do that sometimes, make us feel like they're going to get reamed out by whoever's above them in the pecking order. We're supposed to save them.

And annoyingly, it works.

"It was fun while it lasted," I say, standing up.

Everyone has relocated to the great room and they're on their respective loveseats. I have to make a choice as I take my spot beside Zarine: my pride or my happiness. I snuggle in and tell her, "Don't let them drive us apart. I love you more than anything. It's you and me, baby."

I'm holding my breath until she whispers back, "I'm not ready to let you go." Then she gives me a kiss that makes my vision blur.

There's no time to savor our reunion because as Sam and Dave start to explain it's Parents Day, a time to explore where so many of our issues and patterns originated. I can see the freight train coming. But I don't see how I can get us off the tracks.

The producers did an extensive background check. At my urging, Zarine had been willing to let them invade her life, submitting to a medical exam and filling in about a million bubbles on the personality inventories and psychological tests. She said they could call anyone they wanted except her parents since Zarine hasn't come out to them yet. Marla had given Zarine her word, but what's that really worth?

"No!" I say. "You can't do this!"

Dave and Sam turn to me, all innocence.

"Don't bring them out."

"Bring who out?" Zarine's lost about twenty years of maturity and breeding in a matter of seconds.

"They flew here all the way from India," Dave says. "They want to be part of this experience."

"What would we tell them?" Sam asks.

"Tell them this has all been a mistake. Your mistake." Zarine's on her feet now, headed toward Sam and Dave, ready to appeal to their compassion. It's so naïve and misguided that it's hard to watch. But no one at home will be able to look away.

"You motherfuckers!" I shriek. "You promised!"

"I didn't make any promises," Sam says.

"This is a clinical decision." Dave has pasted this simpering expression on his face, like he aches for Zarine, but really, you know he's relishing the impending crash.

Zarine's unable to speak. I have to do it for her. "You can't," I say. "You're supposed to be helping us. Zarine only signed on because the show doesn't air in India."

Five years ago, her parents had moved back to India. They'd never acclimated to the U.S., and they'd only stayed for Zarine. I've never met them. The whole topic is incredibly painful for Zarine, and to be avoided. This has to be killing her.

"You can't do this," I repeat. "You can't destroy a family."

"They want to be here," Dave says. "They've missed their daughter. My understanding is that she hasn't visited in several years. They have a lot to say."

"This has been a long time coming." Sam turns to Zarine. "You need to tell them who you really are and defend your relationship with Tatiana."

"They know who I really am." But she already sounds defeated, not Zarine-like at all.

"How can they know who you are if they don't know who you love?" Sam asks.

"You and Tatiana have so much conflict because you're in conflict with yourself," Dave tag-teams.

I look to the other cast members. They should stand up for Zarine now because they're next.

"This is vile," The Major pronounces, his lip curling. The others nod with varying degrees of intensity but they can't stop this any more than I can. So much for safety in numbers.

"Tell your parents the truth and set yourself free," Sam says. "You'll be amazed how your insecurities will vanish. You'll be like a new person."

"She's already told them that she's attracted to women," I

say. "She just doesn't flaunt it. Besides, it's totally immoral to out people. What year is this?"

"I'm not outing her; I'm inviting her into a life of truth and authenticity." Sam looks at me with pity. "You do know that you're fighting to keep yourself a dirty secret?"

"This is happening," Dave says gently. "Zarine has a choice to make."

Less than a minute later, two aged people walk into the living room. The man is stooped, his skin dark and weathered, his hair entirely gray, wearing a long shirt over loose-fitting pants. The woman is in a red sari with her gray-black hair in a bun. They're like two burned out bulbs next to Zarine's incandescence. In the pictures I've seen, they're much younger and more vibrant. Now I can see why Zarine is inclined to shield them. It takes a lot out of you to hear a truth that you're not ready for.

And it's evident how much they love her. They've hurried forward to embrace her, smiling and crying.

"We're very excited to meet your significant other!" her father says. They look past me and around the room, trying to figure out which of the men in attendance is here with Zarine.

She stares at the floor. I'm powerless. If I try to help her, I expose our relationship. Sam and Dave are right about one thing: This needs to be her choice.

"You shouldn't have come," she says quietly.

"We wanted to see you," her mother responds. "We wanted to meet the man who is so important to you."

Zarine doesn't lift her head as she says, "It's a woman."

I'm in a skintight leotard with cutouts and a miniskirt. If I'd known they were coming, I would have dressed for the occasion. As it is, I'd hesitate to introduce me, too. But this is what Zarine likes. She wants me to be what she never could.

Because they've inadvertently confined her. Their love has caged her. She chose me to set her free.

I step forward. "I'm Tatiana."

They try not to look shocked, or appalled. "Hello," her father says formally.

"I love your daughter very much."

"They're here to work on their relationship," Sam interjects. "They want to spend their lives together."

"Is this true, Zarine?" her mother says. "You want to marry a woman?"

"We haven't talked about marriage," Zarine says, her eyes on the floor.

"You've hid your life from us." Her mother's disappointment and sadness are palpable. "Why would you do that?"

"It's not about gay or not gay," her father says. "It's about lies."

"How could I tell you? You don't want to hear that I love a woman."

You can tell they're hurting, for themselves and for her. They want to be okay with this, and with me.

I'm filled with anger toward Marla, Sam, and Dave. I won't get another chance to meet Zarine's parents for the first time.

"This is fucked up," I say, startling her parents. "I'm sorry, it just shouldn't have happened this way. You should have visited us in Santa Monica and seen where we live, seen what we're really like together—" I stop short as Zarine glares at me.

"You live together?" her mother asks.

Zarine hangs her head again.

"Tell them about the shame, Zarine," Dave instructs. "Tell them about the insecurity and the jealousy and the fighting."

"That's what your relationship is like?" Her mother seems on the verge of tears.

"We need to get you out of here at once." Her father is also distraught. "You obviously don't belong together."

"We do belong together!" I turn to Zarine. "Tell him. Tell

him how you really feel about me. When we're good, we're so good. We're perfect."

Zarine has tears streaming down her face. She looks from her parents to me and back again and then, seemingly in a daze, she heads for the double doors that lead to the pool area. I watch her jump in fully clothed, half-dazed myself.

When I realize what's happening, I run outside and leap in, finding her at the bottom. I grab her and stroke my way up and over to the side. She doesn't resist but she's not swimming either. I tug her out, calling for help. She's sputtering and lying prone beside me, like she doesn't have any will left in her body. A medic appears and I make room for him.

As he prepares to check her vital signs, I see the other couples gathered by the doors, watching. Zarine's parents are clutching each other, shaken. Sam and Dave are talking to them, probably trying to reassure them that their daughter is in excellent hands. The entire crew—fifty people at least—has assembled on set. This is where the action is. But Marla's nowhere in sight.

"Marla!" I yell. "You bitch! Where are you? Where the fuck are you?"

FIFTEEN

THE MAJOR

Naomi's head is buried in my chest. "What if that were Rebecca or Rachel?" I murmur into her hair.

"Rebecca or Rachel would never..." She doesn't finish the sentence.

"You don't think they could ever be gay, or that they'd ever tell us? Or you don't think they would ever try to kill themselves?"

She steps away as if she fears contagion. "Don't, Cain. Not here."

"Yes. Here."

The one good thing about all the mayhem is that the production team has been deployed outside. Naomi and I can finally really talk since she's got nowhere to hide. No clients to train or friends to see. No more excuses or avoidance tactics.

At dinner last night, I didn't like being shushed, though I understood. She's trying to protect me and our family. She doesn't want me on camera ranting about the end of days. But I've been trying to tell her for months now that it's the world that's crazy, not me. Does she need any more proof than what we've just witnessed?

"Zarine had a breakdown right in front of us," I say. "Because that's what they wanted."

"No one wanted that to happen," Naomi says. "It was an exercise that went wrong, that's all."

"That's all?" I can feel my eyes starting to bulge.

See, this is what she does. She deflects, she punts, she sticks her head in the sand. That's why I end up feeling more alone when she's in bed next to me, why I've been falling asleep on the couch downstairs with the TV on for the past year. I guess I've been hiding, too.

But I'm not anymore. I'd be okay if this conversation aired, same as last night's. The problem isn't the talking, it's when you stop talking. That's where Naomi and I have been for a while.

"This show is the world, writ small. Treating vulnerability like a commodity, everyone scheming and screaming, monetizing the ugly." I'm pleading with her. If she could understand me right now, maybe this could turn out okay. Maybe I wouldn't have to enact the rest of the plan.

Naomi is staring at me like she's got no idea what I'm even talking about. Like she doesn't know who I am.

That's when Sam and Dave reenter the room and take the floor. "Sit down, please," they say. Naomi listens, as do the others. I remain standing.

"I know that was highly upsetting," Sam understates, "but I want to assure you that we've got this. Dave and I aren't the only mental health professionals on staff. At times like this, protocols kick in. There are well-trained, talented therapists doing triage with Zarine and Tatiana right now."

"Where are they?" Lauren asks, since the pool area is now a ghost town.

"At an undisclosed location. They're getting help, I can promise you that."

I let out a derisive snort. Tatiana said that Marla had broken her promise. We can't trust a thing out of these people's mouths.

"We're doing something radical here," Dave says. "That's why it works. It blasts through the entrenched patterns in your life and in your relationships. Cookie-cutter therapy can't break through walls and defenses as thick as Zarine's. You all came here because you needed something extreme."

"You came here because you saw this process work for all your predecessors," Sam adds. "Eight other couples who now have the relationships you want. But to get there, you have to do as we say."

"What's going to happen to Tatiana?" Joshua asks. "Is she coming back?" You know it's bad when even a self-absorbed, superficial tool like Joshua sounds concerned. But then, he was willing to face off with me last night over Tatiana, so he might be capable of feelings after all, just not toward his wife.

"Both Zarine and Tatiana are going to receive full psychological evaluations." Dave's tone is soothing. "They'll need to get medical clearance to return."

"None of you would have been chosen if you weren't strong enough," Sam says. "You can handle what we throw at you."

I catch Lauren's eye. I would have thought she was the least equipped to handle any of this but she's the calmest I've seen her, while Tristan seems rattled. He's actually leaning into her. It's a role reversal I hadn't seen coming. Is it possible that there really is a method to the therapists' madness?

There's no justification for this kind of cruelty. "You will be judged, you know," I tell Sam and Dave.

"Cain, no," Naomi hisses. "Sit down."

I ignore her, taking a step toward Sam and Dave. "Anger is an appropriate response to what we just saw. You don't take those kinds of risks with other people's lives. These two are playing God."

But before they have to answer for it, a voice enters the room. It's coming through hidden speakers, surrounding us.

That voice is mine.

It must be someone impersonating me because I never said those things. No, it's someone impersonating my father. Ever since I grew into my voice, I've sounded like him. I told Marla that; I've told them all too much.

"A man's first duty is to his family. The measure of a man is how he takes care of his wife. You've got to treat her better than you treat yourself because that's what it means to be godly."

Only here I am, living a lie, pretending to work on my marriage.

I know that my dead father isn't speaking to me, and yet, they're just the things he would have said. Where did they get the script? Could Naomi have...?

"A time of upheaval is a time of transformation. You can't become despondent or discouraged. *Discouraged*—that's the opposite of courage. You don't give up."

My rational mind knows it's not really him, that this has Marla's fingerprints all over it.

But the timing, after the spectacle I've just witnessed, the murder of Zarine's family, which I'd done little to stop—no, it's worse than that. I've borne witness. And I'm still here, letting them do this to me and to Naomi. She's a good wife, a good woman, and my father is right, I'm supposed to protect her. Only I can't seem to protect anyone. No one in this whole wide ugly world.

I put my hands over my ears and pray for it to stop.

SIXTEEN

BLANCHE

Give credit where credit's due: Sam and Dave are finally getting to me. This place has turned into a demented funhouse, and no one's immune.

I've weathered my mother's mental instability over the years, including her nine phony suicide attempts. That makes me something of an expert. Since Zarine never previously seemed to have much drama queen in her, I can only conclude that she was so eager to get off this island that she was willing to swim for it. That attempt was real.

Now Tatiana and Zarine are gone, the walls are talking, The Major is out of commission, and the rest of us are wondering who's next. Who'll be next to crack.

"Blanche was a beautiful little girl. She looked like the one who was murdered. You know who I mean? The one with the French-sounding name."

No, no, no.

It can't be. Not when I've been so careful.

I coached my mother for hours, and even then, I left nothing to chance. I made sure that I was always in the house when they interviewed her. No one from casting could have noticed the baby monitor hidden under the couch, though my mother knew it was there to keep her in line.

The producers must have gone back to her apartment without my knowledge. They just showed up, or my mother invited them under the guise of maternal devotion ("There are some pictures you really should see!"). Of course she did. She's been trying to bring me down my whole life.

I keep my face as neutral as I can. Never let them see you sweat.

"With how she looked, Blanche got a lot of attention and she ate it up. When I had a boyfriend, she'd want to put on a show for him and pirouette around. I had to tell her, 'It's not all about you!' Otherwise, you'd never even get to have an adult conversation in her presence. You just can't feed that, you know? You can't feed the 'look at me' stuff."

Nope, you can't let your daughter think you're actually interested in her.

Growing up, I never even heard the word *narcissist*. Now I can't escape the clickbait about how to survive toxic people, emotional vampires, psychological predators—the ones who act on your life like black holes, absorbing all light, with their own terrible gravitational pull. If only I'd learned about that when I was young enough, maybe she wouldn't still be able to do this to me.

"Blanche's parenting? She doesn't want me commenting on that. The thing is, she really needs everything her way. That's why I'm not watching the grandkids while she's on your show, because she'd probably fill her house with nanny cams and watch me from there. I don't envy Joshua's parents. I can't imagine how it'll be for her to be on your show, following your directions, even if it is for her own good. She'll fight you the whole time, I bet."

She isn't watching Kyle and Lily because I never, ever leave them alone with her, not even for a few hours. Who knows what she'd say to them unsupervised, about me or about herself. I don't want them exposed to her myopic disregard. I make sure they always feel important and valued.

But the viewers aren't going to see me with my kids. The average person might not realize that mothers like mine exist, that anyone could do this to their own child. They also don't know that the contract acts as a gag order and stops us from calling the show out on anything, even once we leave the island, even on our private social media. If we blame the editing, we can get fined, or even sued. Defending our honor comes at a steep price.

I can see how gullible I've been, thinking that one simple rule could save us. I'm not an asshole but I was raised by one and now I can't shut her up.

Joshua has been a step ahead of me, and I dismissed him out of hand. He tried to save us the night we arrived, when we thought we were alone and they were already filming. And the hits just keep on coming.

"I'm glad she's going to work on her marriage. They spend practically no time together. It's always about the kids. She gives him no attention. He's a wonderful man from a wonderful family but if she keeps on this way, he's going to leave her for someone who appreciates him. If I were him, I would have left a long time ago. But I'm only saying this because I love her, and I want her to change. I'm just not sure she has that in her."

The walls go silent.

Sam says, "What was it like, growing up with a mother who wouldn't share the spotlight? Having to make sure you never upset her? Taking in the message, *Be good but never as good as me?* Such a double bind."

The shock probably shows in my face, just for a second, before I recover. It's not what I expected to hear. I thought they'd take my mother's word about who I am but instead, Sam is showing actual compassion. Unfortunately, I won't be able to accept it.

I've always been my mother's representative in the world, I have to make her look good, but if I do too well, then I'm full of myself and she has to knock me down so I won't get a swelled head. My whole life, she's undercut me with teachers, friends, and boyfriends. She has a black belt in passive aggression. But if I ever confronted her, she fell apart and that was even worse. The night Joshua proposed, she tried to slit her wrists. Shallow cuts, horizontal rather than vertical, but still, I spent the night in the hospital with her instead of with him. Her fragility is her shield.

I can't risk telling the truth. If it aired, she might cut too deep. That means I have to take the fall, but that's okay. I can handle it. I'm not Lauren.

Holy shit, is this one of those therapy light bulb moments? The reason Lauren annoys me to no end is because she reminds me of my mother.

I've known Tristan mere days and yet he's so tuned in to me that he sees the danger, how I might for a second give in to Sam and Dave and sink down into the quicksand of their empathy. He's gleaned from our precious smoke breaks by the pool what might be at stake if I give them what they want. He's the only one here who gets that. Not Joshua. Never Joshua.

"Leave her alone," Tristan says. Lauren's head snaps toward him, and Sam and Dave can't resist the invitation. They batter him about his compulsion to leap to the aid of every pretty blonde, asking what inadequacy his savior complex is really covering up, and then they taunt him, saying we'll all find that out soon enough, won't we?

But Tristan is my hero. He's bought me time to pull myself together and formulate my plan. I'm full of indescribable gratitude. And resolve.

"I'm not sure what you thought you heard," I tell Sam and Dave, "but my mother loves me and wants the best for me."

"You don't need to pretend," Dave says. "This is a safe space, Blanche."

Ha. "It's not about my mother. It's my dad. He died when I was six in a car accident. I was there. I watched him die."

Six years old, the age Kyle is now. Sometimes I look at him and see how dependent he is and remember how independent I had to be. But Kyle can stay a little boy. He can rely on me totally for as long as he wants.

"When my father died," I say, "my mother was heartbroken." That's her version, anyway, and she'll like hearing it told. "We both missed him so much, and I pulled for a lot of attention to make up for him not being there. We did the best we could. But maybe I became a little too self-sufficient." I turn to Joshua with moist eyes. "Maybe I don't know how to need someone."

Sam and Dave are lapping it up. They almost look like normal therapists.

"Joshua, what's it like for you to see Blanche finally opening up?" Sam asks.

"I'm really proud of her," he says.

His condescension makes my skin crawl. But still, I take his hand. "I know I can be overly fixated on the kids, and I can be hard to please. Now you get where it comes from. You can see that it's not you. Like my mother said, you're a wonderful husband."

Joshua is staring at me with empty eyes. Either he doesn't believe me, or he doesn't care.

"You're not used to seeing her like this," Dave says to Joshua. "It'll take some time for you to trust the transformation."

Good thing I have a strong gag reflex. Joshua and I continue holding hands as the next voiceover starts. I recognize it immediately and am filled with relief. It's Joshua's father. Then a female voice is in the mix, a duet of love and support.

They'd never rag on their son publicly or privately. My father-in-law runs a multimillion-dollar business and my mother-in-law is the perfect housewife and mother. They're talking about how they worried that growing up, Joshua had suffered under the weight of their high expectations. Yawn.

Joshua and I haven't yet told his parents about our financial troubles, and we altered the records we turned over to the preproduction team. No one except for Joshua and me knows that his business is failing and we're swimming in debt and if something doesn't change soon, we'll have to sell our house. This show was the only way we'd see the Caribbean for a long, long time.

It looks like all our castmates are falling asleep around us, except for Tristan. He's searching my face. I've seen enough faux concern in my life to know the real thing. I try to communicate with my eyes that I'm okay, thanks to him.

The next recitation begins, a woman.

"Tristan was a good boy, he really was. But he didn't know his place. He thought he needed to take care of his sisters, be their mother and their father. I told him, they have parents, just worry about yourself. But he was so headstrong. Sure, his father liked to drink sometimes, but he wasn't an alcoholic. You couldn't tell Tristan that, though. Tristan would never admit that he was the angry one. He wanted to think he was the protector."

Tristan stands up, as if that's going to stop the voice. He looks to Sam and Dave, then seems to resign himself to what's about to happen, lowering himself slowly.

If only I could step in and do for him what he did for me, but I can just feel that it would backfire, that the therapists would talk about his hand on my knee and treat our relationship like some tawdry affair. It's so much more than that.

"Tristan started getting into fights. To hear him tell it, they were never his fault. He was taking down a bully or defending someone weaker. He was convincing, too, because it took a long time for the police to do anything about it, even though we called them. We wanted them to stop him because he sure wouldn't listen to his father and me. We wanted to make sure he didn't seriously hurt himself or anyone else. But then he nearly killed someone. He cried in court and got a slap on the wrist. He's always been a very good actor.

"Anyway, he doesn't talk to his dad or me anymore. His sisters tell us that he's doing well. They say he has his anger issues under control. We hope that's true. We love him and we always will."

Poor Tristan, writhing in anguish over there. I, of all people, know parental sabotage when I hear it.

I haven't seen any sign that Tristan can't control his anger. Sam and Dave have hammered away at him and at Lauren again and again, and Tristan has remained a gentleman. He was the peacekeeper between Joshua and The Major when they started to get into it last night. Even now, you can see that he's more pained than angry.

"It's always been like this," he says. "My mother will always take my father's side. Everything I've ever said about my family," he appeals to Lauren, "is true." Lauren is having trouble meeting his eyes.

Well, clearly, he's looking at the wrong woman.

"Do you have a juvenile record?" Sam asks.

"No, I don't."

"Because it's been expunged?"

"If it was expunged, then it doesn't exist."

"This is your chance," Dave says. "Tell us what you did, and why."

Tristan sits back in his seat, crossing his arms across his chest. "I had a violent alcoholic father, and I protected my sisters from him. I'd do the same for anyone I love. End of story."

He's irresistible, the reformed bad boy. And finally, Lauren's stopped resisting. She moves toward him with an energy I haven't seen before.

Joshua's body is tense next to mine. He's watching me watch Tristan.

Everything has been coming at us so fast today that I've barely been able to breathe, let alone metabolize the fact that Tristan had his hand on my leg last night. This might just be mutual.

Sam and Dave are circling Tristan like boxers when The Major commands, "Leave him alone. None of us came here for this."

"This is part of the journey," Sam says.

"It's not my journey. Not anymore. You stand for something or you fall for anything, am I right?" He gets up. "Anyone coming with me?"

He stares around the room at the rest of us. It's a showdown moment. Are we with him or against him? With him and against the therapists?

Naomi clambers to her feet. Lauren is next, and after a second, Tristan follows. I'm torn. Was there a clause in the contract for situations like this? Could we be incurring a penalty that we can't afford to pay?

Joshua grabs my wrist and pulls me up with unusual decisiveness. Maybe he is changing.

His hand is on the small of my back, prodding me forward. We're really doing it, walking out. We've just declared war on production.

Joshua whispers in my ear, "Keep going, up the steps. Just do what I say." Upstairs, he opens a door that I'd never thought to try, assuming it would be locked or someone's room, but it's a walk-in closet full of cleaning supplies. He latches the door behind us and takes off his microphone, putting out a hand for me to give him mine. Then he places them on a high shelf behind bottles of laundry detergent. How did he know about the closet?

He's right in my face. "I told you, we should have gone home when we had the chance." His voice is barely audible yet the blame comes through loud and clear. "We need to do it now."

Tristan had his hand on my leg. I can't leave now. "You mean pay to charter a plane and get sued by Marla?"

"We'll figure it out. I'll ask my parents, if I have to. If we stay here, there might be no going back."

Television has made him so dramatic. "It's only a few more days, and then we can go back at Marla's expense." Suck it up, buttercup. But his parents never taught him that. He's never endured true hardship. Not like me, or like Tristan.

"Listen." I see him struggling against himself. There's something he wants to tell me, and I can feel in my bones that once I hear it, there really might be no going back.

"Not here," I say, reaching up and grabbing for my microphone. "We'll be home soon."

Too soon.

Continuing interview between Detective Sonya Mohr and producer Julie Lindstrom, taking place on Glass Island.

Detective: So the walkout you just described never aired.

Julie: Marla got everyone back under control in record time. Showed why she's a diabolical genius.

Detective: You seem angry.

Julie: Thinking about Parents Day makes me angry, yeah. None of that should have happened. Someone could have died.

Detective: Someone did die.

Julie: Well, yeah, eventually. I just wish I'd tried harder to stop her, or at least quit so I wasn't a part of it. But I kept rationalizing, thinking that it was better for Lauren and Tristan to have me as a producer than anyone else. But then Zarine went into that pool, and I saw that there was no limit to what Marla would do to these people.

Detective: To play devil's advocate, didn't Zarine choose to jump in that pool? She wasn't pushed.

Julie: Not physically, but psychologically she was. The entire shoot was about pushing them, engineering the environment so that they'd behave in ways that benefited the show. I'm not saying Marla's the only one who does it; she's just the best.

Marla was totally stoking the Blanche-Lauren-Tristan love triangle. She did that little trick of putting the cigarettes in

Blanche's room and making sure her smoke breaks overlapped with Tristan's.

If you take people out of their ordinary environments, manage what they see and who they talk to, ply them with alcohol, and dial up their insecurity, they won't know if they're coming or going. Villains aren't born, they're engineered.

Detective: It sounds like you've given this a lot of thought.

Julie: Marla did it with us producers, too. She knew all our buttons and she had no qualms about pushing them.

What I'm still not sure about is why she was so much more brutal this season. Her ratings had been fine the first two seasons.

Detective: Maybe she wanted better than fine.

Julie: Maybe that's all it was. But sometimes it seemed like it might be personal.

Detective: With who?

Julie: With all of them, at varying moments. I could be wrong, it's just a hunch. I got the sense that she really took pleasure in her machinations, and in their reactions. You know the way you can burn ants with a magnifying glass, if you apply singular focus?

Before the show, I didn't really understand what it meant to be a social creature. I thought it meant humans aren't good at being alone for long periods of time. But now I get that it means we're constantly exerting pressure on one another, and if we get enough messages that there's a way we should be, we'll probably start acting like that. So for people like Marla, it's just a matter of finding the right forms of social pressure, both subtle and overt. She knows we're all susceptible.

Detective: It seems like the cast tried to take control back with the walkout.

Julie: They did, but it was short-lived. That night, Marla had a talk with each person individually, off-camera. She knew their levers. They never stood a chance.

SEVENTEEN

LAUREN

Day Five

"Oh... my... God," I pant. It's never been like that before, not with Tristan.

He rolls off and reaches down to pull on his boxers. Did he come? I don't want to ask, I want to applaud.

He heads for the bathroom. I'm hoping he'll come back and cuddle like usual. Instead, I hear the shower running.

If I'm honest, there was something coiled and angry inside Tristan that time. It wasn't lovemaking, that's for sure. It must be the lingering fury from yesterday's exercise, everything he was subjected to. If I had to listen to those kinds of lies from my own mother's mouth, I would have crumbled into a million pieces, but not him.

Besides, Tristan has no reason to be mad at me, based on what Marla told me privately last night. She assured me that he doesn't know about Alexei. Which confirms that she does. But she and I have come to an understanding.

The process might seem harsh, but Marla really does have our best interests in mind, and it's working. Blanche showed her softer side, and Tatiana and Zarine are probably in a better place now, getting help. I have to hope that the Major is okay, or en route to being okay, and that he and Naomi are bonding, like Tristan and I have. I can finally see how we fit together. More than that, I can feel it. Everywhere.

He's back, smelling sweet but looking worried. He crouches by the side of the bed. "Listen," he says, "I don't want you to get the wrong idea."

I stare at him, eyes widening with fear. Could that have been breakup sex?

"I did have a juvenile record, and it was expunged. I was planning to tell you someday, I really was." He averts his eyes. "I just didn't want to give you a reason not to love me. I was embarrassed because, yeah, I got in a lot of fights when I was younger but it wasn't like my mom said. Most of them were just kid stuff. The one my mom was talking about, the guy I really messed up..." He takes a deep breath and closes his eyes, like it hurts to remember. He's just so beautiful. "That guy tried to rape my sister."

"Oh my God."

"She got away but what about other girls? When I went to find him, I was mad but I was only planning to talk to him. With my reputation, I didn't always have to fight. I'd talk and they'd back down and I could walk away." He swallows, bracing himself. "This guy, though, he wouldn't back down. He'd attacked my sister and he said he was only sorry he hadn't finished. So he wound up in the hospital."

"Sounds like he deserved it." I start rubbing my belly, glad that she'll have a protector like her daddy.

"The cops seemed to think so, especially after they talked to my sister. I might have been able to walk away from it except that my parents wanted me in juvie. They argued for it: first to the police, and then to the D.A. They would have testified against their own son! They said it was for my own good but really, they wanted me out of the house. I was the only one standing up to my father and they wanted me gone."

"That's so horrible." Part of me is relieved that he's been keeping a secret, too. I know it doesn't make us exactly even, but at least it makes us closer. I grab his hand and squeeze it, tears in my eyes.

"I spent sixteen months locked up, and maybe it was a good thing because I decided I wasn't going to do anything that could get me sent back to a place like that. That's how I got control over my anger. But I never forgave my parents. I stayed in their house only for as long as I had to so I could watch over my sisters."

I pull him up and into the bed and wrap my arms around him. "I'm sorry," I say. "The way your mom talked about you made me sick, and now that I've heard the whole story, I just want to take care of you. No matter what you do, I'm on your side." I look into his eyes and I almost say those three words.

I don't ever want to leave the room or the bed but after a while of us fantasizing about life after the show, all the amazing things that await us and the baby, there's a knock on the door. Tristan puts on a robe and opens it just a crack. Then he opens it wider to take the breakfast tray. "We've got another hour!" he says, smiling. Maybe that's the deal he struck during his private conversation with Marla, a whole morning for just the two of us.

We sit outside on the balcony, giddy. "This could be every day," he says, gnawing on a slice of bacon. "You, me, and the munchkin in our own mansion."

I laugh. "One blockbuster and we're there!"

"It could happen, you know. I've got this lucky feeling. We came here for a reason, it's meant to change our lives. I bet I'm going to have tons of auditions once we get home. Or maybe I won't even need to audition anymore. The offers will be rolling in."

"I'm feeling lucky, too." I slip my hand under his robe.

He groans. "I'm not twenty-two anymore, babe! You've got to let me rest a while."

"We don't have all day."

That line proves prophetic. Far too soon, we're in our swimsuits, reporting to the pool. Will today's exercise be something to do with Zarine?

Nope, Tatiana and Zarine aren't there, though the other remaining couples have already arrived. Blanche fills out her bikini top way better than I do and has a matching sarong that probably costs more than I make in a day at the salon, and Naomi's body could be sculpted out of iron. I'm the youngest, yet my one-piece is the most conservative and the pregnancy is already causing spidery varicose veins.

My eyes flick toward Tristan with a newfound pride of ownership. A part of me has always felt like he's on loan but not anymore. He's the best looking of the men, and he's all mine.

He and Blanche have started smiling and chatting. I'd approach The Major except for his funereal expression, which contrasts sharply with his Hawaiian shirt and brightly colored swim trunks. There are plenty of crew members around, but no Sam or Dave. It's only junior producers, not the ones who tend to give out instructions. I wish Julie were here.

Then Marla appears. It's her first time on set. Her thick dark hair is piled on top of her head, and she's wearing cat's-eye glasses and a loose-fitting black dress. She doesn't need to be done up like Sam for you to know she's in charge.

"Good to see you all," she says, with a micro-smile. "With all the hard work you've been putting in, you deserve a day off, and I wanted to personally welcome you to your day of relaxation." She does an ironic arm swoop like she's on a game show as Brandon rolls out a machine that is lazily rotating a neon yellow liquid. "Ta-da! Your very own margarita machine."

At 11 a.m.? Great, now I'll have to watch everyone else get wasted. For hours. I flash back to the image of Tristan's hand on

Blanche's leg. He thought it was my leg, though. I have to remember that.

Marla hasn't moved. She's waiting for something. Finally, Blanche says, "Thank you so much, Marla. Who doesn't love a poolside margarita?"

"And who doesn't love a day off?" Naomi adds. "Thank you, Marla."

One by one, we all chime in, until Marla is satisfied with our tributes and exits stage left. Joshua immediately goes up to the machine and begins filling a glass. He sucks it down quickly.

Everyone else seems much more wary. I catch Blanche eyeing me. Marla probably visited everyone's rooms last night, with carrots or sticks. There's definitely distrust in the air. But is it toward Marla, or toward each other?

The Major plops down on a deck chair, pulls the wide brim of a sunhat over his eyes, and appears to instantly fall asleep.

A producer shows up with pineapple juice in a cocktail glass so I don't have to stand there awkwardly with nothing to hold. I will, however, have to exclaim over its virgin delicious-ness at least once for the camera.

So far, it isn't much of a party. Blanche fills a glass halfway, saying she's never been a fan of margaritas. Tristan follows suit, and then Naomi. "I thought we might really be in for it today," I hear Tristan say to Blanche in a low voice, and she laughs like he's kidding. But it does feel like we're getting away with some-thing, and that makes me a touch uneasy.

No one's making any direct comments about the producers or Marla or our missing castmates or the fact that we're basically all strikebreakers. Marla knows my secret and I'm not about to piss her off. Is that true of the others, too?

We all turn at the splash. Joshua is in the pool, his empty glass next to the diving board. "The water's perfect!" he calls. He arranges himself in an inner tube.

I cluster with Naomi and Blanche. They start talking about

how the beach on Glass Island compares to Saint Barts. I'm considering whether to employ my usual tactics for when I'm in the salon dealing with much wealthier women, which include flattering them or asking deferential questions.

Naomi looks over at The Major, who seems to be stirring. "I'll be right back, okay? I'm going to see if a margarita might resuscitate Cain."

I watch as she approaches him and as usual, he seems to be shrugging her off. Maybe she's had enough of the inattention because she dunks herself in the pool and walks toward Joshua in this slow, sinewy way. With her dripping red hair, she's like a mermaid who just grew legs. Joshua seems only too happy to receive her.

When I look back at Blanche, she's watching Tristan. She doesn't even care that her own husband is flirting with a beautiful woman fifteen feet from her.

"Yesterday was rough," I say. I remind myself that Blanche deserves my sympathy, after all she's been through. "What you said about your dad—"

Blanche cuts me off. "I don't think we heard from one of your parents." She runs a finger around the edge of her margarita glass, searching for phantom salt.

"There's only my mom. I don't think it would have been that interesting."

"Did you find my mother interesting?"

I'm feeling uncomfortable, like she's baiting me into offending her. "I'm glad the exercise ended well for you and Joshua. That you were able to get closer." I spy Joshua and Naomi in my peripheral vision. "But like the therapists said, it can be a little while before the change fully takes hold."

"Do you think that change has taken hold for you and Tristan?"

I think of earlier this morning, and my face grows hot. "Yeah, I think it has."

She smiles. "Then I'm glad for you, too. And for your little one." She might really mean it. Tristan seems to like her, and I need to trust his judgment. It'll be easier if we can hang out with the same people, even if it's only for another few days.

"I don't have a lot of girlfriends," I say. "Do you?"

"Plenty. My friend Elle was the one who introduced me to Marla. That's how we ended up here." She looks around, like she can't quite believe it. I'm not sure if she's incredulous at her fortune or misfortune. With me, she tends to keep it surface and opaque. Unreadable. "I find that the connection happens right away or not at all."

Is she hinting that she and I haven't connected, but she and Tristan have? My hand tightens on my glass.

"What would your mother have said? If the walls had talked."

"I'm not sure. She doesn't know any of my secrets." I see my misstep in Blanche's eyes. "What I mean is, we get along, but we don't share anything deep. She sees things in black and white: There's no free lunch. All that glitters isn't gold. You reap what you sow."

"Well"—Blanche finishes her drink—"some platitudes are true."

It's time to admit what's been going on right under my nose. Blanche is never going to like me. I'm an impediment to what— to who—she really wants. But how can she be so obvious about it when she's being filmed? Or is it only obvious to me?

"Not everyone can be friends, that's true," I say. "We should just focus on our own relationships. That's why we're here, right?"

Her laughter is lightly tinged with scorn. "Did you actually just say the biggest platitude in all of reality TV? That you're not here to make friends?"

I don't smile. "I guess I did."

"Then there's nothing to talk about, is there?" She pats my

arm like it's too bad that I've shut down the possibility of us getting to know each other further. Could I have misunderstood her? Was I the rude one?

I watch helplessly as she sashays toward Tristan in his lounge chair, and he smiles up at his new friend.

EIGHTEEN

TATIANA

"Did you get any sleep?" Julie asks.

I shake my head as I stare out the window. My mind is elsewhere, wondering where Zarine is right now and what she's doing. What's being done to her.

"It must be hard, going back to a couples retreat alone," Julie tries again. There's a cameraperson next to her in the limo. She'll probably get a promotion if she can get me crying like those women who've been dumped on *The Bachelor* and are being driven back to the airport, saying things like, "I really thought we were going to spend the rest of our lives together."

Zarine and I really are going to spend the rest of our lives together. That's the truth, not a sound bite.

"I'm a big girl." I smile to let Julie know I'm not going to hold the probing against her. I know exactly who's responsible.

For a delightful touch of sadism, Marla chose to house me in the very same unadorned room where Zarine and I spent our first night on the island. It was what I guessed it would be like in a locked psychiatric ward, with the crew stationed outside my door and a psychologist inside.

She had a no-nonsense manner, like I was just paperwork to her. She explained that she'd be evaluating my mental fitness to return for filming and assured me there were no cameras in the room, that it was just us. As if I'd fall for that.

I said what I needed to say to prove that I was well enough to go back to the villa because I'm hoping Zarine is doing the same. Neither of us can afford to look traumatized right now. Once we're reunited, Zarine will charter a plane and we'll get off this island together. The hell with the contract. The hell with all of them.

"You didn't get to spend much time with Zarine after you pulled her out of the pool," Julie says. "I'm sorry about that."

"I'm sure it wasn't your decision."

"No," she says, her eyes kind, "it wasn't."

My own eyes threaten to moisten but I won't let it happen. I see why Marla sent Julie, though. She's good.

"We're here," Julie says unnecessarily, as we pull into the driveway. "Do you want me to tell you the itinerary?"

"I want you to tell me where Zarine is and how she is and when I'm going to see her again."

"I wish I knew."

"Marla loves the element of surprise." I need to change my tone, she's always listening. I don't want to piss off the woman who's holding Zarine hostage. "I get it, I signed up for this."

Julie looks out the window and sighs. "Yeah, we all did." Then she turns back to me. "There's a pool party, but you don't have to go."

Is Marla completely fucking with me?

"If you're not feeling up to it, you can skip it. Go to your room and get some rest and I'll bring you lunch. Any special requests?"

"I don't have much appetite. But thank you."

"Go straight to your room, okay? Decide whether you want

to be alone or if you'd like to go down and have a drink. There's a margarita machine."

I close my eyes. What is Marla celebrating, I wonder? She is definitely fucking with me.

"It's just a party. No therapy and no exercises. Sam and Dave have the day off. But there are cameras, remember that. If you choose to go, I mean."

Julie is true to her word. I spend the next hour alone in my room uninterrupted. But with no TV, computer, or phone, it feels like solitary confinement. Without distractions, all I can do is berate myself some more. I mean, I did sign up for this. I signed Zarine up. Part of me does want to rejoin the others because my thoughts are a prison.

I put on my lime-green bikini and wind my hair up into two Princess Leia buns on either side of my head. Some waterproof concealer for the bags under my eyes, and voilà, I'm ready to party.

But when I make my entrance from the double doors of the great room, everything goes silent. No, wait, they haven't even noticed me. That means it was already silent. What the…?

Everyone is sipping their margaritas at a glacial pace, and conversation seems stilted. I can understand why they're cautious. But this is a travesty. We are in the Caribbean, after all, for just a few days more. Or less, in my case. I'm out of here just as soon as Zarine walks through those doors.

"Hey, everyone!" I wave all around and then get my margarita. I sip it and make a face. "I can't even taste the alcohol." I gesture to Julie. "Could you get us a bottle of tequila, please?"

She comes close to me. "Are you sure? You've been through a lot in the past twenty-four hours."

"That's exactly why I need the tequila."

Reluctantly, she nods.

"Thanks so much!" I down the rest of my drink and

approach the lounge chairs. Naomi is obviously determined to kill the buzz I'm fighting to accrue by asking about Zarine and how I'm holding up. Blanche and Lauren do the same, and I can't take it. I look around for better options. Tristan is doing laps in the pool, and The Major seems to be asleep, which tells you all you need to know about this soiree.

Joshua, on the other hand, is amped to see me, waving madly from a pool float. He bobs over to the edge. "Grab me another drink, and I'll fill you in on everything you missed," he says.

"Deal." I wink at him. "I'll even top it off for you."

Julie's back with the tequila and I make the rounds to everyone. "Let's face it," I tell them as I pour, "if we don't do something, we're all going to end up like The Major."

Then I return to where Joshua is waiting. He hoists himself out of the water and sits beside me, feet and calves submerged, shimmering droplets still clinging to his chest hair. I'm glad he has chest hair, that he hasn't gone full Ken doll.

"How are you doing, really?" he asks.

"Don't give me that shit." I toss back half my margarita and pour more tequila into what remains. I know it's dangerous, talking to Joshua, given our most likely past association. But I just can't play it safe right now. Under extreme stress, old habits come back to life. "You promised to tell me what I missed."

"There was a walkout."

"You don't say!"

"I do indeed." He smiles. "I was afraid I'd lost you for good."

I have that same fear about Zarine, but I'm trying to ignore it. Be in the here and now. Drink it all away.

I gesture downward. "In the flesh. Now, tell me about this walkout."

"After you and Zarine left, they started playing recordings of our parents talking shit about us. In The Major's case, it was his dead father. Who sounded exactly like The Major. My guess is they hired a voice actor to imitate The Major's speech patterns. It was *sick*. I still don't think he's recovered. Then it was Blanche's mom, going on about how Blanche was JonBenét Ramsey as a kid and that I'm a wonderful man from a wonderful family, and afterward Blanche realized, *Hey, he is!*, so yeah, we're pretty much cured."

I laugh. "You look it." At that moment, Blanche and Lauren are both hanging on Tristan's every word. "What do they see in that guy?"

"I guess you have to be a straight woman to get his appeal." His tone is distinctly less jocular than mine.

"I've had my moments."

"I remember."

I stare at him. I've wracked my brain and I still can't place him, not for sure, which is disconcerting. But this is no time to ask questions. There's a cameraman with his lens trained on us.

"Get this," Joshua says, his eyes lingering on Tristan with no hint of amusement, "Tristan might be a murderer."

"*What?*"

"He hurt someone really bad, maybe killed them, when he was a teenager but he got his record expunged. He wants everyone to think his father was the violent alcoholic and that he had to protect his sisters, but it was the other way around. Tristan's the dangerous one. I've felt since day one that something wasn't right about that guy."

Meanwhile, Blanche has thrown her head back in laughter at something Tristan just said. "Does it bother you that she's over there?"

"I know where I stand." His tone is dark but when our eyes meet, he breaks into another smile. "Where was I? Oh, right, the walkout. So after Tristan's parents had spoken, The Major lost his shit. He basically said that Sam and Dave and Marla were going to hell, and he walked out, and we all followed."

"And then?"

"We all ate separately in our rooms, and I'm guessing that Marla divided and conquered because we all reported for duty this morning. I wasn't sure there was any point in sticking around but now you're back. So cheers." He clinks his glass against mine. "To getting what we deserve."

NINETEEN

THE MAJOR

I'm not asleep; this is passive resistance. Marla won last night's battle, but she hasn't won the war. My intention is to give her as little usable footage as possible. She's calling this a Day of Relaxation, but I suspect a truer name would be Day of Reconnaissance. I'm sure she's gathering intel, gearing up for the next skirmish.

I still have some fight in me, but I have to admit, my spirits are low. I was hoping the party would fizzle quickly, and then Tatiana showed up to dose everyone with tequila and her megawatt smile, letting them know it was okay to have fun. Shouldn't she have a little more respect? Wasn't it yesterday that Zarine tried to kill herself in this very pool?

I don't understand any of these people, not even my own wife. Especially not her. My hat might be pulled low but my eyes are open, and I've caught more than a few glimpses of Naomi whooping it up with Joshua, a man with no discernible character.

But I can't blame everyone else for my own failings. I shouldn't have let Marla bribe me into staying. The indisputable fact is, Naomi and I never should have come here.

I thought I could be a different kind of houseguest, one who defied stereotypes. A unifier. A role model. Instead, I'm probably coming off sanctimonious and belligerent. But how can you be a decent person in this environment? If it's a microcosm of America, then no wonder the country is circling the drain.

Tatiana convinces the producers to play some music and gets Tristan and Lauren to dance with her. Blanche is next, then Joshua; they're all falling like rhythmically challenged dominos. Tatiana is equal opportunity, rubbing up on everyone, with just about no regard for the beat. No regard for Zarine either.

Naomi comes over to me with a smile on her face and her arm outstretched. "Come on, party pooper," she says. "You love to dance."

It's not true. Naomi loves to dance, and she's great at it. But it used to be a lot of fun, being out there with her when she took over the floor. "No, thanks."

She sits on the edge of my chair. "You've said no to everything all day long. You don't want a margarita, you don't want to dance, you don't want to talk to me or anyone else."

"That about sums it up."

"Cain." She tilts her head to give me that look, the twenty-plus-years-of-marriage look. "We've got three more days. Let's make the best of this, please."

"Fine. But no dancing."

"All right, Footloose." She laughs. "You are becoming a crotchety old man, do you know that?"

I laugh in spite of myself. "Becoming? I'm already there."

"Let's do this, all right?" She kisses my cheek, a reminder to follow the plan. Tell the story we came here to tell. We're supposed to look like we're rekindling our flame. "When you're ready, you know where to find me. Three more days, Cain."

Lauren takes the vacated seat next to me, her face flushed with exertion. She lifts off my hat and fans herself with it. "So when are you going to dance with me?"

"One a.m."

"It's not even dinnertime."

"That gives me about six hours to come up with a good excuse."

She laughs and gives my hat back. "Thank you for leading us out of there yesterday. For all I know, they had my sperm donor of a father queued up."

"I wish I'd done it a lot earlier, before they drove Zarine around the bend."

"It could turn out to be a good thing. She finally told her parents the truth, and it's obvious how much they love her. Now it's all out in the open." She looks over at the barbecue area where Tristan and Blanche are dancing. They might not have rhythm but they have chemistry.

"It's just dancing," I say. "It doesn't mean anything. I mean, get a load of Tatiana and Joshua."

She scoots her chair toward mine. "I tried to talk to Blanche earlier and she's definitely into Tristan."

"She said that?"

"Not in those words. I thought Tristan and I made some real strides, only he hasn't been paying me much attention since we got to the party. For the last couple of days, he hasn't been very affectionate either. Is that because of Blanche, or do you think it could be something else?"

"What else could it be?" My tone is rhetorical, but her worry grows more pronounced. "During the first therapy session, he was ready to shout his love from the rooftops. Now, have his feelings changed? Only he knows, so you've got to ask."

"That might drive him away. I'd seem insecure."

"Or you'll seem like an adult capable of a mature conversation."

She glances over toward the makeshift dance floor, biting her lip.

"Speak your mind, Lauren. Because if you don't, then even when he says he loves you, who's he loving?"

"If Blanche would back off, everything would be okay. Way better than okay. We'd be perfect." She's started rubbing her belly like it's an amulet.

"I think it's a mistake to make it about another woman. Can you trust who you're sleeping next to every night? That's the question."

TWENTY
BLANCHE

"Dare!" Tatiana sings out. "In honor of Zarine!"

The other couples assembled on the beach grow quiet. We've picked up Tatiana's cue from earlier and started treating Zarine as a taboo subject, like she's on a plane that went down at sea and we don't yet know if there are any survivors. Meanwhile, Tatiana's been all over the place, literally and figuratively, and even though I'm used to toddler wrangling, my patience is wearing thin.

At first, her presence was energizing. She turned this into a legitimate party. But then she started alternately sobbing to whoever would listen and engaging in sophomoric stunts like cannonballing in the pool and soaking everyone nearby, running topless into the ocean, and demonstrating how well she can walk with a margarita glass on her head (spoiler alert: not well, and production had to sweep up the shards). She's started to wear on everyone except Julie, who's been assigned to babysit, and Joshua, who seems to be volunteering.

Fine by me. While he's occupied, I get to talk to Tristan. I especially appreciated when Lauren was hanging out with The Major. That's it, Lauren. Work out those daddy issues.

Without Tatiana, this party would have continued its death march, so I have to thank her for the time I spent dancing with Tristan. I made sure to keep it clean. No more forgetting about the cameras or pretending we can give Marla the finger with impunity. This is a job. We work for her, and if we accept that, we can enjoy our remaining time in paradise.

"It's not your turn, Tatiana." Even the unflappable Naomi sounds annoyed.

"Oh, right," Tatiana says. "Whose turn is it?"

"Mine," I say. "Truth."

"When did you last masturbate?" Tatiana asks.

I make a show of screwing up my face like I'm trying to remember way back and then answer, "This morning. Next!" Everyone laughs except Joshua.

It's true. Joshua was in the shower, and Tristan was on my mind. But I reach out and give Joshua's thigh a squeeze.

"Dare," he tells the others.

"Surprise Marla in the control room," Tristan says.

Joshua and Tristan stare each other down for a long minute and then Joshua stands up.

"No problem."

As he strides back toward the villa, the rest of us exchange uneasy glances.

"Why so serious?" Tatiana slurs. "Let's have some more drinks!" She starts to get to her feet and then plops back down like gravity is simply too much to contend with.

"The margarita machine broke," Naomi says drily.

"There's plenty of booze inside." Tatiana tries to rise again, with the same result. She starts to pout. "Could somebody help me? Or better yet, could someone go and bring back a few bottles?"

"I'll go," The Major says. You can tell we won't see him for a long time.

Which makes me think of Joshua. Should I go in after him and make sure he's okay?

No, we need to stop acting like Marla's some bogeyman. Joshua will bang on the control room door and be told in no uncertain terms to get back on the beach. That's it. Marla isn't omnipotent. She produces a reality show. We all need to get a grip.

"Truth," Lauren says.

"Are you in love with Tristan yet?" It shoots out of my mouth, unbidden.

"You don't have to answer that," Tristan tells her, and I realize that I haven't just put her on the spot; I've done it to him, too.

Naomi takes pity on them. "How about this one: What are you going to name your baby?"

"Lame!" Tatiana yelps. "Answer the first question! Are you in love, Lauren? You can tell us, we're your best friends!"

Lauren moves close to Tristan and whispers in his ear. He smiles.

"Tell the group! Tell the group!" Tatiana chants.

So Lauren and Tristan really have made progress, whereas Joshua and I have just been putting on a show. I shouldn't feel so crestfallen. Tristan and I met less than a week ago, and I didn't come looking for love. I have a husband.

Speak of the devil. Joshua's back, looking triumphant as he holds something aloft. I squint into the sun and see that it's Marla's glasses.

"She gave them to you?" Tristan looks suspicious.

"To prove I did the deed. He who asks shall receive."

Tatiana leaps to her feet. "Give them to me!" She tries to grab them out of his hand, and then they're wrestling on the sand, laughing.

"Stop," he says, "you'll break them."

"Marla's broken everything else!" Tatiana is really clawing

at Joshua and you can see it's not fun and games anymore. "Give them to me. I'm throwing them in the ocean unless she tells me where Zarine is!"

She continues to struggle, while Joshua is restraining her, telling her it's going to be all right, she should just let it out, she's safe. She dissolves into hysterics and finally her body goes limp like some sort of emotional orgasm. Where did he learn to do that?

He lifts her up onto his shoulder. "I'm going to put her in her room." It's another surprising act of chivalry, once again directed toward Tatiana.

"See," I hear her telling him, all breathy, "you can do caveman style," and then more giggles, and then, "Don't I know you from somewhere?"

I've had enough. "Joshua, put her down. A producer will do that."

"I don't want a producer," Tatiana says petulantly. "I want Joshua!"

"I'll just be a minute, okay?" Joshua tells me.

It's a no-win situation. If I let him carry her away, I look like a dupe; if I insist that he stays, I look like a shrew. And what if he doesn't listen to me anyway?

So I relent, and off they go toward the villa. Is that pity I see on Tristan's face?

I notice that Naomi and Lauren are huddled together, whispering and laughing as they sneak glances at me. It's sophomoric mean-girl shit and I'm irritated by my irritation. I would have thought Naomi was above that, though I've always suspected Lauren's true level. I just hope that Tristan is seeing it, too.

Lauren's not who she pretends to be. Not at all.

Continuing interview between Detective Sonya Mohr and producer Julie Lindstrom, taking place on Glass Island.

Julie: Yeah, the Day of Relaxation. Not for me. I was Tatiana's handmaiden. And I'm pretty sure it set the scene for everything that followed. There was something for everyone at that party, including a motive.

TWENTY-ONE

LAUREN

Day Six

"It's the day you've all been waiting for," Sam announces. "The polygraph exercise."

"You'll be asked questions and as you give your answers, skilled examiners will be measuring your breath rate, pulse, blood pressure, perspiration, and skin conductivity," Dave explains. "Taken together, this data tells us whether deception has been indicated."

"Tatiana!" Sam looks toward the doorway with what seems to be a genuine smile. "Glad you decided to join us!"

Tatiana steps into the room like she's not sure how she'll be received by the rest of us. "Hi, guys," she says, curling up like a cat on the loveseat she'd been sharing with Zarine.

"I have good news," Dave says. "It's an update on Zarine. She's going to remain on the island, though she won't be filming. She'll be having private therapy sessions, while Tatiana will continue the process with the others. We're still working on the relationship, only separately."

Despite the upbeat delivery, Tatiana sinks down farther into the loveseat.

Dave claps his hands together. "Lauren, you're up first."

It's a little bit of a walk of shame, returning to the same small white room where I'd seen Alexei's dick pic. Another woman staring at a laptop, and this time, the electrode is on my finger instead of my temples. I also have a blood pressure cuff attached to my arm and two black straps wound around my chest.

My nerves are starting to jangle, though Marla had assured me I didn't need to worry about the lie detector; my secret's safe with her. She'd even given me some useful tips. She said there would be control questions to establish a baseline, and from those, the examiner would try to determine if I was lying in response to the relevant questions. "What will the relevant questions be?" I'd asked. When Marla hesitated, I pressed my advantage. "You said that I'm the reason people are tuning in. That without Tristan and me, there's no show. I need those questions."

It's easy to spot the control questions. They're about minor transgressions like whether I've ever shoplifted or cheated on a test. I answer clearly and calmly. In between are the questions Marla fed me. Most of them are about Tristan: whether he's ever been violent, whether I've caught him in a lie, whether I believe his mother, and finally, whether I love him. For that final question, I say confidently, "Yes, I do." I'm smiling as I begin to remove the cuff from my arm.

The examiner stops me. "One more question. Have you ever been unfaithful to Tristan?"

That bitch.

I instantly break out in a sweat. I should probably lie. Maybe I'll get away with it and the examiner won't catch me. But even if they call me out, I can tell Tristan that it was a mistake or that the producers are the real liars.

He's already been betrayed by his own parents. He's had to listen to his mother accuse him of being a violent criminal. Talk about trust issues. What if he doesn't believe me when I blame the producers? Or if he does believe me and the truth comes out later in some way that I can't plausibly deny?

The island was supposed to help us. It was supposed to help his career. Yet I came here with a secret that could blow it all up. He's never going to forgive me.

"Have you ever been unfaithful to Tristan?"

I stand up and take off all the equipment, slowly and deliberately. Then I walk down the hall to find Tristan in the kitchen, standing closer to Blanche than I'd like. But as The Major said, this isn't about her. It's about Tristan and me and our baby. It's about the life we're going to have, and no one— not Marla, and certainly not Blanche—is going to take it from us.

I grab Tristan's hand and start to run, pulling him with me, out through the front door and then toward the beach. I rip my microphone off and tell him to do the same. I say we have to keep going. We need to catch them all off-guard so we can get a head start.

"Just trust me!" I shout, and he does.

When we're far enough down the beach, I stop, breathing hard, and I tell him almost everything. That I'm in love with him. That I'm terrified of losing him. That months ago, I did the stupidest thing, and I will never ever do it again.

I'm crying as my hair whips my face. "I love you, and I know that when I said that it was supposed to be your happiest day, the beginning of everything, and I've ruined that, but can it still be the beginning of everything? I want to marry you. I want to be only yours, forever. Please? Can we still have that?"

He's staring at me, the realization of all that I've said dawning on him. Conflicting emotions kaleidoscope across his face, like a sunrise and a sunset all at once.

"I'm so sorry, but there's no time," I say. "They're going to be here soon. You have to decide."

He digs his fingers into my upper arm, and it hurts, but it's not like I can protest, after what I've done. "Come with me," he says roughly.

TWENTY-TWO

TATIANA

There's some kind of commotion going on. The production team appears equal parts frenetic and purposeless, striding about and talking into their headsets, probably waiting to find out whether to amplify or contain the drama, whatever it may be. I hope this means that my polygraph test has been delayed or better yet, called off.

No such luck. I'm up next.

I never should have gone to that pool party. I'm too old for nights I can't remember.

My heart is beating triple time just walking down the hall. I'm not planning to lie, but I can't rule anything out at this point. I have a theory of how Joshua and I first met, but I still don't know for sure. I've been keeping myself in the dark so that if I'm asked about it, I can tell the truth.

I just have to hope that Marla doesn't know, and that there are no questions for Joshua that might expose our prior association, if that's what you want to call it.

The technician is detailing how the test is going to work, but I'm not listening. I keep picturing Zarine's cadaverous face as I dragged her from the pool, wondering where she is right now and if someone is about to stick some electrodes on her and ask questions and measure her responses. If they'll even get a pulse. I don't want to imagine what they could be doing to her in a place with no cameras.

As the chest strap is tightened around me, I feel myself seize up. I see the tech's lips moving, grotesquely magnified, but I can't hear a thing. Then it all goes dark.

TWENTY-THREE

THE MAJOR

I am not messing around with these people anymore. I will beat that lie detector.

After we were cast, I flew over to Scottsdale and took a three-day course from a guy who used to work for the FBI. I logged hours of practice in how to establish a phony baseline during the control questions in order to fake them out on the real ones. This time I'm prepared for what Marla is going to throw at me. Not that I can stop Sam and Dave from reading false results anyway, but it's satisfying to know in my own mind that I am not to be trifled with.

I worry about Naomi, though. She claims she'll be fine, she's got her ways, but she chose not to take the course. That could mean she's at their mercy.

This morning, we had it out in a way we haven't in—well, ever. It started innocently enough. "Take a shower with me," I said, and she smiled, though it wasn't that kind of a shower.

I made sure we left our microphones in the other room. If we talked low with the water running, it would be nearly impossible for the producers to hear us.

"I'm sorry I haven't been much fun," I whispered. "I'm

trying to get my head in the game. Based on the previous two seasons, the lie detector is today. So we need to prep."

"Didn't you say something about fun?" She smiled. Then she was soaping me up instead of herself.

As we started to kiss, my body didn't want to stop, but my mind knew it wasn't right to continue. My key doesn't belong in her lock anymore.

"It would feel good," I said, "but it would confuse everything."

She acted like she hadn't heard. She started to go down to her knees, and when I grabbed her by the shoulders to pull her up, she slipped. She was on the shower floor looking up at me a little dazed, like she couldn't believe what was happening. I'd never turned that down before.

"I'm sorry," I said. "We just don't fit together."

"How would you know? When's the last time you tried?" She got to her feet, her voice rising. I put a finger to my lips but she did the opposite, almost like she wanted the producers to hear.

"It's not about the physical." I mean, look at this woman. If it could be purely physical, I wouldn't be holding back. But I respect her too much. I can't have sex with my wife with how I'm feeling.

Then she lost her mind, screaming, "Physical, spiritual, emotional, we've been the whole package for twenty-three years! Is this what it's come to?!?"

I stared at her, shocked.

She started washing her hair with agitated motions, fighting to get herself back under control. "Just keep doing what you're doing, Cain. Sit alone and pull your hat down and check out. You don't like the game? You don't have to play. You don't like the world? You don't have to live in it."

"That was one party."

She shook her head vigorously as she rinsed her hair. "Go ahead, tell yourself you've done all you could."

There was nothing I could say, she was too irrational. "I'll see you at breakfast." She didn't answer as I stepped out and toweled off.

She never did come down for breakfast and she's off doing her lie detector now. I don't even know what kind of measurements they're getting when her blood pressure must be sky high. I hate seeing her upset but we need to learn how to exist separately.

I've been outside by the pool for a long time, and no one's come to get me. Not Naomi, not the producers. Behind the glass doors, I can see people rushing to and fro. More chaos manufactured by Marla, I'm sure. I'm not about to get caught up in it.

But I have to admit, it's lonely out here.

TWENTY-FOUR

BLANCHE

"Please," Brandon says, with a note of exasperation. He seems like he could use a different assignment. Being in the confessional has clearly wiped him out. "Work with me here."

"I am working with you. Ever since I got here, I've answered every question you asked."

"In the most superficial, boring way possible." Now he actually seems angry. Well, this is new. He moves closer and speaks through gritted teeth. "You need to follow my instructions to a T. I'll tell you when to cry—preferably an ugly cry because that reads as more genuine—and then maybe, just maybe, people will give you another look. Right now, the viewers hate you. With a passion."

I study his face. He has to be lying. The ugly cry would be some kind of coup for him, a feather in his cap. Maybe he'd win a bet or he wants to humiliate me for kicks.

"If you want to turn it around, one vulnerable moment in therapy isn't going to be enough," he says. "That only makes you look more insincere. You've got to be full on. Now, should we go through the questions again?"

Who does he think he is, talking to me like this? Why would

I believe he'd help me when it's apparent that he's the one who really hates me?

"I don't have anything to cry about," I say.

"How about the fact that America loves Lauren, and so does Tristan?"

I glare at him. Then I stand up. "Thanks for nothing."

I huff my way to the great room, where The Major, Naomi, Joshua, and Tatiana are already waiting. My friend Elle had told me that there are no villains on *Relationship Rescue*, that Marla picks a cast the viewers will fall in love with and edits accordingly. But what if America has fallen in hate with me despite Marla's best intentions?

"Now that everyone's here, we should go ahead and get started," Sam says.

I look over at Tristan and Lauren's empty loveseat, recalling her interruption in the kitchen this morning, how she yanked him away. I figured something was wrong but then, something is always wrong with Lauren.

Fresh sweat is breaking out on Dave's forehead. "We can't tell you anything about Lauren and Tristan's whereabouts right now but we'll give you information as soon as we can. What we can say is that we have it all under control."

If Tristan's gone home, will I ever see him again?

I shouldn't. What happens on the island should stay on the island.

But we do live in the same city. I mean, nothing in the contract forbids us from getting together.

No. I have kids. Their father is sitting next to me, holding my hand. Constantly. I'm no suicide bomber. You don't go blowing up a family (two families, given Lauren's pregnancy) based on a crush.

But I'm afraid that what I've been feeling can't be contained. In spite of myself, I've been learning and growing. For the first few days, alarm bells had gone off inside me when I was supposed to be giving Kyle and Lily their baths or reading to them or tucking them in at night. Since then, though, the alarms have grown fainter. I adore my children and relish every video chat. But the distance is about more than geography, and now I can see that so much of my desire for physical touch—desires that Joshua used to fill earlier in our relationship—has been transferred to the kids, because caring for children this little is such a tactile experience. Sex with Joshua has become another obligation, and maybe he feels that because he rarely initiates anymore.

What I feel for Tristan is different. It's a true drive, with force and velocity and momentum, and I couldn't feel such intensity without some degree of reciprocity. It's painful to imagine going back to life without it, becoming only a mother again. I can't wait to see Kyle and Lily, but I also can't ignore the fact that part of me has been reawakened.

Once I'm home, I imagine that I'll again be subsumed by motherhood. My social schedule will be full and intertwined with the kids in terms of playdates and birthday parties and school volunteering and committees and fundraisers. Then there's the book club that's really a wine club and all the local-business-owner schmoozing where I need to support Joshua. I feel tired just thinking about it. I haven't even been gone a week and it already seems like another life, and honestly, not the one I meant to have. Parenthood, yes. The obliteration of self, no.

On island time, I feel like a whole person. With Tristan. Not with Joshua.

And now Tristan is gone.

"Let's move on to the polygraph," Sam says. "We don't have everyone's test results. Per medical advice, Tatiana was unable to participate."

We all laser in on Tatiana, who does look pale and sickly with an afghan over her shoulders, but there isn't much sympathy headed her way. Envy tinged with suspicion seems to be the prevailing sentiment, except for Joshua, who appears truly compassionate. I don't understand his soft spot for that woman.

"We don't have Tatiana's results, and Zarine didn't take the test. Tristan left suddenly before his turn." Dave sounds like he's disappointed in the whole lot of us. "Of the remaining tests, one of them has been invalidated."

After a somber pause, Sam takes over. "One of you used countermeasures. You tried to defeat the test. We want to give that person a chance to admit it now and retest. Otherwise, we'll be forced to expose you. Think how that'll impact the trust you have with your partner, and all the other participants."

My first thought is how I should behave. Would an innocent person stare directly at Sam, or look down, or look around for the true culprit? Is it possible everyone at home really does hate me and they'll all assume my guilt?

"Where's the proof?" Naomi asks in that composed way of hers. But the question itself makes her look a little bit suspect.

"Our polygraph examiners are some of the best in the world," Sam says. "They know countermeasures when they see them. So who's ready to come clean?"

Silence.

Sam turns toward my loveseat. "Joshua, you used counter-measures and as a result, all your answers have to be considered inconclusive."

"I've never even heard of countermeasures," he says blandly, "so how could I use them?"

"There's a lot of debate as to whether polygraph tests are legitimate," The Major says. "Like you all said yourselves, they're not lie detector tests; they're monitoring physical responses. You don't know what our physical responses mean. It's just an educated guess."

"Very educated," Dave says. "These are well-trained, licensed—"

"An educated guess is still a guess," Naomi interrupts. "Are we going to trust a machine over what a person is sitting right here telling us?"

"Joshua says he didn't do it," Tatiana says, "and I believe him."

I realize they're all looking at me now, Joshua included. I'm the only one who hasn't joined the chorus. I dutifully chime in: "He didn't do this. He's the most honest man I know."

I can't help thinking of our fight the night we arrived. When he'd panicked and wanted to go home, I asked point blank if he had anything to tell me before the cameras started rolling. He said no, and I believed him. But since being here, he's become so... unbelievable. There was all that flirting at the pool party with both Naomi and Tatiana, not to mention his knight-in-shining-armor routine. When he pulled me into the closet, who knows what I might have found out if I hadn't stopped him. And how did he know that closet wasn't wired?

Sam launches into the list of questions Joshua had been asked. There's fire in her eyes. She doesn't appreciate us uniting against her and had probably been assured by Marla that we'd been housebroken. "Do you genuinely love Blanche? He said yes. Do you believe Blanche has been unfaithful? He said no. Have you been unfaithful? He said no. Do you have romantic feelings toward any other cast member? He said no." Sam looks at Joshua coldly. "Every single answer was inconclusive."

"I told the truth," Joshua says. "I love my wife, I trust her, and she should trust me."

Dave doesn't even dignify that. "Time to hear Blanche's results. She was asked if she genuinely loves Joshua. She said yes. No deception indicated. She was asked if she has ever thought seriously of leaving him. She said no. No deception indicated. She was asked if she stays only because of the children. She said no. There was deception indicated. She was asked if she has romantic feelings for another cast member. She said no. There was deception indicated."

Damn. That sounds about accurate.

"Anything you'd like to say?" Sam asks me.

"I don't stay only because of the children. But one of the reasons I've stayed is because of my children, that's true. It's a complicated answer. How can a machine understand the nuances, ambiguities, and ambivalences in a long-term relationship?" I'm pleading my case to the room. They've just come to Joshua's aid, so I assume I'll find support, too. Instead, crickets. "And obviously I have feelings for the other cast members. We've been through a lot this week. I didn't hear the word *romantic*."

"I believe you," Joshua says robotically.

It's time to get honest with myself. Joshua has been a disappointment for years. I'd married him expecting a version of his father: a family man who would worship me and be entirely involved in his kids' lives. But maybe Joshua's parents stayed too involved. They'd put in all the seed money for his business, never really let him fail. Joshua hasn't learned to work for anything. Kids are too much effort, so he's abdicated all responsibility, showing up as little as possible, and I haven't argued because I don't particularly like his company. I like him gone.

"Cain and Naomi," Sam says, "you both answered yes to being one another's true love and to having been faithful. There was no deception indicated. Naomi was asked if she lusted for women and she said no. There was no deception indicated." So apparently Marla's dropping that whole closeted-lesbian storyline. "Cain was asked if he lusted for other women. He said no, and there was no deception indicated. But here's the puzzling part. Naomi was asked if she and Cain have had sex in the past year and she answered no. There was no deception indicated. Cain was asked if he and Naomi had sex in the past year and he answered yes. There was no deception indicated."

"How do you explain that discrepancy?" Dave asks. "Neither of you are lying, yet only one of those answers could be the truth."

"Maybe we define sex differently," The Major says.

"That must be it," Naomi adds.

"Moving on," Dave says, like he can't be bothered anymore. "Tristan would have been asked whether he's ever been violent toward women, if he's committed any crimes for which he hasn't been caught, if he's been unfaithful, if he thinks Lauren has been unfaithful, if he's sure that the baby Lauren's carrying is his, and if he has romantic feelings for any other cast member. Meanwhile, Lauren ran out of the test when asked if she'd been unfaithful to Tristan."

Hold the phone. Lauren's been cheating?!? And the baby might not be Tristan's??!!??

"A lot of information comes from the questions people refuse to answer," Dave says, his eyes on Joshua. But I can't think about Joshua right now; my mind is solely on Tristan.

Continuing interview between Detective Sonya Mohr and producer Julie Lindstrom, taking place on Glass Island.

Detective: Marla clearly had a knack for making things happen, and for keeping things from happening. Which begs the question, did she want Tristan and Lauren to run away?

Julie: I highly doubt it. She went ballistic. Then again, she spent so long freaking out on the crew that she might have bought them time to get further. There were contingency plans for things like this but she took forever to find them and print out maps of the island and organize the crew into search parties. We finally got it together and spent hours scouring the beaches and every house on the island and the crew bunkers plus the airport, twice. But after we'd tromped around the most accessible parts of the rainforest for the second time, we started to get really afraid.

If they'd gone deep into the rainforest, the crew definitely wasn't going to follow, not at night. We didn't want to get lost in there ourselves since there were no trails and none of us were trained in rescue operations. There weren't even any seasoned hikers on staff. And there were no emergency services on the island.

If Marla had called for outside help, it likely would have made news and been really embarrassing for the show. Failing to keep your cast safe, with some of them being that desperate to get away—not a good look for her.

Detective: So she was deciding between the welfare of her cast and her reputation and she chose her reputation?

Julie: She was gambling that they'd turn up, unharmed.

Detective: Were there dangerous animals in the rainforest?

Julie: Not as many as you might think. Like there were no jaguars waiting to attack or anything. But there were poisonous frogs and snakes, so you needed to keep your eyes open. The insects could be brutal, though they liked feasting on some people more than others, and they didn't seem to enjoy the taste of Lauren and Tristan all that much.

The most dangerous animals on the island are actually in the water: jellyfish, sea urchins, certain types of coral. We told them things to look for and avoid, but it's a little daunting, which is why you almost never see anyone take a swim in the ocean.

Detective: Did Marla often gamble with the cast? And did she often freak out?

Julie: No, and no. She was either in control, or sure she'd be back in control soon.

Detective: I'm guessing it was no accident that her winning record got broken this season.

Julie: That's right. Only it was the wrong couple.

Detective: She obviously wanted to destroy Tristan and Lauren.

Julie: No, they were the couple she most wanted to stay together.

Detective: But what she put them through... it was practically biblical.

Julie: That was part of her plan. Well, her rewritten plan, after we found out about Alexei. At first, Lauren and Tristan were supposed to be the darlings of the show, and after Alexei, Marla was even more convinced they were her stars. The story editors thought she was nuts. They said the storyboards should be completely redone to cast Lauren as the villain.

Detective: But the show doesn't have villains, right?

Julie: It never did before this season, but Marla had it out for Blanche from day one. Marla never called Blanche by name; it was always the Prom Queen. I felt bad for Blanche because whatever she did, the editing was going to ruin her. No wonder everyone at home despised her. It was preordained.

Detective: Tell me about Tristan and Lauren's rewritten storyboards.

Julie: A pregnant fallen angel, redeemed by the love of a reha-bilitated good man. Marla was going to make them suffer because the greater the obstacles to be overcome, the greater the love story.

Detective: Let's wrap things up for today. I may be in touch with additional questions. Thank you, Julie. You've been extremely helpful.

TWENTY-FIVE

LAUREN

Day Seven

Being on the lam with Tristan turned out to be the most romantic experience of my entire life. Not that it started out that way, and there were some touch-and-go moments in the middle but by the end, it was magic. Best of all, there were no cameras. That meant it was 100 percent real for both of us.

The thing that's so crazy about the island is that once you run away from the villa and into the trees, it becomes *Survivor*. There's nothing manmade, no people; it's just this lush jungle butting up against the sand. Walk into the trees and you get swallowed up. You can't see the beach anymore. You're in the wild.

I was following Tristan, who was too furious to speak. I mean, who wouldn't be, with what he'd just found out about Alexei and me? He was moving quickly and I could barely keep up but we needed to elude production. I assumed they'd come looking for us soon. Tristan and I needed to work this out all alone, in what felt like the right setting: an enchanted forest.

The foliage wasn't too thick to walk through, it wasn't like we needed a machete or anything, and fortunately I was wearing sneakers with my maxi-dress, given all the things that skittered and slithered. There was an omnipresent rustling of leaves and the occasional burst of monkey chatter. We never saw the monkeys or any other large animals. I probably should have been scared since I've got no actual survival skills. But even under such trying circumstances, I couldn't help being in awe of what I was seeing: so many butterflies—with wings of stained glass, some iridescent, some neon—and lime-green frogs with bright red eyes and so many brilliant birds flitting around, hummingbirds and macaws and I didn't know what all else. I didn't have names for what I was seeing. I didn't have a name for what I was feeling.

There was terror and exhilaration and relief and dread. The sense that our entire relationship had been building to this and that in such an extreme environment, it could only go one of two ways. We'd combust or we'd become indestructible.

Early on, we heard the crew calling our names but it stopped fairly quickly. It seemed like they didn't trek in very far. They probably figured that we'd turn up soon enough, before it got dark.

But we didn't turn up. We kept going. Even with the sun's power muted by trees, I could feel I was getting burned. I wasn't going to complain, though. Tristan had barely turned around to check on me; he was probably still too angry, which I totally got. I thought soon we'd have to come out on the other side and reach the road, the only one I'd seen, the one that had taken us from the airport to the crew headquarters and then from the headquarters to the villa. Only somehow, we didn't. We might have been walking in circles. My feet were hot and blistered, and I was getting scraped up around my ankles. I had a scratch on my cheek from an errant branch but I kept up with him. I had to show him what I was made of, that I'd go through jungle —or fire—for him. We didn't speak for the longest time.

Then we did, out where no one could hear us scream. And eventually, we made love with leaves as our mattress. I've never before been so conscious that we're all just animals beneath the surface, that the wild is inside of us.

Somehow, with no compass and almost no time to spare before dusk, he got us back to the beach. I was relieved because I wouldn't have wanted to sleep on the forest floor with all the snakes and the spiders.

We came out onto the sand near one of the other houses. It was like a miniaturized version of the villa: another great room, just slightly less great, and the pool was smaller. We assumed it was occupied by one of the higher-ranking members of the crew and we'd soon be found.

In our last moments of freedom, we went for a swim in the ocean, the first skinny dip of my life and my first baptism.

We were starving and exhausted as we lay down on the lounge chairs, which were identical to the ones by the villa pool. We slept like rocks. The surprise was that production never found us.

Now it's daybreak. Tristan and I agree that it's time to head back to the villa and face the music, hand in hand.

I feel myself slowing down the closer we get. I want to stay with Tristan in this pristine moment, with four shades of purple striping the sky. Only us and our baby, outlined against the horizon. Just as it should be.

He wraps his arms around me from behind. I flinch, just a little. Then I lean back into him.

"I love you, Lauren," he says, "so much. I want you to marry me."

I always thought when he said it, we'd be looking into each other's eyes, but somehow, this is better. We're looking out, toward our future, and it's brightening by the second.

I start crying. He knows (practically) everything, and he still wants me. He's different from everyone who's come before; this is different. Like Marla said, true love really can conquer all, and it can change you. I'm not the same person I was even yesterday.

"I can't wait to marry you," I say.

"The ring's back in our room."

"You brought a ring with you? You were that sure?"

"The show had me meet with a jeweler. They're going to want to see a proposal, and we'll give them one on Decision Day, but this moment is just for us."

We pause, savoring, and then by mutual silent agreement, we start walking again. We come up the back way, past the pool, where Brandon is sleeping in one of the loungers. He's probably supposed to sweep us back into the confessional immediately and have us account for everything that happened last night. Fat chance of that. Some stories will never be told.

"Those loungers really are comfortable," Tristan says in my ear. "We should know."

I stifle a laugh. "Let's not disturb him. He needs his beauty rest."

We let ourselves in to find Julie waiting on a loveseat in the great room with grooves under her eyes, wearing yesterday's clothes. I have the impression she's been awake all night.

"You're back!" she says, leaping up and giving me a hug. Then she starts speaking rapidly into her headset. Brandon comes rushing in from the pool area. He tells Tristan that they're overdue for a one-on-one. Tristan kisses my cheek and goes with him, but I'm not worried. We both know how to keep a secret.

I'm left with Julie. "You won't believe what happened," I say, grinning.

"I'm sure I won't!" Her voice is startlingly loud.

"I don't have my microphone on," I whisper. "I'm only going to tell this to you but—"

"What happened? I want to hear all the details!" She

remains at maximum volume. I've never heard her sound like this before, so phony. "Wait, is that a scratch on your face? Is it infected? Will makeup be able to cover it up? Decision Day is practically here."

My face falls. I'd been so happy and I'd wanted to share it with my friend Julie but instead she's my producer.

"Actually, I don't feel like talking." As I walk away, heading up the stairs, I'm hoping she'll come after me to explain or apologize. But of course she doesn't.

It's stupid to feel hurt. I should have known this whole time that she wasn't really on my side. Blanche would have known.

Julie doesn't matter, Blanche doesn't matter. This is almost over, and then it will be Tristan and me forever. Like I said, I didn't come here to make friends.

I take a long shower, washing away the rainforest and the sand and my interaction with Julie. I relive my favorite memories from my escape with Tristan. The hot water soothes my mosquito bites.

Afterward, while I'm trying in vain to cover up the scratch on my cheek, Tristan dashes past me into the shower. "Brandon had lots of questions!" he calls over the running water. I assume my confessional will have to wait because Julie knocks and tells us to report to the great room in ten minutes. What is it with these people and ten minutes? She's brought us a few protein bars since we missed breakfast. I mutter thanks.

Tristan and I look better rested and a whole lot happier than everyone else. Tatiana, especially, is a wreck. Her hair is up in a messy bun, she's in cutoff shorts and a white T-shirt (I'm surprised she even brought clothes that plain), and there's no light in her eyes. The Major and Naomi are neatly dressed but they look wrung out. Blanche and Joshua are just themselves. I'm not sure anything short of a full demolition could ever change them. Blanche is done up as ever, in full makeup and hair and jewelry, and you know what? I've got nothing to worry about, no matter how excited she clearly is to see Tristan.

Sam and Dave survey the group. When Sam gets to Tristan and me, she says without a smile, "Welcome back. In our next therapy session, we'll have to process where you've been. But for now, we have an exercise to get to." She addresses the group. "It's a reprise from season one: the couple swap."

I try to meet Tristan's eyes but he's focused on the therapists. This is the first I'm hearing of it, and I don't like the sound.

"We're going to match you with a partner and send you out on overnight dates," Dave says. "You won't have any contact with your current partner until tomorrow when you'll decide if that's who you'll be leaving with."

I'm not going to see Tristan for twenty-four hours until Decision Day? Meanwhile he'll be with...? No way. They wouldn't.

"The pairings are Naomi and Lauren, Joshua and Tatiana, and Blanche and Tristan. With Zarine still absent, we have an odd number. That means that Cain has no partner. You'll be on your own, trying out life as a single man."

I raise my hand. "I'm not sure about these pairings."

Sam ignores me. "You all need to gain new perspective on your old relationship by seeing what life could be like with someone else. See if the grass really is greener."

So I've been paired with Naomi to keep me out of Tristan's hair while he's off seeing what the grass is like with Blanche? She can barely contain her joy, and I'm seething. As she glances over, I feel like she can tell, and her smile widens.

"Say your goodbyes," Sam tells us. "The limos are outside, waiting to take you to your personalized destinations."

I give Tristan the most passionate kiss I can muster under the circumstances. "Be good," I tell him, and he laughs like it's a joke.

"Have fun," he says, and then he heads over to Blanche, who's just been released from a pro forma embrace with Joshua.

"You ready to go?" Naomi asks me.

I'm watching Tristan and Blanche, her hand on his arm, and no, I am not ready. I feel like stamping my feet and shouting how unfair this is.

Instead, I nod and force a smile, and Julie ushers us outside into the first of three limos. Then she takes the seat across from us, next to a cameraman. I stare out the back window, wanting one more glimpse of Tristan.

"Don't worry," Naomi says. "I'll keep my hands to myself." She turns to Julie. "Does being paired with a woman for the couple swap mean Sam and Dave still think I'm gay?"

"You and Lauren were matched for clinical reasons."

"Mm-hmm." Naomi isn't buying it. "Because if the show hurts my brand, they're going to have a lawsuit on their hands."

It's the first I've heard about Naomi's "brand." I assume she's talking about the gym she and The Major own. It's also the first time I've heard that tone from her, like she's the talent and Julie is the help.

"Where are we going, anyway?" Naomi taps her fingernails impatiently.

"You'll see in a few minutes."

"You like romantic dinners and long walks on the beach?" Naomi says to me. "Piña coladas and getting caught in the rain? You know that song?" I shake my head. Then she asks Julie, who also shakes her head. "Way back in the Pleistocene era, there was a song about a guy who places a personal ad—which you've probably never heard of but it's like Tinder only in a newspaper and with no pictures—and this guy, he names all the things he wants to do with someone special, like drinking piña coladas and getting caught in the rain, and he hears from the perfect woman, who turns out to be the one he's already with."

I scrunch my nose. "So basically, they meant to cheat but then caught each other? And it's a love song?"

"I guess people can have pretty strange notions of love." Naomi shifts toward me in the seat, her expression growing thoughtful. "You and Cain seem to have gotten close. Has he said anything to you about our marriage?"

"Not really."

Naomi does an efficient nod, like she's glad we've gotten that out of the way. "Tristan and I haven't had any heart-to-hearts but from what I can tell, he's crazy about you."

I glance at my naked ring finger, which will soon be clothed, and smile. But then I think where he'll soon be heading. "Blanche seems crazy about him."

"You don't need to worry about that if you trust him."

"That's what The Major—I mean Cain—told me."

"Then he and I agree on something. Lately, he doesn't like that many people, but he took an immediate liking to you." She turns thoughtful. "So I didn't mind helping you out on the beach, getting catty, making Blanche uncomfortable." I widen my eyes. I hadn't realized I'd been so transparent about wanting to stick it to Blanche like she'd stuck it to me during truth or dare. "Maybe someday you'll be able to repay the favor."

I look again out the back window of our limo. Tristan and Blanche are now getting into theirs right behind us. They're so caught up in conversation that he doesn't even bother looking around for me. When we arrived on this island, his eyes were a heat-seeking missile, and I was fire. *What the fuck? Doesn't he care that I'm still right fucking here?*

I need to calm down. Those are my pregnancy hormones talking. Tristan has just affirmed our love in the absolute boldest, most emphatic way possible. No one can touch us.

Naomi follows my eyes. I don't like how sympathetic she looks as she says, "Yes, you really are going to need a friend, aren't you?"

TWENTY-SIX

TATIANA

"Think of it as an experiment," Joshua says.

"This isn't science class."

"Then think of it as an experience."

I'm sick of that word. Sick of all their words.

I stare out the limo window. I've been missing Zarine bad, and it's only getting worse. I want to crawl out of my skin.

Maybe Zarine will be waiting at our destination for a rendezvous. During the first two seasons, there were surprises that made people happy.

Poor Joshua, stuck here with me while his wife is obviously dying to jump Tristan's bones.

"It's going to be great," Joshua says. "All we need are some ground rules." He's trying hard to make up for the enthusiasm gap between us. It's a little bit cute. Futile, but cute. The camera operator sitting beside him seems to think so, too, which is irritating.

"I hate rules," I say, though I might be better off if I sometimes had to color inside the lines.

"I do, too, actually. Okay, it's not a rule. It's more of a

premise. Imagine there's time travel, and we've gone back ten years to before we knew our current partners."

"Pretend to be twenty-two again?" I groan. "So much angst. So much eyeliner." So many drugs to wake me up and to put me to sleep and to help me forget.

He grins. "Be yourself, at any age so long as you're single. Because for today, Zarine and Blanche don't exist." I frown. "I mean, neither of them exists yet for us, as someone we know. They exist out there in the world. They're just fine out there in the world."

He knows that about Blanche, but we can't know that about Zarine. "I don't feel like playing games." I close my eyes. "I need a nap."

"Well, if that's an option wherever we're going, then okay."

"You don't care if I fall asleep on our 'date'?" The air quotes are strongly implied.

"You do whatever you want to do. I'm just glad we're together." He leans toward me, talking lower. "I have to confess, this time-travel idea didn't come out of nowhere. I've been thinking about it for the last few days, hoping they'd do the couple swap and I'd get you. For obvious reasons."

He means our history. Would that be clear to anyone watching? Are viewers starting to dig into my past? The hive mind can solve all kinds of mysteries.

"It's not that obvious to me," I say, looking out the window, telegraphing that I'd prefer ignorance. He's acting like we're not being filmed, and like we're not miked up. Moreover, he really is acting like he's single. He truly could not give a fuck less about his wife and whether she exists. But I love my girl. "I'm going to be terrible company. I already am."

"Why do you have to put yourself down? You do it more than you think."

"Okay, I have a rule: No probing insights. No psychoanalysis." The last thing I need is him referencing anything I told him during our conversation the other day in my room. I'm still holding out hope that it'll be too dull to air. When he made Zarine sound unsupportive, I should have defended her. She's my person, no matter what.

No, scratch that. The absolute last thing I need is my past getting out. Zarine would be mortified, and she's already been through enough with her parents.

"Agreed," he says.

"And just so you know, I don't have any whimsy in me today. I'm not here to entertain you, if that's the reason you were hoping I'd be your swap partner. Even if there was a margarita machine, I'd still be miserable."

"Maybe I'm planning to entertain you."

I laugh sardonically. "Good luck with that."

"I remember the first time I heard you laugh."

He must mean years ago when we first met. Will the viewers pick up the allusion that time? The camera operator is sitting up straighter in recognition, ready to zoom in. It's like Joshua's trying to get us in trouble. Just because his marriage is trash doesn't give him the right to mess with my relationship. It's like he said the other day: He wishes he had what I have. Plenty of people would kill to be in my shoes.

"Zip it," I say.

"Tatiana—"

"Not another word." I look out the window and he must be able to feel that it's a command and not a request because he complies.

When the limo comes to a halt, I stomp out. We're on a deserted beach, and there are horses, saddled and waiting. A blanket has been laid out with a picnic basket and a bottle of champagne sweating on ice. I walk over, pop the cork, and swig from the bottle. Because fuck him.

Joshua comes up behind me. "I'm sorry," he says.

I hiss in his ear, "Not one more word about our past, do you understand? Or you will regret it." Then I step away from him and let my voice ring out so that it'll surely be captured by the microphone, and by the camera crew that's followed us. "Zarine's the best partner I've ever had, and all I want is to have her back." He nods, unconvinced. "What, you don't think she's good for me?"

"That's what this exercise is about. Seeing if what you have is what you need. It's not about anyone telling you their opinion. You decide for yourself."

He's so earnest, so unargumentative, that my anger falls away. I'm suddenly exhausted from all the emotional upheaval —not just since Zarine's been gone, but when she was around, too. I put the champagne bottle back in the ice bucket. "You hungry?" I say. "You want to see what they packed for us?"

We sit on the blanket, taking out fried chicken, biscuits, corn on the cob, and brownies. Then we stuff our faces with such urgency that we don't even stop to talk. I haven't been eating, and I haven't showered today either. The sun is intense, so I walk into the ocean in my T-shirt and shorts. I lie down where it's shallow and let the waves wash over me.

Joshua joins me, and we're on our backs, staring up at the sky. "When I was little," I say, "my dad and I always played that game where you look at clouds and say what you see. It's basically a Rorschach test, isn't it? You know, the ink blots where a therapist tells you if you're crazy or not." The show psychologist did a few of them with me while assessing my "fitness" to return to the villa.

"You're not crazy."

"You're not a therapist."

"I'd love to play that game with you, only there are no clouds in our sky." No clouds, but a camera operator lurking nearby.

"We can use our imaginations." I lower my eyelids. "No, it doesn't work. That makes me want to go to sleep."

"So do it."

Just like that time in my room, I find it's easy to be with him one-on-one. Alone, he's such a warm and accepting presence. When Blanche is around, he turns into her mirror image, as plastic as she is. I hope he leaves her on Decision Day. Not that I have any vested interest in the outcome.

"Thanks for letting me be a boring date," I say. "I've never thought it was okay to be boring."

He returns his gaze to the sky. "Well, I'm not bored."

I laugh. "Yeah, who wouldn't love lying on the beach in soggy clothes with some crazy bitch, trying to spot nonexistent clouds?"

"Don't call yourself names. If you only follow one rule, follow that one, okay?"

"I've got a rule for you."

"Yeah?" His blue eyes are far too intent on mine.

"Stop looking at me like that."

"Like what?"

But he knows. And I know that what happened between us once upon a time can never happen again. I want Zarine back—I need her back—and nothing's going to stand in my way.

TWENTY-SEVEN

THE MAJOR

"Hi, Daddy!" Rachel says.

"Where's Mom?" Rebecca asks. They're in their dorm room, crowded in together around the phone. Even though there's only a three-hour time difference between Glass Island and L.A., we've had a hard time syncing up our schedules. When Naomi and I have access to our cell phones, the twins are almost always in class or at practice.

"I'm so happy to see you," I tell them. "Mom's off on an exercise."

"What kind of exercise?" Rachel looks worried. I've seen that expression too much over the past months.

"I'm not allowed to tell you that. And you're not allowed to tell me what you've seen on the episodes. Which means we need to keep the focus on you."

I can tell they don't want to, though. Whatever they've been watching has them concerned.

"How are you doing, really?" Rachel looks so much like Naomi when she pivots to being the grown-up who needs to take care of me.

"To be honest, today's been a little rough. I guess I'm not

used to solitude." Unlike, say, Lauren or Joshua, I don't have to worry what my better half is doing.

"You miss Mom." I can tell that while they don't like me having a rough day, they like the idea of me missing their mom. We told them that this was just going to be a tune-up for our marriage, but who knows what Marla's been showing them each night?

Part of the reason Naomi and I signed up for this was so that when we split up down the line, the girls would have seen with their own eyes that we'd left no stone unturned. Then in three months or six months or a year, after the business has gotten enough of a boost that we can sell it off and split the proceeds, we'll sit them down and tell them we fought nobly and lost. Divorce was inevitable.

It wasn't fair, the way Naomi looked at me in the shower, like I'm a quitter for wanting to move forward with our shared plan. Why does she make me reject her over and over?

She and I just don't see the world the same way anymore. She's spent the last couple of years trying to stifle me, to turn me back into the man she married. But there's no going back, so we're better off moving forward without each other.

I don't want to have to keep hurting her. That's why we have to go through with the plan, even if I am feeling some momentary reservations. We've been a unit for so long that of course there will be some death spasms.

We already know the decision we're going to make on that beach tomorrow. No suspense there. But I can't predict anything beyond that, least of all myself.

TWENTY-EIGHT

BLANCHE

I let out a little moan of pleasure. I can't help it, with this kind of touch. Then I glance at Tristan to see if he's heard.

No, he's too busy getting the tension pounded out of his shoulder muscles. I almost moan again. Those shoulders. That smooth olive skin. He is a sight to behold, and I never would have thought we'd be here together, on side-by-side tables, having a couples massage.

The show took us by boat to a different island, where they'd rented out an entire spa. Tristan and I had all manner of pampering with facials and detoxes and wraps and dips in whirlpools of varying temperatures. In between, we were served a gourmet meal, multiple courses with wine pairings, on a veranda overlooking the ocean. We haven't talked about Joshua or Lauren once since we arrived, and the conversation has never flagged.

The spa is also a hotel, and we'll be staying overnight in separate rooms. I like to imagine myself knocking on his door; I can see him opening it, and then a little wider. What if this were our honeymoon?

After the massage, we return to the same veranda. It's night-time, the air cooling and the stars just beginning to peek out. Because we're the only guests, we get to stay in our robes, which makes it feel incredibly intimate. Except for the crew and what I have to talk to Tristan about, it's perfect.

Decision Day is tomorrow so it's my last chance to make sure he has all the necessary information. Given how lovey-dovey he and Lauren were this morning, he must not know about the lie detector questions. Marla might intend to blind-side him tomorrow, in which case he'll be humiliated, but worse than that would be if she intends to protect her track record and let him go ahead and propose. Lauren's only going to betray him in some new way down the line. A woman like that can't help herself.

As we're sipping cucumber water and taking in the view and I'm screwing up my courage, Tristan smiles over. "There's no better swap partner than you, Blanche."

"I wouldn't want to be here with anyone else."

He holds my gaze, and I feel like it really might happen. He might kiss me. But if he does, I can't kiss him back, can I? I can't commit adultery, not on camera.

I almost told him about Lauren a hundred times today but kept delaying because the second I did, it would shift the focus from what he might feel for me to what he feels for her. Once I tell him, he'll associate me with something horribly painful. But he has to know who she really is.

"Where did you and Lauren sleep last night?" It's not as artful as I might have hoped, but it could still get the job done. "I mean, after you ran off."

He cocks his head. "Where'd that come from?"

"I was just wondering, since tonight, you'll be sleeping here, with me. I mean, not with me, but you know, right down the hall." I'm stammering. I never stammer.

"It'll be good for me to spend the night alone. Big day tomorrow."

"Huge." I hesitate. He has to know. But I don't want to be the one to tell him.

"What are you going to do? Go home with Joshua, back to your life, like none of this ever happened?"

Is he offering an alternative? "I'm not exactly sure what's happening."

"What do you want to happen?" He's staring into my eyes and I feel faint.

"I don't know. What do you want to happen?"

It's a game of intimacy chicken, and he breaks eye contact, looking out toward the ocean which is navy blue in the half-light. "I think you and your kids deserve better. Joshua's not a good guy."

I didn't want to hear his name just then. "Well, he's not a bad guy."

"Are you sure about that?"

"Are you sure about Lauren?" That's not how I wanted to kick it off. But now I have to go through with it. "Did she tell you what she was asked during the lie detector test? Why she ran out?"

"We talked a lot while we were gone." It's the first time he's been cagey with me. We've always been so unguarded with one another.

"Sam and Dave read us Lauren's lie detector questions, and yours, too." I start playing with the cucumber floating in my water.

"And?"

I take a deep breath. "Do you know Lauren cheated on you?"

He contemplates the ocean for a full minute. In profile, I can't tell if he's sad or angry or both. If it's at Lauren or me or both. He says, "Thank you." Then he stands up, kisses me on the forehead, and walks inside.

The thing I've forgotten, since it's been so many years, is

that a big part of me hates being in love. The powerlessness of it. That someone else can make or break you with a look or a touch.

I'm not sure I want to feel that again. But it seems I have no choice.

TWENTY-NINE

LAUREN

Decision Day

Naomi and I spent a lovely day on a glass-bottomed boat, watching exotic fish darting beneath our feet as we sipped mimosas. Whatever we were supposed to learn, we didn't.

Afterward, I went to sleep in our room; Tristan didn't. Which meant a fitful night punctuated by images of him and Blanche on the dance floor. That had been in front of everyone. What would they do once they were alone?

I remind myself they haven't been alone, there's a crew tailing them, soon to be converted into millions of viewers. More importantly, I know how Tristan feels about me, and I know he's not a cheater.

It's scary, though, having told him about Alexei and then spending time apart. He forgave me but he could always reconsider, especially if he's chosen to make Blanche his confidante.

Julie brings me a muffin and juice. Hot on her heels are my esthetician, makeup person, and hairstylist. It upsets me to look at Julie but she's not looking at me, either. Since we finish filming today and the cast flies home first thing tomorrow, I've nearly outlived my usefulness for her.

I'm not going to think about Julie; I'm going to think about Tristan and the second proposal that's coming my way. I have a very specific vision of an intricate chignon to go with the white spaghetti-strap dress (the required uniform for Decision Day) that's hanging on the back of the door. It accentuates my baby bump in a way that I don't love but Tristan will. There's nothing holding me back and nothing to fear. We've already decided on one another.

After I'm dolled up, Julie escorts me outside. The Decision Day ceremony will be filmed on the beach underneath a floral arch festooned with white lilies. Sam and Dave are already positioned there like ministers, and a drill sergeant producer is ordering us around, putting us in two lines, men in one, women in the other. Tristan and I are sent to the front of our lines, we'll be up first.

I keep trying to catch Tristan's eye for reassurance that we're just as we were yesterday morning, that a night with Blanche has only confirmed that he and I are made for each other. But he's dialed in, the consummate professional, focused entirely on the drill sergeant.

When we're given the cue, Tristan and I will move in front of Sam and Dave and clasp hands and state whether our intentions are to leave the island together or alone. In the previous seasons, couples always chose to stay together and rings were always exchanged. (According to Tristan, either couples got engaged or they pledged their love anew with heftier rocks.) This season promises to be more suspenseful, but not for me. After Tristan and I have publicly committed, we'll move to the back of the line and become the substitute bridesmaid and groomsman as the next couple comes forward, and so on. It's a revolving door wedding party, with all the women in their identical spaghetti-strap dresses and the men in their tuxedos. Tatiana is in line, alone and antsy. Zarine hasn't shown up yet.

As the ceremony begins, Sam delivers a speech that sounds slightly canned, like she has to repeat it every season. It ends with a line about how our future starts *now*. She shimmers in red satin, and the curtain of her dark hair is arranged around the rose behind her ear. It's matrimony, flamenco style.

As Tristan and I approach the altar, he smiles over at me, and I beam back. He's so handsome in his pearl-gray tuxedo, and I love him so much that it's hard to believe I ever had doubts, that we ever needed to come here at all.

He takes my hands in his. "I'm not perfect," he says, "and you're not perfect but our time here has shown me that we're perfect together. We can get through anything. I love you, Lauren, and I love our baby, and if you love me, if you'll have me..." He gets down on one knee in the sand, producing a ring from his vest pocket.

I knew it was going to happen, I know that it's all for show, all for *the* show but I'm not acting when my eyes fill with tears. I'm not acting when I say, "I love you, too, Tristan. Thank you for being so patient with me while I figured out that you're the best thing in my life and I never want to be without you."

"Is that a yes?"

He's grinning, and I'm laughing and crying at once. "Yes, yes, yes!"

As he slips the ring on my finger, as he lifts me up into his arms and kisses me, I'm almost the happiest I've ever been in my life, second only to our true sunrise proposal.

He's twirling me around when I'm suddenly gripped by terror. Can I really get this kind of fairy-tale ending after what I've done?

THIRTY

TATIANA

Another cloudless day. It's full-on tropical swelter and I should be sweating, but I'm a block of ice. I feel frozen in every way as I stand before Sam and Dave in my white slip dress, same as the ones worn by Naomi, Lauren, and Blanche, though it looks very different on me than it does on them, Naomi being so strong and toned and Lauren pregnant and Blanche with her perfect boobs/boob job. I've lost five pounds this week that I could ill afford, you can see ribs. Will Zarine be here, or am I essentially being left at the altar?

Sam and Dave reveal nothing. For all I know, they've already told Zarine about my past and they're about to somehow produce a television screen from the sky and roll footage of her leaving for the airport in a limo. Or she's going to walk up and tell me that she's disgusted by me. Or she's planning to come out and profess her love and then they'll tell her what I never have, zooming in for a close-up.

Unless Marla doesn't know. Unless Joshua wasn't a plant at all.

I can't look at Joshua. I'm well aware of what he thinks I should do, he made that abundantly clear last night, but I need to trust my own mind and heart. He doesn't know me like he thinks he does, and he certainly doesn't know Zarine. He's the one who should be ending a relationship, not me.

I wait. And wait. And wait. It's probably only five minutes, but it's nearly intolerable. I notice that producers are talking on their headsets, and it occurs to me that maybe Marla isn't calling all the shots. Zarine could have pulled a fast one. I'm starting to think that all is lost and then...

For a second, it seems like a mirage, but no, she's here, gliding toward me in her slip dress. My heart nearly stops from relief and fear and pure, unadulterated love.

I grab her hands fervently, saying how happy I am to see her. She doesn't pull away but her face is placid and impossible to read. "Are you okay?" I ask. She nods. I want to know what they've done to her but that'll have to wait until later. Not much later, thankfully. This'll all be over soon.

It's clear that she's waiting for me to make my declaration first. So I dive in, just as I did that day at the pool, telling her how much I've missed her and how awful I feel about the situation with her parents and my role in it. I can see my wrongs and my faults, and I'm ready to grow up and be the partner she deserves. We don't need to fight anymore, because in the most important ways, we're the same: two women who need to accept ourselves and be accepted. That's what love is, right?

"I understand if you can't forgive me now," I say, "but I hope you will someday, after I prove to you that I've changed. Come home with me, please."

A tear trickles down Zarine's face. Such a goddess. My goddess, and I'm going to worship her, always. If she'll let me. If she'll have me.

"I forgive you now," she says. "And I hope in time you can forgive me."

My heart sinks. "Zarine, please, I—"

"I take responsibility for all the pain I've caused you, all the times I doubted your intentions. I should have trusted you. Because I love you more than anything, and I believe in your love for me. I'm going to prove that I've changed, too."

I break out into an enormous smile, and she smiles, too, much less broadly but just as sincerely. A study in contrasts.

"Sam and Dave," Zarine says, "I need to thank you. You were right to bring my parents here. I might never have been honest if I hadn't been forced into it, and without honesty, I could never feel as free as I do now."

Dave gives her a big smile and a thank you. Sam is more reticent. Maybe she's one of those people who can't take a compliment.

A producer approaches and I think, *Oh no, what now?* Then I see that he's acting as a ringbearer.

Zarine takes the box from him and opens it. I gasp. The platinum band is adorned with a huge sapphire, the most vivid and saturated of blues. On our best day on the island, Zarine and I had compared the shade of the Caribbean to the Pacific Ocean, and at that moment, it had been precisely the color of the stone that's before me.

"Will you please, please marry me?" Zarine asks.

It's not something we've discussed before, and it has special significance after what happened with her parents. This proposal means that she's choosing me, come what may. It's us against the world.

Zarine's changed, the ring is epic, and the moment demands a yes.

I don't look at Joshua. I refuse to look at anyone but Zarine. I'm shocked by the weight of the ring on my finger but I'm sure I'll get used to it. I'm going to have to.

Zarine starts kissing me and that's when I feel the chill, that's when I know: Not all change on this island is for the better.

THIRTY-ONE
THE MAJOR

Naomi's a vision in white. Beautiful, smart, kind, accomplished, my wife is a truly righteous woman, in every way.

One of the things I told myself when I first hatched this plan was that we'd send the message to millions of midlife couples that they should never give up; we'd inspire people to rediscover one another. Then by the time Naomi and I quietly divorced months later, the good would have already been done and it could help cancel out some of the bad. Divorce is a sin, yes, but there are far worse ones.

"Naomi," I say, taking her hand, trying to channel all the feelings from our wedding, all the hope and excitement and disbelief that a woman this incredible was going to yoke herself to me for life. "You are unparalleled." When I look into her eyes, I begin to falter. "I want to tell you... You need to know..."

She gently removes her hand from mine and holds it up. Stop.

"I love you, Naomi." That will always be true. I'm too old for one knee as I reach into my pocket for the ring the show has provided, much more ostentatious than I'd been able to afford all those years ago. "I want to marry you all over again. When we get home, let's renew our vows. In front of our girls, in front of—"

"No."

I stare at her, sure I must have misunderstood.

"This relationship has been all I could have asked for," she says. "It's produced two beautiful girls and many wonderful memories. But after being here on the island, I've realized that it's time to move on."

I'm speechless.

The only woman I've ever loved has just blindsided me on reality television.

THIRTY-TWO

BLANCHE

After the shock of Naomi and The Major's split, it suddenly seems much more possible. More doable. You can follow your heart, even if it takes you in the other direction.

Joshua and I stand before Sam and Dave.

Both our lie detector tests have left us with more questions than answers. I still don't know if Joshua really used counter-measures, and if he did, why. Since I already know where the bodies are buried (metaphorically speaking, of course), what could he possibly be concealing? Surely it isn't hidden depths. And he can't know if I'm still in love with him or if *love* has become a synonym for *obligation*, what I'd do if there were no children involved. Neither of us knows what the other did last night, while we were out dating other people.

But I know that I have completely fallen for Tristan. Watching him lift Lauren up and spin her around, a tableau of young giddy exhilaration, knowing their whole lives are ahead of them—it was excruciating.

In coming to the island, I hadn't thought Joshua and I were risking much. It didn't seem like either of us could ever walk away, not with all we have waiting for us at home, two little people whose trust is blind and absolute. They need us.

Or do they just need me?

Joshua puts his sweaty hand on my cheek, and my first thought is whether it will ruin my makeup.

He begins to profess his love, sounding like AI that's spent the last week learning to be human. He says he knows he hasn't always been the best talker or the best listener and he's going to do better, he's going to be a more attentive husband and father. It's a regurgitation of everything Sam and Dave scoffed at from the first day. And has he mentioned how much he loves me?

If I didn't know better, I'd think his proposal had been calculated to increase the odds of refusal. There's no intimacy in it, no romance. Nothing like what I felt last night with Tristan.

"Blanche, do you still take this man to be your husband?" Sam asks. "To have and to hold, in sickness and in health, for as long as you both shall live?"

I'm fighting not to glance back at Tristan. He was the one who asked me if I'd be going back to my life like nothing had ever happened. Was that him admitting that there's something between us?

I can feel everyone's eyes on my back, imploring me to finish up. I'm the last one. They're all puddling, they want to get to the wrap party and be rid of these cameras. They're ready to go back to their lives, even if I'm not.

What am I waiting for? There's no new information. I have it all.

Now I just have to say it.

THIRTY-THREE

LAUREN

Blanche took her sweet melodramatic time but she did say yes. Now we can celebrate. The end of filming, the beginning of everything.

Tristan smiles over at me from his row. My understanding is that all that's left is to get our champagne and toast the future. Close this chapter, start writing the next. Pick out a name for our baby, decorate her room, enjoy these last months before everything changes again.

I mouth the words, "I love you." Tristan mouths them back.

I'm trying not to flaunt my happiness. I can't believe what happened to The Major, that a piano basically fell on his head and now he has to stand in his line with Naomi a few arm's lengths away. I hadn't seen that coming, she really seemed to love him. He probably needs a drink more than any of us. Where are those trays?

The longer we stand, the more it seems like something is wrong. No, like something is being orchestrated. Marla might have one last trick up her sleeve.

But it can't touch Tristan and me. He's already proposed. Twice.

I see Tristan smiling at Blanche, and I don't even care. I mean, she's stuck with Joshua while I've got Tristan. Once we're back in L.A., if Tristan wants to be friends with her, I can deal with that. I have no reason not to trust him. And if Blanche and I can bury the hatchet at tonight's wrap party, so much the better. We really have nothing to fight over. I've already won.

How much longer are they going to make us stand here? I'm about to make a joke about how we should stage another walkout when I see something that knocks the wind out of me. Tristan is quickly at my side, asking if I'm okay, if it's a bout of morning sickness or heat stroke.

I shake my head as Alexei—all six-foot-four of him—goes right up to Sam and Dave, who are still positioned under the flower awning. That was the tip-off, I guess, how they never moved.

Sam asks Tristan and me to step forward. I can feel him looking at me curiously, but I've got my eyes on Dave, who's produced an envelope from the inside pocket of his tuxedo.

"Lauren, you and Alexei already know each other. Tristan, have you two met?" Dave asks.

"No," Tristan says, his voice tight, "we haven't."

"You do know about Alexei, though? That he and Lauren were intimate during your relationship?"

"She told me."

"I knew about you the whole time, and I didn't care," Alexei says. "Sorry, man."

Tristan keeps his eyes on Dave. "Why's he here?"

"Inside this envelope are the results of a DNA test," Dave says. "During preproduction, you both submitted to medical tests, and authorized us to do additional tests with the blood samples as we saw fit. Alexei agreed to be tested."

"Why would he need to be tested?" Tristan says. "It was once."

Alexei adopts a pitying expression. "Try ten, maybe fifteen times, bro, and I didn't always wrap it up. Again, sorry about that."

Tristan drops my hand but he still turns to me wanting to hear that it's not true. Only I can't lie to him anymore.

My confession had been carefully worded to give the impression it was just one time, though I never said that directly. Since Tristan never asked, I figured he didn't really want to know. Anyone in his position would be eager to forgive.

"No," Tristan tells me. They might not be able to see it on TV but he's shaking even as he's trying to sound certain. "You're an honest person. You wouldn't even say you loved me until you were sure."

"And now I am sure," I say. I'm shaking, too. "I couldn't love you more."

"If it's my baby, I'll do the right thing," Alexei says, and I want to scrape my lacquered nails down his face. He's never done the right thing in his life.

I see something come over Tristan, his hands involuntarily balling into fists, and I fear that he might actually kill Alexei. I step in between them for Tristan's safety, not Alexei's.

"You didn't even use a condom," Tristan says, his eyes on me. "Did you respect yourself at all? Did you respect me?"

"I haven't always." Tears are running down my cheeks. "But it's different now."

"Open the envelope," Tristan orders Dave.

Even Sam can't stomach much more. "Open the envelope," she commands.

Dave complies. "With 99.9 percent accuracy, Tristan is the father."

My shoulders sag with relief. I turn to Tristan but he's walking away, back toward the villa, ripping his microphone off. Brandon's chasing him because I'm sure they want an interview while the agony is fresh. Tristan gives Brandon a look that sends him scurrying.

He can't scare me off no matter what he does. I chase after him, my runaway groom. I have to make him understand.

He's already through the great room and into the foyer and is about to open the front door. "Please don't go," I beg. "Let me explain."

"Get away from us," he says menacingly to the camera team that's followed. "I'm warning you."

Then he yanks open the door, ushers me outside onto the circular driveway, and shuts it behind us. He leans back against it, holding on to the knob in case anyone tries to open it. No one does but that's probably because they're just going to come for us the other way. In other words, we don't have much time.

"I'm so sorry, Tristan. But I didn't lie to you. Everything I said was true. I just didn't say how many times it had been."

"Or that he could have been the father." His words are coming out with difficulty.

"I knew he wasn't the father. The dates didn't match up. I always knew in my heart that this was your baby." The disgust in his face almost stops me but I soldier on. "It's not like I was with him fifteen different nights. It was more like six or seven nights. We just..."

"You just did it more than one time, every time." His eyes are blazing but there are tears in them. He's probably thinking that before this island, we'd never done it more than once in a day.

"Things were so different between you and me then. Look at my face. Can't you see how I feel about you now?"

But he won't look at me. "We were all alone, with no cameras. You had your chance. Why didn't you tell me everything then?"

Speaking of cameras, a crew is approaching from the direction of the beach.

"Get back!" Tristan yells. "I swear to God, get back!" Whether it's out of decency or fear, they come to a halt.

"I thought that if you forgave me once, it would be easier for you to do it again," I say. "I could tell you the rest at home when we'd have all the time in the world."

"So we'd get engaged and then go home and you would have told me the rest?"

"Yes."

He lets go of the door and turns his back to me. "I don't believe you."

I want to think that saying "yes, yes, yes" to his proposal would make an honest woman of me, but I might have been able to rationalize my lies right up through "I do." And beyond, really, since I wouldn't want to risk my baby's family. Because if I never did anything like that again, if I was always going to be faithful, then how would it help for him to know every sordid detail?

"I was so ashamed, Tristan," I say, "and terrified that it would change the way you looked at me. Since we've been here, I've learned to look at you that same way: with total love and devotion." He doesn't turn around but he must be listening. He's still here, isn't he? "Like when you told me your secret, you were afraid, too. But I only loved you more for what you've been through, and for sharing it with me."

He spins around. "Are you comparing what I did when I was a teenager to what you did over the past year? I was a kid! Are you using that against me, like collateral or extortion or something?"

"No, I wouldn't do that!" But I do need him. There's no way I can raise this baby alone. Tristan is the steadying force in my life, and I can't let him walk away, no matter what.

He advances on me. "We are nothing alike. I was defending my sister and you don't know the meaning of loyalty."

"I'd never—"

"You pretended to come clean, but you'll always be dirty."

He stalks away. I crumple to the ground, and that's when I hear the whoops from the beach.

It's a wrap.

THIRTY-FOUR

LAUREN

Day Nine

Tristan and I are packing in silence. I don't know where he slept, and there's no point in asking. He won't speak to me.

Last night at the wrap party, I was devastated and desperate. I kept following him around—thinking if we talked a little longer, if I could explain in different words, if I apologized again, if I reminded him just one more time how much he loves me and how much I love him and that we're almost a family—until he told me to stay away for good. For my own good, since he didn't want to do anything he'd regret.

I'll find a way to prove my loyalty. I won't give up on us, ever.

Tristan might not want to talk now, but I can wait him out. After all, we'll be connected to each other for the rest of our lives. Away from here, he'll see reason. We just have to get off this island, and fast.

Or not so fast. I hear Marla's voice over the intercom: "Please report to the great room." In ten minutes? "Now." It's all the more chilling because she never does announcements.

I stop stuffing clothes into my suitcase and look over at Tristan. Is it my imagination, or is he frozen in fear, too?

We're under Marla's jurisdiction for just a few hours longer. Then we'll fly home and I'll do my penance away from the cameras. Tristan forgave me once, he can do it again. He'll want to for our little girl. And because he loves me, so much. He used to tell me that all the time before we arrived. It's this black magic island, that's all. We're caught in its grasp.

At the wrap party, we'd gotten our phones back, without restrictions. The cast members barely lifted their heads for hours. I didn't have the stamina to binge-watch all the episodes, so I relied on social media and recaps to fill me in. My cheating had actually been revealed in one of the early episodes. Marla included the conversation I had with Julie in the hall after I'd ripped off my microphone, not realizing that Julie was still wearing hers and there was also a stationary camera taking video. It was an obviously unstaged moment, and the viewers had really responded to my vulnerability. Now I have hundreds of thousands of followers/defenders who want me to know I'm worthy and deserving of love. They're really pulling for Tristan and me. Coming off the worst night of my life, their support feels like salvation.

I was relieved to find that there were no surprises where Tristan's concerned. What you see is what you get. Blanche came off badly in a very accurate way. Viewers saw right through her, realizing she's phony and self-centered, primarily to blame for her loveless marriage. They could see she'd been after Tristan and they loathed her for it.

The real shocker was Joshua and all he was doing behind closed doors, from his pursuit of both Tatiana and Naomi to his candid (and drunken) confessional videos. He'd proven highly meme-able and hilariously irreverent, a total fan favorite. I wasn't the only star who'd been born. Joshua was the prom king to my prom queen.

But when Tristan and I go downstairs for the farewell therapy session, Joshua and Blanche's loveseat is empty. The other cast members are in attendance, though The Major and Naomi are sitting at the farthest ends of their loveseat. Marla and Dave are wearing exaggeratedly grave expressions, and Sam looks like she's barely holding it together. And while the wrap party was last night, there are three camera crews, poised to document the participants from every angle. But we're not participants anymore, are we? What's going on here?

"There's no good way to say this," Dave says. "I can't possibly prepare you for the news. Joshua's body was discovered on the beach early this morning."

We all sit in stunned silence.

"The details haven't been released yet," Marla adds calmly, "but what we do know is that detectives are on their way here from Los Angeles to investigate. No one will be able to leave until the investigation has concluded."

"No one?" The Major sputters. After his public heartbreak last night, he must want to get out of here as much as I do.

"No one," Marla confirms. "Not the cast or the crew."

"We have kids!" Naomi says.

"In college. Blanche's are three and six, and they've lost their father." Dave sounds reproving.

The Major stares at Marla. "Why the hell are you filming this?"

"It's about the integrity of the production," Marla says, and I don't know what she means but she seems to think the phrase provides airtight cover.

"I'm very sorry for Blanche's loss," Zarine says, not sounding particularly sorry, "but I don't see what this has to do with the rest of us. And some of us are needed at home quite urgently. We have important jobs, and businesses to run." She looks toward The Major and Naomi in solidarity, and then back at Marla.

"I'm not in charge here," Marla says. "I have to stay, too."

"What happened to him?" Tatiana is speaking just above a whisper. "Was it an accident or did he...?" She squeezes her eyes shut and a single telegenic tear escapes.

It occurs to me that I should be plastering the right look on my face, too. But I'm not an actress and besides, I haven't had any scenes alone with him. I mean, how distraught can I be without seeming phony as Blanche?

I get that it's tragic, I just can't feel it. Is that what shock really means?

"The details haven't been released," Marla repeats, seeming a little irritated. She definitely didn't miss her calling as a therapist.

"So no one on the island right now can leave? Including Alexei?" Tristan's lip curls when he says the name in a way that makes you think Alexei might be the next to go home in a body bag. But I know that Tristan didn't have anything to do with Joshua's death; he's not the person his mother made him out to be.

"No one," Marla says.

"Is Blanche staying, too?" Tristan asks.

I know they're friends, I know that she's just had a terrible shock, but still. Given the current state of our relationship, how he won't even look at me, it's hard to hear the note of concern in his question.

"Yes, Blanche is here," Marla says.

"Wait, if we're not allowed to leave until the investigation's concluded, doesn't that mean Joshua was murdered?" The Major asks.

"And we're all suspects?" Naomi adds, appearing faint.

Now everyone's staring at one another in dawning horror. We came to the island in pairs. How are we going to leave?

THIRTY-FIVE

TATIANA

We're all silent. Not out of respect for Joshua—none of these fuckers gave a shit about him, did they?—but in computation.

Joshua's dead.

Drowned.

Murdered.

By someone in this room.

As in, someone in this room is a murderer.

Which means we're trapped on this island with a murderer.

Trapped, while the cameras are still rolling.

Now it's pandemonium, with everyone talking at once (except for me). They've all finished the math equation, and come up with the same answer: We're fucked, every last one of us.

I feel like I might faint again, like I did with the lie detector. This island has turned me into a consumptive in a Victorian novel.

No, a consumptive in an Agatha Christie novel. And then there were seven. Or six, with Blanche tucked away upstairs. I can't even imagine what she's going through.

No, actually, I can. It's ridiculous to say—and I won't say it, not with Zarine here—but I feel bereaved. My life with Joshua, such as it was, is flashing before my eyes. There's way back when, the distant past he kept trying to evoke, and then there's the time I spent with him on this island. I'm besieged by the contradictory mess of feelings I had for him, what I acted on, what I didn't, and now it's too late. Then there's this ring. I'm not sure if anyone's ever complained about too many carats before but I've got skinny fingers and every second I'm painfully aware of the heft. The burden.

Everyone else is standing up and huddling and walking and talking. Zarine is pleading her case to Marla. She didn't block this out of her schedule; she has important surgeries. People's lives—their feet—hang in the balance. Marla is saying that this isn't her doing, that we need to take it up with the police, but she looks far more self-satisfied than she should, given that one of the participants is dead, on her watch.

This is the Zarine I know, the one who doesn't think anyone could possibly be in control besides her. The one who could just leave me on this loveseat alone, shriveling, melting, pooling into the cushions.

But then she shocks me. She comes back. She takes me in her arms and says it'll be all right, we'll get through this together.

I should appreciate this softer side of my fiancée. But New Zarine scares me in some way that I can't quite explain. It's like she's been replaced by a pod, and some might say the pod is an improvement but still. I want to know what they did to her when she was locked away in her own island compound. I asked at one point last night and all she said was, "Therapy."

Can therapy reconfigure a personality? Last night, when we all had our phones back, she learned what I'd been up to with her out of the house. While she'd been "working on herself" as she put it, I'd been... not working on myself. She and I found out at the same time that the night of the pool party, when

Joshua carried me upstairs, I tried to pull him down into the bed with me. I told Zarine the truth: that I'd been blackout drunk and missing her and, well, I don't know what else. I truly can't recall.

Not a good look when you're thirty-two and your soon-to-be fiancée is off in an undisclosed location but amazingly, Zarine hadn't been judgmental or jealous. She hadn't even seemed surprised. She put her arms around me and said, "We all have our own responses to stress." I asked, "What are you on?" and she just laughed. Then I said, "No, really, what happened while you were gone?" She never did answer, beyond that vague "therapy" comment.

I'm glad that she didn't lose her shit entirely but she should have lost her shit a little. She has a certain Stepford wife quality that I find unsettling. I know what Sam and Dave would say: That I'm resisting a healthy relationship, that I'm afraid of boredom, that I'm sabotaging myself. Joshua would have had a very different take.

Now Zarine is rubbing my back, her eyes full of compassion, as if she's not even bothered by my distress over Joshua's death. But then, why should she worry? The competition's dead.

Everyone has started to settle down. They've burned themselves out; there's nothing to be done but wait. Wait to be interrogated by the police; wait to find out about the killer in our midst. Dave starts reviewing the stages of grief while Sam looks like she's a million miles away and Marla is stifling a yawn.

Denial, anger, bargaining, depression, acceptance...

I wonder about a few choice others. Remorse. Regret. Guilt.

THIRTY-SIX

THE MAJOR

After Dave's public service announcement on grief, Marla takes over again. "Thank you, Dave and Sam." Though Sam hasn't said a word, not even when we'd all been talking at once. We'd been milling around but now we've all returned to our loveseats because it's not yet clear where else we can go. Do we have the run of the island or are we essentially under house arrest, confined to this building? Marla claims that she doesn't know the parameters yet, either. "What I do know is that you're all fortunate to have such talented therapists here to help you process Joshua's loss. In other words, your journey isn't over."

No.

She wouldn't.

She can't.

But look at her face as she talks about this being an opportunity to strengthen ourselves and our relationships. She's glowing like a jack-o'-lantern.

Instinctively, I turn to Naomi, and then I remember and turn away. There's no one with whom I can share my horrified realization: We're trapped, with no end (and no mercy) in sight.

Marla hasn't stopped talking. "...in case you're concerned

about the legality, I'd refer you to page forty-seven of your contract. As long as we continue to provide compensation at the agreed-upon rate, the show is permitted to document throughout any unforeseen extension, including"—she does the slightest smirk in my direction—"acts of God."

She's batting us around like a cat with a ball of yarn. This is fun for her. We're in her clutches until an arrest is made. She claims she can't leave, either, she's not in charge, but everything about her belies that.

"In my case, there's nothing for you to document," Naomi says. "Cain and I split on Decision Day."

"Which means you're both in mourning. That dovetails perfectly with what Blanche is going through. We'll be supporting all of you as—"

"*Supporting* us?" I look to my castmates, expecting them to share my umbrage.

Yet Tristan seems flattened, while Lauren only has eyes for him. She might really believe this is a chance to repair all the damage she's done; she might actually buy that Sam and Dave are the people for the job. Tatiana is dazed and Zarine is ministering to her. And Naomi? We're finally on the same page. She can't stomach the idea of more time together at the scene of the crime, the place where our marriage came to die. Where Joshua came to die.

"We're going to help all of you," Dave patronizes. Silent Sam looks a touch green. "You've been engaged in a very intense experience with Joshua for more than a week. So this news is going to bring up a lot of emotions for all of you."

"Especially since someone here killed him," Tatiana says. No one responds because what do you say to that? For all the rest of us know, she was the one who did it and she's just playing for the cameras. "Fuck you all. I don't want to be here with any of you." She crosses her arms sullenly, shaking off Zarine.

"Remember, anger is one of the stages," Dave says. "And paranoia would not be uncommon in a situation like this."

"You've been in situations like this before?" Naomi shoots back. With her, sass represents full-on panic.

You know what's funny? Anger barely makes my top three right now.

There's an undercurrent of fear and dread running through the room. And of course paranoia. People are alternately locking eyes and averting them. No one knows who they can trust right now.

Everyone has to be wondering who had a motive to kill Joshua. The most likely suspect, Blanche, isn't here, but then, it's hard to imagine her mustering the requisite level of feeling for a crime of passion. But once she found out at the wrap party what he'd been up to behind her back, her humiliation must have been boundless.

Who else had a motive to kill Joshua? Even if you don't care about him—and it wouldn't even be wise for me to pretend to, not after what I learned last night about him and Naomi—you have to wonder who killed him and why. Joshua hadn't been pursuing only Naomi; there was Tatiana, too, which could have sent Zarine into a tailspin. When those hypercontrolled types lose control, watch out! Tristan and Lauren—not sure they've got a dog in the fight. But Joshua was pretty active in the shadows so... I wouldn't put anything past him, after what I saw. The man had no conscience. He had no soul.

So no, I'm not sorry Joshua is dead. He doesn't deserve to rest in peace. But we all have to care who killed him.

Because someone who killed once could kill again.

"All feelings are legitimate," Dave says.

Marla casts him the quickest look of disdain ever recorded. Will she actually show her face on tonight's episode, take responsibility for this vile circus? I can't believe the network agreed to this. Can't believe it's legal to hold us captive and watch us wriggle like worms on a hook. Or maybe it's only too believable. This is what I've been trying to tell Naomi about a world that's not just gone mad but is devoid of any sort of moral compass. What's right is what you can get away with.

"It won't be all grief," Marla says. No, that would be a downer! "You still have plenty to work on as couples. Lauren and Tristan, Decision Day turned into a cliffhanger for the two of you. Zarine and Tatiana, you're newly engaged but you've also just been reunited and a lot happened while you were apart. And Naomi and Cain, there's clearly a lot of love between you and so much history. Is this really the end of the road?"

"I'll put in the work," Lauren says. "I'll do anything." Marla rewards her with a smile. Tristan moves to the very edge of the loveseat, indicating his stance on the matter.

"Given the extreme circumstances, I've decided to bend the rules," Marla says. "We're going to give you much greater access to your phones, including social media privileges." Marla looks around like she expects us to thank her. "But don't forget: There's an ongoing investigation. I'm no lawyer but I imagine anything you say publicly can be used against you."

I've never felt such pure, potent hatred for a person before. For her to take advantage of these "extreme circumstances" to get an extra however many days or weeks of footage... it's unconscionable. It should be illegal but apparently, page forty-seven gives her the right to do anything she wants to us. We have no protections.

I glance at Naomi. What she did on the beach, and what she did after—that's unconscionable, too.

They called it a wrap and Naomi came over to me, the champagne glass still in her hand. She apologized, saying she could explain, but I wasn't about to hear her out. Life's about what we do, not what we say. Then she turned around and confirmed her true colors on social media. "Following" my own wife, this is what it's come to.

The season finale airs just a few hours after the Decision Day ceremony (closer to real time than any of the other episodes). It had never even occurred to me she'd be live tweeting but the woman apparently has no shame. Naomi's always been capable when it comes to social media for the gym but this wasn't about the gym. Not one mention of our business; no, she's the product. By promoting herself as a strong Christian woman who refused to settle, she's racked up 200K followers already. Only Lauren and Joshua have more.

From what I can tell, Naomi's main demographic seems to be divorced Christian women who want to validate their own choices. They love when she tweets things like: "Just because you came from Adam's rib doesn't mean you have to be under any man's thumb." She's encouraging people to leave their marriages if they need to, which is the opposite of what she and I said we would do by appearing on the show.

What about our girls? They just watched her treat me as disposable. Does she really think that's good for them? Maybe she thinks she's some sort of feminist icon now.

I stare at her through narrowed eyes. I never would have thought it was possible for me to have hate in my heart for Naomi.

But she didn't only humiliate me. Our kids have had to watch her carry on with Joshua, flirting up a storm in her sports bra every morning. I don't know how she's going to explain away her behavior to them. At least they haven't witnessed everything. I'm the only one who's had to see it all.

She tried to feed me a bullshit sandwich last night. She insists that she'd been standing at the altar on Decision Day, expecting to say, "I do." Rejecting me had been spur of the moment, a spontaneous explosion of hurt and anger from all my rejections of her. She didn't want to live a lie, blah, blah. But I think she might have had her own plan all along.

Could she have been in cahoots with Marla, the ultimate planner?

Nothing seems farfetched anymore. After all, a man is dead and we're marooned on a desert island run by a sociopath.

I look around the room. I can't trust a single person here. Lauren's the best of them, and even she slept with one man while pregnant with another man's child.

This is madness, me being locked inside this clown car. One of these things does not belong, and I am that thing. Unlike Tristan, I've got no history of violence. I'm not impulsive like Tatiana nor jealous like Zarine. I've never cheated like Lauren nor double-crossed like Naomi. I'm not an alcoholic like Joshua, and I don't know what's up with Blanche but I'm not that either.

"I can see how upset some of you are." Marla is practically cooing, and looking right at me. "You thought your emotional work was done. But really, it's just beginning."

"We're never done growing," Dave says. "I'm here to make sure that you move from anger all the way to acceptance in a healthy way so no one snaps again."

"How do you know someone snapped?" I ask. "How do you know it wasn't premeditated?"

"No one knows what happened." Marla's expression is full-on Cheshire cat. "We're all going to find out together, in real time."

THIRTY-SEVEN

BLANCHE

I wish I could switch rooms; I can smell Joshua in every cranny of this one. But all the other rooms are still occupied and while I could pull the widow card and insist, how would that look to the viewers at home? They're going to see everything, in due time, and I need to get them on my side. The influencer lifestyle, post-*Relationship Rescue*, can be very lucrative.

It's not for me; it's for my kids. Joshua's left us with all his debts and a legacy of dishonesty and betrayal. I'm just grateful that they're still so young. I can shield them from what he's done and from what everyone's saying about him. Someday they'll probably find out the truth, and when they do, I hope it won't be as brutal as it was for me last night.

I thought I had no illusions about him coming into this. It turns out that I didn't know the half of what he was capable of. A quarter. An eighth.

I want to feel sad. Sadness seems appropriate. But Joshua was so much worse than inappropriate. He was... He was...

I can't even find the words.

I need to think about my future. Mine and my children's. It's my job to provide for them, and in his own bizarre way,

Joshua might have provided a launching pad. Some would call me mercenary; I call myself a survivor. Keep moving, always. *Opportunism* isn't a dirty word.

I'm sure Lauren intends to cash in.

Fucking Lauren.

I cannot believe the edit that woman received, compared with the hatchet job I've endured. No wonder they all hate me. I'd hate me.

I want to scream: *I am not an asshole! Joshua's the asshole!*

And yet, they love him. It's misogyny in full bloom. I develop genuine feelings for another man and they want my head on a stick, whereas he...

We had one rule, and he broke it, flagrantly, behind my back, while knowing it would be in my face soon enough. That must be what made it so much fun for him. Because that's part of what the viewers love about him: He's so evidently having fun.

It's not only the viewers who hate me, apparently. My own husband did, too.

And now I have to sleep in this room that stinks of him. It hasn't helped to change the sheets, or even to have the crew remove all his belongings and store them elsewhere (I explained that the police would be here soon and there could be evidence in there). They have to be thinking homicide, since I'm not the only one Joshua betrayed. This island is full of suspects.

I have the day off from filming and I need to use every minute of it. This is no ordinary bereavement. There's no time for feelings. It's all about strategy. Damage control. He's always been a disappointment. I accepted that a long time ago. He was a mess that I had to clean up, and I did, willingly, for my kids. But even I didn't know who I was really dealing with.

When Marla came to me first thing this morning to tell me he was dead, she was surprisingly kind, and her eyes were red-rimmed. The police arrived by the afternoon. I know there's a whole team but I've only met one, a Detective Mohr. The group therapy room already looked like an interrogation room so now it's been turned into one officially. It's like Marla knew it would come to this someday.

Detective Mohr's a petite woman with short white-blonde hair and plain features. She seems sharp, competent, and not without compassion for my loss. She apologized numerous times for having to ask certain questions, yet that didn't stop her from asking them. She'd already watched the episodes forensically, looking for clues, and was also reviewing additional footage that hadn't "made the cut." I shudder to imagine Joshua's outtakes. The detective said that after she gets the medical examiner's complete report, she'll be able to confirm the official cause of death. Then we'll talk again.

The wrap party had been a bizarre affair, and maybe that's been true every season. After all, unlike other reality TV shows where you go home and wait weeks or even months to see how you've been edited and how you'll be received by the viewers, *Relationship Rescue*'s format is merciless. It allows the cast no distance or time for mental preparation or perspective. It's like we were already playing catch-up, since everyone at home began passing judgment on us almost a week ago.

So last night, we'd all been chomping at the bit. Sure, there'd been a little buzzing about the Decision Day surprises: Zarine's return and proposal; Naomi's cold-blooded mowing down of The Major (I quipped that after that, he should be renamed The Minor, and I'd been planning to hashtag it); and of course, Alexei's appearance and the revelation of just how treacherous Lauren really is (I had no quips for that one, seeing Tristan in that kind of pain). I approached Tristan numerous times to see if he wanted to talk but he never did. I knew that once we were back in L.A., there would be plenty of time to help him pick up the pieces.

What I didn't know was that in mere minutes, I would be intimately familiar with intimate betrayal myself.

The phones were distributed, and I went straight to the recaps. Episode One more or less adhered to the formula from the first two seasons. But then...

TV Tonite: Relationship Rescue, Episode Two

I'm not going to lie: In the past, I haven't been the biggest fan of *Relationship Rescue*. That's because I tend to want my reality TV to pick a side. Is it going to be soft and fuzzy like the stuff on TLC or Lifetime where you know that you're rooting for the participants to overcome their particular brand of adversity, or are you allowed to dehumanize them on Twitter and IG, guilt-free? The queasy middle ground is where *Relationship Rescue* resided for the first two seasons, wanting to have its cake and eat it, too. But this season's gone to the dark side and I, for one, couldn't be more thrilled.

Sam and Dave have dispensed with all pretense of responsible therapy. They won't accept any of those tired old problems like communication issues or empty-nest syndrome. And they have zingers now, like when The Major says that he and Naomi are only there for a tune-up and Dave says they came an awful long way for a lube job. But bro had that coming (pun intended) for showing up with some BS problem and calling himself "The Major." My money's on erectile dysfunction. Or maybe roid rage.

I like Tatiana even though she's a blatant gold-digger. Zarine's phony accent reminds me of one of my other reality TV faves' phony accents (here's looking at you, Georgia, from Season Five of *Hot to Trot*!) Speaking of hot to trot... But that was pretty much all their screen time since the rest was taken up by the remaining two couples, and deservedly so.

I am obsessed with Blanche and Joshua (#RealityKenand-Barbie). It's not just about their dead eyes, or that creepy constant handholding. It's that you know they despise each other as they declaim the most banal issues ever. It's not just Botox gone wrong, these two are secretly, utterly bonkers. *Finally*, we have a couple we can root against without a lick of guilt. Hallelujah!

Since Blanche and Joshua are a love-to-hate, it has to be balanced out by a couple we'll love to love. That comes in the personages of Snow White (I mean Lauren) and her brave huntsman, Tristan. Lauren's always been into dirtbags. She can't seem to fall for anyone as wonderful as Tristan, and she says it's 100 percent her own fault. But Sam and Dave say Tristan's smothering poor Lauren. Note to self: Loving someone deeply is a mental health issue.

After they've all filed out, Sam says, "Their walls have walls. We've got our work cut out for us," and Dave replies, "The ends justify the means." (!!!) I'm hooked. Are you?

TV Tonite: Relationship Rescue, Episode Three

The show begins where it ended last night, with our mustache-twirling therapists. Dave says (again), "The end justifies the means," and we're about to see the means.

It's one of those behind-the-scenes reenactments that I love, where the show pretends it's pulling back the curtain to show us what really goes on with the producers. In this case, senior producer Brandon is talking into the camera, explaining how they always have to take the cast members' phones away for safekeeping, and then it's producer Julie's turn. She looks all of sixteen and seems incredibly uncomfortable as she takes us back to the night in question: "A text came in on Lauren's phone. It was from a guy asking to get together, with a naked selfie." What, "dick pic" still can't make it past the censors?

Sam and Dave revamped the day's exercise because why ask a direct question when you can elaborately trick someone? They say they'll need to "induce a confession," as if it's early labor and delivery.

They don't make us wait for the good stuff, either. Right away, there's a close-up on Lauren's absurdly beautiful angelic face (it's a soft-focus lens so it's already kind of porny). There are electrodes stuck to her temples to measure her "physiological responses to a series of images." She's smiling as she watches a TV monitor with Tristan's face. But then there's a blurred photo—presumably, the dick pic in question—and her reaction to the blurred photo, with her face quite literally drained of color.

We get a quick montage of the other cast members getting their results from the exercise. No one cares, in the therapy room or at home. Then it's Lauren's turn.

Let me just say that I was unprepared for the vicious takedown by Sam and Dave. They basically did a compare and contrast between Lauren and Tristan: He is totally ready for love, commitment, and family, as proven through the airtight science of his arousal levels. I repeat, his arousal levels. Whereas Lauren's arousal levels showed that in the best-case scenario, she's ambivalent about monogamy and much more likely, destined to fail at it.

It's obvious that Lauren knows nothing about reality television because she took off her microphone and thought she could no longer be seen or heard while talking to producer Julie. She basically confesses to cheating, talking about her self-hatred and inability to be part of any club that would have someone like her for a member. It's sincere and genuinely heartbreaking. Jaded as I am, I actually misted up.

Then it's dinner, where the entire cast is getting drunk off their asses, except for abstaining, tormented Lauren.

Cut to the confessional where Joshua's bombed out of his

mind, and you get the impression he's been there a long time because the editors are doing that thing where they fade out on one line and fade in on a whole different subject.

Drunken Joshua is a treat for the ages. Here are some choice snippets:

"...Tatiana's funny. And smarter and more interesting than she knows. Which I would know better than anyone. She's cool and she's hot. And there's nothing better than women who are, like, both temperatures..."

"...The Major pisses me off a little because he doesn't know what he's got. Naomi is a gem. A cut gem, if you know what I mean. Have you seen her work out? Those abs are unreal! Jesus Christ did good when he made her, I'll tell you that."

"...Wait, did I fight with The Major at dinner? I don't really remember that."

"...Yeah, Tristan's definitely the one who bugs me the most. Not because I think Blanche is into him, nothing like that. Why would she want dog meat when she's got prime rib at home, right?" Awkward/insecure laugh. "Listen, he's not an actor. He's a bartender. I know people. I can break his career. I'll break him, if he's not careful...."

"...Blanche better watch her step, because she's on thin ice. She's my wife, so of course I know stuff she doesn't want out there. I'm just saying she knows that I know, and I know that she knows, and if she knows that I know that she knows... fuck, it's just a lot of knowing, all right?"

I can't wait to know either! If you're not hooked yet, you must be dead.

I'd looked up from my phone, gobsmacked. In the center of the great room, Joshua was doing his trademarked crazy dance with producer Julie, spinning her around like a top. In one moment of horrifying clarity, it all came together. I realized that for our entire marriage, he'd been hiding in plain sight. All this time, I assumed he was a man-child who didn't quite have his shit together and so of course I had to cover for him. Of course I had to keep up appearances while I was also taking care of pretty much every domestic task and coordinating every aspect of our lives.

That motherfucker tricked me. He used his weakness against me. He manipulated me.

Just like my mother. Just like Lauren.

Cheating on someone like Tristan should have done her in, but instead, they're all talking about how awful it is that a girl so sweet and beautiful never learned to love herself. They want to elevate and protect her, just like Tristan did.

She has everyone's sympathy. And me? I get their antipathy.

At first, both Joshua and I did. We were #RealityKenand-Barbie. But after the drunken rant, Joshua was born again. He became #NewKenDoll, beloved antihero. In the rest of the recaps, he's known as the GIF that keeps on giving.

I'm convinced that what really turned it around for him wasn't just the zany quotes; it was the way he so cannily strung them along. Everyone was sure that he would nuke me before the series ended. After all, the producers wouldn't leave in a line about what he knew if they weren't going to get it out of him somehow. They'd have to deliver, no matter what it took. And Joshua sure looked like a willing accomplice.

Every remaining episode featured at least a little drunken Joshua and people leaned close to their screens and hoped and prayed. But miraculously, it didn't happen.

Now it never will.

Next to me on the loveseat and in the marital confessionals, Joshua portrayed himself as neutered and henpecked; behind my back, he was pulling out all the stops with two of my cast-mates. Viewers were delighted by his double life, how he let me think I was in control while he ran wild behind my back. He appeared to lust for Naomi (dirty-talking her during their morning workouts) and to love Tatiana (all that courtly bullshit and talk about her potential), though really, who knows? The man's certainly capable of subterfuge and misdirection. I'm not even sure what he was trying to pull, though, if he was seeking popularity or a truly spectacular way out of our marriage that would sink me right along with him or if he'd been too drunk to know what he was saying. I just don't know.

And now I never will.

The consensus among viewers was that I deserved it for pursuing Lauren's beloved so brazenly, which wasn't what happened at all. The editors chose to splice together shots of me practically salivating over Tristan while the heart-to-hearts on our smoke breaks never aired. Those talks would have human-ized me and proven that my feelings for Tristan were actually reciprocated. Of course they weren't shown and I was instead painted as a deluded crusty cougar. And Lauren was Bambi.

I've always had good self-esteem but last night, watching clips and reading recaps, I was low as I've ever been. Legions of strangers had a head start; for a week, they'd been gathering online to revile me. There were GIFs mocking my facial expres-sions (or lack thereof), nasty rumors about my open marriage (lies), stories from people claiming they've had run-ins with me and that I'm just as awful in person (more lies). They don't have to be truthful or even witty. They win by being incessant and numerous. And cruel, so unrelentingly cruel. Say what you will about me, I've never had the slightest inclination to partake in that myself. My social media has always been positive, which my detractors point to as evidence of how fake I am.

So many strangers telling me I should kill myself and do the world a favor. Those aren't just public comments either; there were hundreds of direct messages waiting for me. As in, people I've never met were telling me to die.

But I'm still alive. It's their antihero who's gone.

Detective Mohr can't know that last night, after I'd caught up on my reading and watching, Joshua and I had it out. His first words when I pulled him out of the wrap party and down to the beach to confront him about all he'd said and done? "It wasn't my fault."

What do you even say to that?

"Brandon kept giving me drinks in the confessional. Then he basically locked me in. It could have happened to any of us."

"It only happened to you."

Joshua wasn't done whining on his own behalf. "He kept me in there for hours, asking the same question over and over until I gave the answer he wanted. I just wanted to go to sleep. Finally I broke, all right?"

His parents, who'd seemed so wonderful to me back in the day? I blame them. They never taught him proper values. Hard work. Decency. Loyalty. Responsibility. You own up to what you've done. You apologize to the people you've hurt. You take care of your family.

"Brandon acted like he was my friend," Joshua said.

"You don't sell out everyone around you to be liked."

Only it worked. He was #NewKenDoll, I'm still #RealityBarbie.

"You loved it in the confessional," I said. "Everyone could see it. You enjoyed slagging the rest of us, but me most of all."

I'm not gullible, yet I'd made the biggest mistake there is in reality TV: I managed to vastly underestimate the power of editing. But then, Marla and her team could never have done that to me without Joshua's gleefully passive-aggressive collusion.

What still confuses me, though, is that he'd warned me the night we arrived. He was the one who wanted to leave before it all went to shit. And then days ago, he'd tried again to get us out of here, but I wouldn't budge. Had he been subject to periodic attacks of conscience? Of clairvoyance?

The contract is so airtight that I would have been in breach if I'd refused to film but Marla's given me the option to stop; after all, I'm not in a couple anymore and maybe she's not a total monster. But I'm stuck on this island regardless. I don't want to spend my time in isolation, not when Tristan's still here, and filming. Not when I have a reputation to rehabilitate. I can't let the internet trolls speculate in my absence. I need to turn it all around, allow them to see me in a more sympathetic light. So I've made my decision. Once I leave this room, I'm back onscreen.

I won't tell the kids about Joshua yet. I'll do that in person so they know that I'll never abandon them, that I'll never leave again. They're safe. Mommy's here.

I check online. It's late, and the news of Joshua's death has just been released. By tomorrow, I assume it'll have broken the internet. Which means that I have the unpleasant task of breaking the news first to Joshua's parents and then making sure that they protect the kids from all outside influences. Unfortunately, my family will need to be in lockdown, too, until I can get everything taken care of.

I can hope that most people won't be so callous as to attack a new widow, and Marla did seem awfully guilty when we last spoke. A kinder edit is the least she can do. After I start filming again, I'll likely have a grace period to win everyone over (cast, crew, and viewers alike). And then there's Tristan, who could use a true friend and a shoulder to cry on.

I may be an opportunist but contrary to popular opinion, I'm no asshole.

THIRTY-EIGHT

LAUREN

Day Ten

"Major," I say. He doesn't respond so I say it a little louder. "Major." What is he doing? It's like he's in some sort of trance. "Major!" Finally, he looks over at me from his balcony.

"Morning," he says, without a smile.

"I feel you. I'm pretty unhappy about being here, too."

"You didn't seem so unhappy yesterday." He sounds suspicious.

"I'm going to try to make the most of this, see if they really can help Tristan forgive me. But that's not the same as wanting to be here."

"So you'll give them their footage."

"Tristan and I can definitely use more couples therapy. Maybe you and Naomi—" He shakes his head so forcefully that I stop.

He stares out at the ocean moodily. "She's got me over a barrel."

"Naomi?"

"Marla. I think she did it."

"Did what?"

"Killed Joshua."

He's really losing it. Marla's the executive producer of her own show. Why would she kill one of the cast? "I don't know why everyone's so convinced that it was murder. All we know for sure is that he drowned. It could have been a drunken accident. It could even have been suicide."

"It had to be murder. It had to be Marla. And this is her island. She could strike again."

I've never seen this side of The Major before. He does kind of seem like he could use some therapy. "Aren't accidents and suicides a lot more common than murder?"

"I'll go and google that. Oh wait, I can't. I haven't been given my phone yet today." He lifts his arm as if he's about to pound on the balcony in frustration and then lowers it again. "It's like we're children. No, it's worse than that. We're prisoners."

"They'll bring our phones soon." At least, I hope so. I never thought I'd say this, but social media is keeping me sane. "It's nice of Marla to let us speak for ourselves."

"Nice? Every time you tweet, you're promoting the show! She's using you. Don't you get that?"

"I'm just saying, things could be worse."

"I can't really look on the bright side. I understand if you need to do that but leave me out of it. We are most definitely on the dark side."

I see his point. While I want to believe we're in the hands of a benevolent ruler, Marla's already fooled me twice: on Lie Detector Day and then again on Decision Day, with that DNA test. I scan to my left and to my right. All I see is jungle ringing the beach but I know Alexei's around somewhere. Is he being filmed right now, giving a play-by-play of what went on between us?

Damn right I'll give Marla footage of my own. If I can

keep my popularity up, if the viewers want a happy ending for Tristan and me, then Marla might be inclined to pull strings in my favor. Always stay on the puppet master's good side. Also, if the viewers are on my side, that could start to sway Tristan. He's got to be susceptible to peer pressure. He's only human.

While I haven't had an Alexei sighting yet, he must be skulking around because he's been ceaselessly posting photos and videos. It's unnerving, knowing he's camouflaged and on the prowl. He's getting reamed online but he doesn't seem to mind. It's all a chance for him to reference #BourbonBarber, his pop-up business where you can get a shave and a haircut while drinking artisanal whiskey.

I'm sure his presence is making it impossible for Tristan to think about anything other than my cheating and lying. And not to excuse cheating and lying, but there's a lot more to me than that. My fans and followers can see it, when will Tristan?

He still hasn't spoken to me, and last night, he slept on the floor rather than in the bed next to me. So maybe therapy is my best bet.

"I'm just trying to stay hopeful," I say. "Marla's all about the show but Sam and Dave are actual medical professionals."

"I worry about you, Lauren. I truly do."

"Well, I'm worried about you. You're so cynical."

"I'd say cynicism is warranted at this point. A man's dead. I'm stuck here in the same bedroom with a wife I can't trust. For all I know, she's been scheming with Marla—"

"Do you hear how crazy that sounds?" I really like The Major. And I like Naomi. If I can play matchmaker, maybe it'll start to even out my cosmic ledger. Plus, I owe Naomi for taking my side on the beach that time against Blanche, and I might need to call in another favor one of these days. "I'm sure it hurt you a lot to find out about Naomi's workout sessions with Joshua, but that doesn't mean—"

"Neither of us know what it means. That's between her, a dead man, and God."

I plow ahead. "She must have been hurt, too, and that's why she was flirting with Joshua to begin with. It might have seemed really sexual, the workouts, but it was still just flirting. And you did blow her off a lot."

"Turns out I was right to blow her off." He's staring down at the pool below, chin set stubbornly. "She's not the woman I married, I'll tell you that much."

"I've seen how she looks at you. All the love in her eyes. She said no on Decision Day but she could change her mind. Have you really talked to her since then?"

He laughs bitterly. "Of course *you* want to believe forgiveness is always possible."

It's the first truly biting thing he's said to me but he's right, I do believe that. I find that I'm rubbing my belly compulsively. My baby girl needs me to keep the faith.

"You know they don't even have proper emergency services on this island?" he says. "When you and Tristan took off, it was just production organizing themselves into search parties. Utterly useless. You had to come back on your own."

I'm grateful for that, actually. That experience with Tristan is what gives me hope even now.

"They've got medics but there's no hospital. One airport, all chartered flights. I don't even know how to charter a flight, do you?"

"No. I couldn't afford it anyway." Not that I want to go anywhere. At home, Tristan's no longer a captive audience.

The Major is peering over the sides of the balcony, frowning. "Look how thick that rainforest is. A person could get lost in there and never find their way out. If you're in trouble, you can't call the police, can you?"

"There are police on the island right now."

"There are *detectives* on the island. But you dial 911 and no one's going to come. Not that we've got phones most hours of the day anyway. And who's going to come if you scream? We're sitting ducks, Lauren."

He's starting to freak me out with that ominous expression on his face and how he keeps scanning the island slowly. "Tristan will protect me," I say.

The Major doesn't answer; his eyes are fixed on the ground below. When I peer over, I can't tell what he's staring at. I really didn't think he'd be the first person from the cast to crack up. Not by a long shot.

"Maybe you should talk to Sam and Dave?" I suggest.

He shakes his head. "I truly worry about you, Lauren," he says again.

Right back at you, Major. But at this point, all I can do is excuse myself. I've got my own worries, like the fact that Tristan is currently being interrogated.

I'm concerned that he might seem like the most obvious suspect, given his juvenile record and all the nasty things Joshua said in the confessional, which could make it look like a feud. Also, that bit from the show where his hand was on Blanche's knee could give the impression that Tristan was interested in Joshua's wife, which I and the rest of America realize is idiotic. But I don't know how investigations work. Don't innocent people sometimes get railroaded?

What I do know is that I'm going to protect Tristan no matter what. I have to believe he'd do the same for me.

THIRTY-NINE

TATIANA

I'm not usually up at this hour, let alone swimming, but last night Zarine and I went to bed early after a thoroughly disturbing dinner with the rest of the cast. Blanche was absent and the other two couples aren't really couples right now. Lauren was on her best behavior, trying to win Tristan back, and he looked like he wanted to dematerialize. Naomi and The Major were both tense as piano wire. Then there's Zarine and me, the least turbulent we've ever been, and she was being super nice to everyone. It was eerie. There were frequent silences, no one daring to mention Joshua's name or the circumstances that have trapped us here. An underlying distrust permeated the entire gathering, people casting surreptitious sidelong glances, looking for clues. Trying to suss out who the killer is. Maybe trying to gauge if they could be next.

It was almost as strange once Zarine and I were alone in our room, and just as silent. We haven't even consummated our engagement yet. Neither of us has tried to get things going, even though we're newly reunited and betrothed. We're also supposed to be turned on by the reminder of our mortality. Doesn't everybody fuck after a funeral?

Joshua's death is huge news. All the earlier episodes have been pulled out of respect for his untimely passing so I couldn't watch now even if I wanted to, which I definitely don't. What I've gleaned from social media is that my date with Joshua received less than four minutes of airtime. Some are wondering whether #missingdate could have anything to do with #WhatReallyHappenedtoJoshua. Inquiring minds want to know: Accident, suicide, or murder? True crime fans and reality TV fans have converged, with a vengeance. When the new episode drops tonight, the whole world will be watching.

I refuse to "like" or comment on anything. I can't believe I used to spend so much time on these sites. But then, what else did I have to do, really? I'm the one who can easily stay on this island forever. If I were gone, it wouldn't leave so much as a ripple.

I switch from the crawl to the breaststroke, thinking of #missingdate. After horseback riding, Joshua and I were taken to this super-cute little love shack. There was food in the fridge and he cooked me a big Italian meal. He had one glass of red wine, and I finished the bottle. I was a little tipsy but I remember everything.

He already knew my history—not that I was going to mention it with a producer and a camera crew right there—and he was totally accepting of it. Accepting of my totality. I could belch and unbutton my jeans shorts (I'd eaten too much crusty bread dripping with olive oil) and make acerbic remarks and he just plain liked me. I never felt that tinge of evaluation that's so often present with Zarine, so I didn't have to stave it off with some form of performative sex or exhibitionism.

In fact, it never felt sexual at all between Joshua and me. I wonder if that was because I wasn't trying to prove myself, if a sense of inadequacy is my greatest aphrodisiac. Because I haven't made a move on kinder, gentler Zarine, have I?

But then I got a little too comfortable with Joshua. I started revealing details about Zarine and me that I never should have.

And suddenly, I was in one of those interventions, or whatever it's called when a deprogrammer comes in to rescue you from a cult. He started talking about how emotional abuse is domestic violence, too, because it's all about control and coercion. It's about keeping someone down, messing with their self-esteem until they think they need you just to exist. That they literally can't survive without you.

"I know a little something about that," he said.

"I can't live without her," I said. "I mean, I don't want to."

"Zarine doesn't want you to feel confident. And you know how she doesn't encourage you to get a job? That's because she wants you to be financially dependent on her."

"You don't know her!"

"Don't you find that strange? All these days on the island and she speaks only when necessary, and even then, she's talking down to us. She wants you all to herself. Is she like that at home, too? Do you notice that you have fewer friends than you did before she came along?"

"You're way off." I didn't sound convincing. "She talks to people she likes. She just doesn't happen to like you."

"I'm crushed."

The truth is, I'm not sure what to think about Zarine as she is now, but he wasn't entirely wrong about the toxic elements of our relationship. I wouldn't listen and now he's gone and I barely had a chance to know him.

So I go underwater, way under, down deep where no one can see me cry.

FORTY

THE MAJOR

Walking back inside the room after my talk with Lauren, I see that Naomi is still in bed, staring blankly at the ceiling. I'm probably supposed to feel bad for her because she's normally up and at 'em but all I can think is how she's lost her desire for exercise since she lost her workout partner. All I can see is an image of Joshua looming and leering above her as she bench presses.

I need to get out of here. Maybe I'll finally exercise myself, exorcise myself, try to release everything that's pent up inside me all day and all night. A constant simmer feels worse than boiling over.

"Who were you talking to?" Naomi asks, her voice sad and faraway.

"None of your business." I keep my hand on the doorknob. She doesn't get to slow me down after what she did.

"Could you please stop freezing me out? Will you finally let me tell you my side of the story?"

I rotate toward her and speak through gritted teeth. "That's what's wrong with the world. Everyone pushing their side of the story instead of telling the whole truth."

"Please, just listen—"

"The truth is, you have stabbed me through the heart." My voice is rising. "You have dishonored yourself, and you have brought shame on our family." Now she's sobbing, and I should care, I know I should, but I yank open the door and I'm storming down the hall.

Oof.

I slam straight into Tatiana and the force of it sends her flying into the nearest wall. "I'm so sorry," I say. "Are you okay?"

She's slid down to the floor, looking dazed but I don't think it's really from the force of our collision. Her hair is wet and her towel has slipped to reveal her bikini top. Her eyes meet mine. "I'm as okay as I can be."

I sit down beside her. "Did you watch the episodes? Looks like Marla decided not to portray me as a homophobe after all. Instead, I'm a hypocritical misogynist, withholding sex and affection from my wife. No wonder she needed ego strokes from a..." I'm not going to name-call the dead guy but, man, I want to.

"I wish I were you. You know all those stereotypes about how bisexuals can't make up their minds, that they want to fuck everyone and can't be trusted?" She points to herself. Then she points up at the camera.

I get it. Marla's always watching, ready to turn us into whatever best serves her purposes.

Tatiana moves closer to whisper, "Joshua and Naomi weren't anything. It was just flirting."

"How do you know?"

Tatiana doesn't want to answer, but she looks troubled. And young, without all the makeup and the hair extensions. I feel a hundred years older than everyone these days. "He didn't love Naomi. Or Blanche. He's loved me, since way back when."

Wait, Tatiana knew Joshua before this island? Did Zarine know that? Did Marla?

A whole host of suspects is opening up right before my eyes.

"Well, I'm glad things are working out for at least one

couple," I tell Tatiana. "It seems like Zarine's made her peace with everything." Something in her expression makes me add, "You preferred making war?"

Tatiana sighs and closes her eyes. "We've got grief therapy soon."

"And if we play hooky?"

"I don't think I'm ready to find out."

I'm not either, not with the footage Marla might very well have from the night we wrapped—a.k.a. the night Joshua died.

FORTY-ONE
BLANCHE

This must be what it feels like to be a debutante just before the ball. I'm about to be reintroduced to America. Time for them to set aside all their prior assumptions. All I need to do is descend the staircase.

I have to admit, even I'm surprised by how quickly I've been able to steady myself and move on. Sure, I've always known I'm a survivor, but we're talking about the death of the man I loved, once. The father of my children, though there are certainly other, better fathers out there. I'm irreplaceable but he's not.

I keep waiting for the sadness to kick in but Joshua's betrayal was so complete that it seems to have severed all attachment to him. I'm free.

Still, I have to be very careful about the image I'm about to portray.

One step at a time, that's it. Tristan's already down there, so that's one friendly face. Sure, Lauren will be next to him on his loveseat, while mine will be half empty. But half empty is better than full of shit.

There's a dedicated cameraperson to capture my entrance. I don't know if Marla will include my hesitation, or if I want her to. Viewers love that stuff when Lauren does it, I'm not sure about me.

Today, though, I'm the star.

As I enter the great room, every face turns to look at me as if choreographed. Dave starts to clap, and then Sam, and then the rest of the cast has no choice but to applaud my bravery.

I give a courageously pained smile as I move to my loveseat. "Thanks," I say, keeping it modest. The clapping dies out.

I notice that Sam is standing several feet behind Dave when she usually likes to be out in front. Her makeup's on point but she still looks tired. And are those *flats* she's wearing? Something is definitely up.

"How are you, Blanche?" Dave simpers.

"I'm holding it together."

"With little kids at home," Naomi says, all sympathy. "I can't even imagine."

And I couldn't have imagined she'd be ogling my husband's glistening muscles every morning in the gym, but here we are.

"This is a safe space," Dave says. He said that to me on Parents Day, too, and it was just as much of a lie then. Sam lets out what sounds very much like a guffaw, which Dave ignores. "We're all here for you, Blanche."

I look at Lauren, who is most definitely not here for me, and then at Tristan, who really seems torn up (on my behalf? On his own?). Lauren sidles a bit closer to him, which he barely registers. Really, I wish I could seem as distraught as he does. But then, I don't have any acting training. One improv class doesn't exactly prepare you for a performance like this.

"We've been talking about where we are in the stages of grief," Dave says. "Denial, anger, bargaining, depression, acceptance. Where are you, Blanche?"

"I know Joshua's gone but it doesn't feel real. Does that mean I'm denying it?"

"Not necessarily—" Sam starts.

"I've got to be honest, Blanche," Dave interrupts. "If I were you, I'd be enraged. All the things he said, all the things he did. Let's call a spade a spade. He disrespected your marriage to the nth degree."

Everyone's visibly uncomfortable. They didn't know you could speak ill of the dead right in front of his new widow. Not to mention, some of the people in here were the vehicle for Joshua to disrespect my marriage.

"I'm still processing," I say.

"If you'd rather process alone, you can be excused at any time," Sam says. Dave shoots her a look, and now she's the one ignoring him. The tension is as thick between them as it is between The Major and Naomi.

I actually appreciate what Dave's said. I want Joshua's betrayal in the room with us. Everyone—here and at home—needs to remember what he's done. They thought it was so entertaining at the time but I was the victim then. I'd argue that I still am now.

"I can't even tell you how sorry I am," Tatiana says.

She looks plenty sorry, and she should. During the pool party episode, when Joshua carried her drunk ass inside, she tried to get him in bed with her. Then when he said, "No, not this way," it was yet another act of chivalry toward her, not me.

What way did you have in mind, Joshua? Guess we'll never find out.

My face goes up in flames just thinking about it, and I don't have him to attack, so Tatiana will have to do. "Are you sorry he's dead or sorry for what you did while he was alive?" America has to be cheering me on. The online response to Tatiana has been decidedly mixed, with much speculation that she has something to hide. What's up with #missingdate? People hate a homewrecker, right?

I'm expecting Tatiana to fire back but instead she goes pale. Then she bursts into tears. Zarine wraps her arms around

Tatiana and says to me, "I know you're grieving but is it really necessary to be cruel?"

As if I'm the bully! I look to Tristan, my friendly face, but he's looking down at his hands. Lauren is staring right at me a bit smugly. I don't have a clue how to get the viewers on my side, while for her, it's effortless.

I remember what Brandon said in the confessional about how I need to be willing to ugly cry. Shed my vanity, and they'll believe. I doubted his intentions at the time but he was actually telling the truth about me being the villain. I can't trust my instincts so I'll have to follow his advice.

I think of my children back at home, and the tears come hard and fast and ugly.

I'm crying because their lives won't change much at all. Because I don't think they love their father any more than I do, and that means as careful as I was when I picked a husband, I still managed to choose wrong.

He hasn't been home to tuck them in for months; he doesn't know the names of their teachers or their friends. My gut has known that it's not because he's working late. He's been out drinking or with other women. Drinking with other women. His "disrespect for our marriage" didn't start on this island, but this is where it ended.

I chose the wrong man, and I ceased to love him a long time ago. What I haven't wanted to face is the shame of my mistake. I feel it now, and I'm letting it out. I am actually grieving—not for the man I had, but for the life I failed to create for my kids.

There's still time to turn it around, though. Tristan would make an excellent father.

The torrent passes. I see eyes on me and eyes averted and I have the overwhelming sense that my catharsis has backfired. No one's willing to say it—who'd call out a widow for weeping? —but some of the people in this room definitely think I'm a fake. Is it because they saw the reaction to me on social media, or did that only reinforce what they already felt? Has Tristan changed his mind about me because of what he's read?

A box of tissues has appeared on the loveseat beside me and I start to clean myself up, blowing my nose and wiping at my smeared makeup. Finally, Tristan's looking right at me, his gray eyes limpid. It really is like a movie, how everything else falls away, and I know I sound like a fifteen-year-old when I say this but it is completely true: He gets me.

I'm right to be here, I'm right to fight for us. Lauren is clamped to his side but he wants out. He just doesn't know how to escape. Well, I'm free and I can show him the way. I'll save him, and he'll save me. That's what love is. Mutual rescue, a relationship of equals. He could never have that with Lauren.

But this isn't about Lauren, as much as she's tried to steal the show. She wants everyone to think it's her love story. Fuck that, it's a mystery, and I'm at the center. Who killed my husband? No one's getting off this island until the right person pays for their crime.

FORTY-TWO

LAUREN

Day Eleven

"I saw online that it's now officially a murder investigation," I say. "Is that true?"

"That should never have been leaked." Detective Mohr is slight but alpha. A table's been brought into what was formerly the group therapy room and she's leaning back from it, studying me.

Social media's blown up. A new game has launched and millions want to play. I guess after Joshua's antics, how he basically caricatured himself, no one's been able to treat his death with any degree of seriousness. I'm pleased to see that #BlancheDidIt is trending the highest, bolstered by that bizarre crying jag yesterday. (No one at home bought it any more than I did, which is really saying something given that her husband's the one who just died. Now that's a true credibility crisis.) After Blanche, it's #TristanDidIt, which I'm not happy about at all. In descending order from there, it's #TatianaDidIt, #NaomiDidIt, #LaurenDidIt, #ZarineDidIt, and #TheMajorDidIt. Some people think #JoshuaDidIt, that he faked his death to frame Blanche.

"Did you have any individual interactions with Joshua? Did you ever talk with him outside of group dinners, group therapy, or exercises?" Detective Mohr asks.

"No, we were never alone."

"Do you know if Tristan had any individual interactions with Joshua?"

"I don't think so."

"But you were aware of enmity between the two men?" she says. "Enmity means hostility. Antagonism."

I know exactly what it means. But if she thinks I'm dumb, that's fine. It's worked to my advantage before. "Joshua hated Tristan. But Tristan didn't give any real thought to Joshua."

"Tristan was having a relationship with Joshua's wife, Blanche, though, isn't that right? A friendship, I mean. They did spend time together individually, Blanche and Tristan."

"They took smoke breaks at the same time." I try to look unconcerned. "Blanche has a crush on Tristan but again, Tristan didn't give much thought to her."

"Did she tell you that?"

"I could see it, and so can all the viewers." Hasn't she watched the episodes? Now who's dumb?

The episodes confirmed all my instincts: that Blanche didn't care about her husband and was openly pursuing Tristan with absolutely no regard for my baby. On the overnight date, she deliberately tried to break us up by telling Tristan about my lie detector questions. In other words, Blanche is one of the worst people I've ever met. It's agony, sitting in group and at meals with her, having to watch her phony grief performance. The only relief is knowing that she'll get excoriated later by my followers. It's incredible how much their support has been buoying me up. They've validated my entire experience on this island. I know I can't retweet #BlancheDidIt but, oh, my fingers ache to.

"Was Tristan aware of Joshua's hostility?"

"Not while we were filming. Joshua was a shady guy, Detective Mohr. He had one face he showed the world and then behind closed doors, he was obviously someone else. Tristan's nothing like that."

Detective Mohr is staring at my belly, which I've started to rub unconsciously. I stop, with effort.

"You and Tristan left the set the day of the lie detector, is that correct?" she asks.

"We needed some alone time, and it was amazing."

"You were almost through with your test, having walked out before answering the final question about being faithful to Tristan."

"Right."

"Lauren, did you have sex with Joshua?"

I can't help it, I burst out laughing. Hopefully, she can see how genuine my reaction is. The thought is absurd, and repulsive.

"Is that a no?"

"That's a hell no."

"But you did have sex with people other than Tristan during your relationship?"

"Only Alexei. I don't know what I was thinking. It was wrong, and I've let Tristan know again and again how sorry I am."

"Has he forgiven you? It looked pretty bad between you in the Decision Day episode."

So she has watched. "Not yet, but he will. He loves me. He loves our baby." I look her right in the eyes and make sure to sound as certain as possible.

"Would you say he's the forgiving type? Or is he the type to hold a grudge?"

"Is this because of what he did as a kid? Beating someone up? Because lots of kids get in fights. He was defending his sister. He's very loyal."

She nods slowly, like she's hearing something other than what I've said. "Tristan's lie detector questions were about whether he'd been violent toward you. By running away, he avoided answering."

"I'm the one who ran out; I made him come with me."

"Has he been violent toward you, Lauren?"

"Never."

When I'm finally free to go, I see Julie's waiting outside the door for me. There's no camera crew though I'm well aware that I'm still being captured on film, and on microphone. Julie has me take my microphone off and follow her through the house into a sort of pantry.

"They can't hear us in here," she says. "I've been wanting to apologize to you. I feel really awful about everything you and Tristan went through. I wish I'd never shown Marla that picture of Alexei on your phone."

"It's your job." Of course her job meant more to her than some girl she'd just met. "We're not friends, I get it."

"But we are! I mean, we were, and I'd like to be again. The thing is, I didn't want to abuse that friendship, which there was a lot of pressure to do. The day you and Tristan came back, the reason I acted so rude was because I was trying to tip you off. I wanted you to know you shouldn't go spilling everything about the time you'd been gone, that you should keep private things private."

"So when I thought you were acting like you weren't my friend, it was because you actually were?" She nods, and I grab her in a delirious hug. "Thank you! You are 100 percent forgiven!"

I can feel her relief, and I'm relieved, too. A friend in this place, and an insider to boot? I just hit the jackpot.

FORTY-THREE
TATIANA

"There are a lot of rumors going around," Dave says, "so we want to give you the facts." He and Sam have their own wing chairs and are sitting down with us in the great room, like it's a high school rap session. We're about to be scared straight. "Joshua's body was initially discovered on the beach and the medical examiner needed a little time to determine the cause of death. She's concluded that it was murder."

The air whooshes out of me. I sag back against the loveseat and Zarine goes to comfort me yet again, but I can't trust her touch, or anything else. She still won't tell me what happened when she was on the other side of the island, how or why she's been transformed.

"Reactions?" Dave is looking around our loveseat circle. "Maybe we should start with Blanche."

"I guess I'd assumed—I'd hoped—that it was an accidental drowning. He's never been that strong of a swimmer. Or maybe suicide, because of shame and guilt. Because Joshua may have put his foot in his mouth sometimes but why would anyone want to kill him?" Blanche sounds so matter of fact that it makes me cringe. I'm more of a widow than she is.

But then, what do any of us want from her? If she cries, we judge; if she's stoic, we judge. I could tell her that I see how unfair it is, only she might try to bite my head off again. Not that I can blame her. Her husband wanted me and I liked it, even as I told myself I didn't. Maybe what Joshua wanted was the push-pull, and he and Zarine aren't so different after all. Maybe I bring that out in everyone.

"You see what you're ready to see," Naomi says. "I've always thought of denial as a gift from God. He's making sure you don't have more than you can handle. He's titrating the pain for you."

"I don't think God's on this island," The Major says. "I'm beginning to think He might not be anywhere." Naomi gives him an appalled look but he's unfazed. "Maybe He's washing his hands of humanity because do you know what I saw this morning? People are scheduling viewing parties. *Viewing parties!*" His eyes are blazing as he takes us all in, wanting our outrage to match his. "So they can drink rosé while they do some amateur sleuthing, like this is *Murder, She Wrote.*" The Major really needs to update his references. "To them, we're characters, not people. Meanwhile, they're getting ready, putting up corkboards. Like on police procedurals where they pushpin index cards into the wall with the suspects' names and pictures and then connect them with string?"

"They're called link charts," Zarine says.

"No one seems to care that a man's dead," The Major says, "while we're all trapped here with a killer!"

Lauren adopts a frightened expression and moves closer to Tristan. He doesn't move away.

So he's starting to thaw. That makes sense. The lock and the key. Lauren needs to be protected and Tristan needs to protect. They're going to find their way back together, it's inevitable. Murder might just speed it up.

"Let's not panic," Zarine says. "Murder is the crime with the lowest recidivism rate."

"What does that mean?" Lauren asks.

"Once someone kills, they don't usually kill again."

"Recidivism is about who reoffends after they've been to prison," The Major says. "What about the ones who aren't caught? They can just keep going."

"You think there could be a serial killer on the island?" Now Lauren's closed the gap with Tristan even farther and she's rubbing her baby bump anxiously.

"There could be." The Major looks around. "I wouldn't put it past any of you."

"Cain!" Naomi says. It's like she wants to protest further but then realizes that she's in a court where she has no standing.

"I'm just saying, none of us know what anyone else is capable of," The Major says. "My jaw was on the floor watching that first week of episodes. I didn't suspect what any of you were up to."

"The Major's right," I say. "We've all been lying in some way."

"Lies are one thing," Naomi counters. "Murder is another."

The Major shakes his head. "People test the waters. They figure out what they can get away with, and each time, they go a little further. That's why our society is—"

"Oh, shut up, Cain!" Naomi says sharply. "Do you even hear yourself? You sound crazy."

"I don't think it's crazy," I say.

"Let's stop using that word," Dave says. Sam suddenly stands up and walks out. "She's been a little under the weather lately."

"She doesn't have to be here anymore but the rest of us do?" The Major says.

"This is your journey, not ours."

"The journey needs to end," Naomi says wearily. "Cain and I are over. We ought to be excused."

"I'm not going to be tortured anymore." The Major stands up. "I'm done. I'm ready to make my guess. I know who the killer is. Marla did it."

"It's not a game of *Clue!*" Naomi is clearly frayed and exasperated. But also frightened.

"I know it's not a game," The Major says. "Not to us. But have you noticed there's no #MarlaDidIt? Or a #DaveDidIt? But there's a hashtag for every other person in this room."

"Because the most likely suspect is in this room." Lauren looks at all of us while pointedly ignoring Blanche, which is the same as pointing right at her.

"I'm going to come to an island so I can murder my husband in front of a hundred cameras? Wouldn't it be easier to do it at home?" Blanche realizes how that sounds and adds, "Not that I wanted him dead."

"He was killed after the cameras had been turned off," Lauren says.

"Lauren." It's the first word that Tristan's spoken today.

But Lauren is unstoppable. "Let's be real. We barely knew Joshua. Why would any of us kill him?"

"Yes, let's be real." Blanche's tone is icy. "This was likely a crime of passion, and there are at least two other women in here who were more passionate about my husband than I was."

"It wasn't like that," I say weakly. But how was it? I don't even understand it myself.

"He was my workout partner, that's all," Naomi says. "I'm very sorry you lost your husband, Blanche, but I had nothing to do with it."

"I didn't 'lose' my husband; he was taken."

"This is what Marla wants," The Major says. "For us to turn on each other. It's what she's wanted the whole time, and we swore we wouldn't give it to her. Don't you all remember making that pact?"

"I do," Blanche says. "I also remember how quickly we broke it."

"Because Marla broke us!" The Major looks electrified. "That's what I'm saying about going a little further if no one stops you. We staged a walkout, and we should have kept on going. If we had, we'd all still be alive today."

I don't know about anyone else, but I'm finding him pretty persuasive. Following his reasoning one step further: Will we all still be alive tomorrow?

FORTY-FOUR

THE MAJOR

"We've got to do our part to solve this crime," I say. "That's the quickest way off this island."

Blanche nods brusquely. "Everyone should write down everything they remember from the party. Account for every minute. Who they talked to. What they saw. When they saw Joshua and with who. Then it's time to compare notes to look for corroboration and for inconsistencies."

"We look for facts!" I declare excitedly. "For the truth!"

"Aren't you going to do it, too?" Lauren asks Blanche. "Because you said 'they,' as in, all of us. Not 'we.'"

"I meant *we*, okay?"

These women truly hate each other. Some men might enjoy being fought over, under some circumstances, but Tristan is not that man and these are not those circumstances. He clearly wants to make a run for it. But he tried that once and look where it's gotten him.

"I don't get why Blanche is calling the shots," Lauren complains to Dave. "Don't you have an exercise planned or something?"

Someone is sure feeling herself.

Without Sam here, Dave seems hapless. "Nothing specific. Just, you know, more processing. Blanche's idea could be a good one. As you write out your timeline, let yourself feel what you felt that night."

"Why?" Zarine asks.

"So you can learn about yourselves."

"This isn't about feelings," Blanche says. "It's about helping Detective Mohr find the killer. Is there anyone who doesn't want to do that?"

Once she's put it that way, we have no choice but to agree. There's a faint whiff of reluctance, which gives credence to my earlier read that we're all hiding something. Dave starts distributing clipboards, paper, and pens.

"I was pretty drunk," Tatiana says, "so there are going to be holes."

"We were all drunk," Blanche says, "except for Lauren."

"Just do your best!" Dave has turned into a kindergarten teacher. Next up: finger painting!

Everyone works in silence for about fifteen minutes and then Dave claps his hands. "Who's first?"

We go around the circle. The party was largely in the great room with the furniture pushed to the side and the French doors open, the revelry spilling out into the pool area. We all account for most of our time by saying we were mingling with the crew—Julie, apparently, was the belle of the ball—or checking social media and watching the episodes in whole or part, learning what the world thought of us. We all claim to have gone to our respective bedrooms for breathers. None of us admits to any trips to the beach.

"Since we're all missing chunks of that night, are we all killers?" I say. "I'd argue the opposite, that none of us is." I don't need to say Marla's name again, they get my drift.

Tatiana has her eyes closed and when she speaks, it's in this strange voice like she's channeling a spirit. "I did talk to Joshua on the beach that night. I don't know exactly when it was or what we said but things have been coming back to me. And I don't think I was the only one."

"The only one what?" Dave prompts.

"The only one on the beach with Joshua." Her eyes fly open and she looks at Dave. "If Marla or the LAPD want to pay for a hypnotist, I could probably crack the case." It's a vestige of the Tatiana I first met: provocative in a way where you're not sure if she's kidding or not. Dave cocks his head like he's considering, though the real decisionmaker isn't here. But I know she's watching. She's always watching.

I get to my feet. We can walk out for real this time; we can make it stick. What's the worst Marla can do, sue us? The court of public opinion would be on our side, given recent events. Maybe we could countersue her for emotional distress. "Anyone care to come with me?"

Nobody moves.

Are they that hungry for more camera time? Or stupid enough to think Sam and Dave really can help us? What does Marla have on these people? What is it going to take, another dead body?

I'm about to start screaming when the answer comes to me. The reason the walkout didn't stick the first time, the reason they're all silent and motionless.

None of them want to be aligned with me. They think I've lost my mind, and you know what?

They just might be right. I have not been myself since I got to this island, and thank God for that.

FORTY-FIVE

BLANCHE

I take a deep drag on my cigarette. Tristan does the same. We're back on our old stomping ground, the loungers by the pool. Even though we've been through the wringer, I feel elevated by his presence. But I can't show it, not with the camera crew right there.

Tristan doesn't seem very talkative anyway. His beautiful gray eyes are pensive with dark shadows beneath.

"Detective Mohr thinks it's me." He says it quietly, like he's hoping it won't be heard, but we both know these mics pick up everything.

"How can you tell?"

"I've dealt with cops before. It's just obvious from the kind of questions she was asking. I'm her number one suspect."

"She'll find out she's wrong soon enough."

He lifts his eyes hopefully. "Do you know something?"

"You heard everyone in there. No one had a solid alibi. And Tatiana just admitted she was on the beach with Joshua. We gave Detective Mohr some other suspects for sure." I'm trying to buck him up but it's clearly not working. I had the total opposite experience with the detective. She'd basically been eating out of my hand. "Let's talk about something else. Tell me what's going on with you and Lauren."

He stares down at his cigarette like he can't remember what to do with it.

"That bad, huh?"

"I'm trying to get past what happened. For the baby's sake, and because I really did love her. I've never been good at forgiving people. A part of me feels like if you cross me once, you'll do it again. I'm not going to be her sucker, you know?"

I nod, encouraging him to go on, the world's most sympathetic bobblehead.

While I could never enjoy seeing him this upset, I'm aware that to be in this position is an honor and a validation. A vindication. All those people on social media are saying he could never be interested in me but this conversation proves otherwise. This, you trolls, is what emotional intimacy looks like.

"She says she would have told me the whole truth once we got home." He stamps on his cigarette emphatically, which lets me know that he doesn't believe that any more than I do. "All that time I was falling for her, she was fucking him. And he's here, on this island."

"That sounds like absolute torture."

Tristan must feel that because he looks like he could cry with gratitude. I had that same feeling when he caught the bullet for me on Parents Day. It's a heady thing, being truly understood.

"I shouldn't be going on about Lauren when you're the one who's lost your husband."

"Some losses are greater than others." I lean toward him. "When you and I first met, I never would have guessed that we were living parallel lives, that Joshua and Lauren were both—" I stop when I see how his face has hardened.

"Don't compare Lauren to Joshua. They're not the same."

"Because Lauren's alive and Joshua's dead?"

He breaks eye contact. "I'm sorry. It's just that some part of me still doesn't want to accept what she did."

"I get that but you don't want to live in denial. Don't be like me. I think The Major was right about testing the waters. How deep will Lauren go?" Lauren's entire existence is a manipulation, and she only has enough bandwidth to care about herself. Narcissists make lousy mothers, I should know.

"I'm pretty sure she's told me everything. She's always crying and begging forgiveness. She says she'll do anything."

"Exactly."

He seems to fold in on himself. I just need him to see that Lauren has been right about one thing: He's definitely too good for her.

"You're going to figure this out," I say. "You'll make the right decision. Take it from an older, wiser woman."

He doesn't smile. Ouch.

I need to take a risk, even if I go splat, like that bug on the windshield the day we arrived. (How prophetic that turned out to be.) Tristan's responded to Lauren's vulnerability, everyone has, so let's see what he makes of mine.

"I'm a cautionary tale." My smile is wry, my hurt barely peeking out underneath. "Ignore all the red flags, go against your instincts, and you end up where I am. Alone and afraid." I've got his attention, that's for sure. I tell him the shameful truth about my life off the island: Joshua's escalating drinking, the obvious signs of infidelity that went unremarked upon, how he was rarely around and never actually present when he was. Maybe this'll air and people will finally see my side. "There were apologies and promises to do better but people don't change, Tristan. Therapy's an optical illusion."

"I appreciate you sharing all that about Joshua," he says, "but I already knew."

I stare at him. "How?"

"I just had a feeling. My dad was an alcoholic sack of shit.

That's why I said what I did when you and I were on the couples swap, about Joshua not being a good guy."

"Is there something more to it? Something you're not telling me?"

"Well, I do have kind of a secret," he says. "Before I came here, Rick Gloucester contacted me. Have you heard of him?" I shake my head no. "My acting agent hooked me up. Rick's one of the top talent agents in L.A. for social media influencers. He reps all the highest-earning alumni from *The Bachelor*. He liked the sound of Lauren and me but wanted to see how we were represented on the show before he made us an offer.

"I told him I wouldn't mind getting free money for paid posts as long as they're companies I believe in. I wasn't counting on it and I didn't mention it to Lauren because she was nervous enough about how she was going to come across on television. But yesterday, I heard from him again. With Lauren's social media reach, he thinks we could make millions on baby gear alone. But that's only if Lauren and I can make things work. If we leave here as happy as the couples did on the other seasons."

Shit. Just when I thought we were getting somewhere. "Couldn't you be a social media influencer on your own, without Lauren?"

"We're a lot more valuable together. It could be the difference between a hundred thousand, if I'm lucky, and a couple of million. We're talking life-changing money here, the kind of money I've never seen. And it's not just my life, it's my daughter's."

"You can't stay with Lauren for the money. That's not you."

"I do love her, though."

I notice it's back to present tense. "You want to be an influencer that badly?"

"Who wouldn't? You get free gear and dinners and trips. It's a lot easier than acting, and I wouldn't have to spend all my time racing around to auditions. I could spend more time with my baby."

I have the impression he's more invested in the baby and the influencing than he is in Lauren. Which is music to my ears.

"But none of it's going to happen from prison anyway," Tristan says. "Detective Mohr's got it out for me, I can tell."

"Well, I'll set her straight. You never did a thing to Joshua. He just had some sort of vendetta because he thought you and I had chemistry."

I'm hoping Tristan will agree that yes, there is chemistry, but instead he's lighting up another cigarette.

It's hard to hear that Lauren's popularity on social media might actually save her relationship, especially when people I've never met are being just as vicious as they ever were. No, more vicious. Number one is always #BlancheDidIt, even as the other cast members rise or fall.

Tristan's lowered his head and is crying silently. I take the risk of reaching out and touching his hair. I'm rejoicing in the fact that he hasn't moved or pushed me away when I see in my peripheral vision that Lauren's approaching, a camera crew in tow. Has she been spying, waiting to pounce? I pull my hand back.

"America's watching, you know," she tells me. "They see everything." Tristan looks up at her, tears clinging to his beautiful thick lashes, and her entire countenance changes. He's still on the lounger and she's around him like a boa constrictor, angling so that his head is cradled between her breasts and her bump. Oh, she's good all right. She knows just what she's doing, lining up that shot for the camera.

Now I feel like I'm intruding on them. "We'll talk later," I say to Tristan as I head toward the house.

I wish I could tell Lauren that America sees who she is, too, only they don't. Not yet. But they will. I'll make sure of it.

FORTY-SIX

LAUREN

Day Twelve

"Where's Brandon?"

"I'll be the one asking the questions today." Alexei gives me the smile that used to make my panties wet.

"You shouldn't be here."

"Are you afraid to be alone with me?" Now his smile is practically a leer.

"You're the one who should be afraid." If Tristan finds him...

As Alexei walks toward me, all I feel is disgust. I once thought I loved him and I was willing to debase myself in order to gain his love in return. But I've since learned my worth.

He takes the red velvet upholstered seat next to me, the one usually occupied by Tristan when we do our joint confessional interviews. "Now it's my throne."

"I'm leaving." I go to stand up but he grabs my arm.

"Let me just tell you what I came here for."

"There's no mystery. You came here to ruin everything for Tristan and me."

"I needed to know if the baby you're carrying is mine. You'd been avoiding me and if it hadn't been for Julie, I wouldn't have known why. Were you going to avoid me for the rest of your pregnancy?"

"For the rest of my life, actually."

He squints at me. "When did you become such an angry person?"

"I just know what I want, and it's not you."

"Are you sure about that? Can I refresh your memory?" That leer again. I don't know how I'd ever allowed him within three feet of me.

"Go home."

"I can't." He's got me there. "You should be marrying me, not Tristan."

My eyes fly to my ring. I haven't taken it off since Decision Day, though Tristan may be sorry he gave it to me. "You don't want me. You want my followers." I'm up to a million now. "You want my fame."

"No, I've always wanted you."

"Bullshit. You've never cared about me. Not when we were a couple, and not when I was doing the stupidest thing ever."

"You mean the fifteen times you did the stupidest thing ever?"

I feel like slapping him but instead, I get to my feet. "You might not be able to leave the island, but you stay the fuck away from me."

"Or what?" He remains seated. What I want has never mattered to him at all.

I can't believe that there was a time when I didn't think I could do better than Alexei, when I was so busy waiting for the other shoe to drop with Tristan that I dropped it myself. The reason I have so many followers is because women see themselves in me; they're making the same mistakes that I did. They need to hear what I'm about to say, and so does Tristan.

"You treated me like crap and I thought that was all I deserved. Then when I was with you behind Tristan's back, it was about me being terrified that I was finally on the verge of something real." I see Alexei's eyes are already starting to glaze over but this speech isn't for him. "I deserve someone who'd never cheat on me, or cheat with me. I want someone I can respect, who'll respect me. I have that now. Tristan and I are going to come back from this stronger than ever. There are no more secrets and no more lies. I've found the love of my life and I won't lose him, no matter what."

Alexei claps his hands against his thighs. "Well, you can't blame a guy for trying."

"Yes, you can."

As he exits the confessional, I can practically hear the cheers; I can see the memes. My fans just want the best for me. They want me to love myself like they love me, and you know what? I think I finally do.

FORTY-SEVEN

TATIANA

Naomi's waiting for me by the side of the pool. Waiting me out, is more like it. I don't know how much longer I can pretend not to see her.

She must be on her way to or from the gym since she's in her workout gear. It's more demure now that Joshua's not around.

It's not like I'm jealous, or even that I dislike her. I just want to get in another ten laps. Swimming's the only thing that soothes me these days, and it has the added benefit of killing those pesky morning minutes before therapy, the time when Zarine might start asking questions I don't want to answer. But I'm not only avoiding her questions; I'm evading the ones I should be asking her. I don't even mind staying on this island because then I can delay making any real decisions about the rest of my life for a little while longer. Unlike the others, I'm not afraid of what could happen to me here.

Naomi is stretching out on the concrete, giving the definite impression she could stay there all day. She's a determined lady. I've never possessed that quality myself. It's pathetic to admit, but I'm fairly easily thwarted.

Which is why I give in after only five laps.

"Good morning," I say as I squeeze out my hair and wrap myself in a towel.

"Morning." She smiles but it's less friendly than purposeful. She's on her feet now, balancing on one leg, the other pointed skyward. Show-off. "I was hoping to talk to you."

"Without the cameras or the microphones?"

"I don't mind if you don't."

It seems like the crews have gotten pretty lax since Joshua's death. The producers drag their feet; the camerapeople take so long to arrive or to set up that a conversation ends before filming begins. Privacy is much easier to come by now. But sometimes I think the only thing that's keeping us safe—keeping us from our worst selves—is being filmed. After all, Joshua died when the cameras stopped rolling.

"What do you want to talk about?" I ask.

"Did Joshua say much about me?"

"Not really." It's the truth, though her eyebrows are knitted. Why ask the question if you won't believe the answer? That's part of what's keeping my conversations with Zarine so minimal. "Did he tell you anything about me?"

"Not really." I'm pretty sure she's lying. "He was obviously playing both of us."

Speak for yourself. "I probably shouldn't have tried to kiss him the night of the pool party but otherwise, I'm okay with everything that happened."

"Everything that happened, or everything that was aired?"

"Everything," I lie.

"What about your missing date?"

"What about it?"

She steps just the teensiest bit closer to me, and I'm not sure if it's an implied threat or I'm being paranoid. The latter is definitely true but that doesn't discount the former. "Aren't you the one who said there's strength in numbers?"

"Safety in numbers."

"I really am sorry for Joshua's kids, but you and I both know what kind of sicko he was."

I rear back. "I don't know that."

"Wake up, Tatiana. He was whispering sweet nothings in your ear and sexy nothings in mine. He saw what we both needed and he gave it to us just so he could get what he wanted. He didn't care who got hurt as long as it wasn't him."

"He was confused. He didn't expect to find me here."

"He knew you from way back when." It's a statement, not a question.

"I thought you said he didn't talk about me." Now she's rearing back. She doesn't like getting caught in a lie. "You and I have barely talked this whole time, so what is it you really want?"

"I thought we were in the same boat, that's all."

She wants us to throw Joshua under the same bus. Blame the victim, act like he's some sort of predator. Does Naomi have something to hide and she wants me to help her conceal it? I'm not about to be part of some smear campaign.

"No," I say, "we're in different boats."

"Is everything all right, sweetie?"

I look over and see Zarine. How long has she been standing there?

"I need to take a shower," Naomi says. "Excuse me."

She goes inside and Zarine comes over. She combs the wet hair back from my forehead, raking it with her fingers just a little too hard. But I don't tell her no.

"Joshua's two conquests," she says. "Were you comparing notes?"

"It wasn't like that." She's scaring me a little but I'm also turned on for the first time since she came back.

"You're not wearing your ring."

I'm relieved every night when I take it off and dread putting it on the next day. "Because of the chlorine."

"Before we get married, is there anything you need to tell me, Tati?" She does a little smile. "Speak now or forever hold your peace."

I meet her eyes. "Anything you need to tell me, Zarine?" The air between us crackles for the first time in quite a while.

"Not a thing." She's holding that smile. "Have you been texting anyone at home, Tati?"

"No. I've been keeping to myself." It's true; in the limited times I do have my phone, I haven't felt compelled to be in touch with anyone. I couldn't begin to convey what this has been like.

"Maybe Bryce?"

"Bryce? You mean my massage therapist?" I feel my chest tighten. I had been meeting with him behind Zarine's back some months ago but that's only to pick his brain about maybe, finally, opening up my own practice. Maybe, finally, doing something with my life. I wanted to see if it was really something I was interested in doing before I broached the subject with Zarine and asked her for startup costs.

"He's not just your massage therapist, is he?"

"Of course he is."

She nods slowly, like I've said something revealing.

"Did you think something was going on with him?" I stare at her, a light bulb brightening. She doesn't answer. "You did. Is that why you were so keen to come on this show? To get me away from him?"

"I thought you could use a vacation, that's all."

Doing this show is completely out of character for Zarine, and she must have agreed to it only as a way to control me rather than admitting to her feelings of insecurity—i.e., she'd rather manipulate me than talk to me. It seems to confirm

Joshua's contention about this being a toxic and abusive relationship.

Did Zarine know that Joshua was onto her? What would she have done if she had known?

"Run along," she says, "or you'll be late for therapy."

My blood runs cold, and I head upstairs to take an extra-hot shower. When I slide in beside her on the loveseat twenty minutes later, I notice that the recent edge is gone. She's Stepford Zarine again.

"Where's Blanche?" I ask Dave, worried. Not because it's Blanche in particular but because I don't want anyone else disappearing. Though come to think of it, Sam hasn't come back either.

"Blanche has been excused," Dave says. "Today is for couples only. She'll rejoin the group tomorrow, which is when the hypnotist will be here for Tatiana."

"That was a joke," I say, heart racing. I never thought they'd actually take me up on the offer.

"Marla and I thought it was a great idea."

"You don't have to do it if you don't want to, Tati," Zarine says quickly.

But I don't see how I can back out now without looking suspicious.

"We've spent a lot of time on the dead," Dave says. "Today is for the living. Our relationships are living, breathing organisms and we have to tend to them. I'm going to ring a bell, and you'll stare deeply and silently into your partner's eyes, the windows of the soul. Don't stop until I ring the bell again."

"Naomi and I are going to excuse ourselves," The Major says. "We're done staring into each other's souls."

Naomi doesn't disagree. She hasn't looked over at me once.

"You still share children," Dave tells them. "You've had a life together. This is a way for you to release some of the anger and distrust. Let go of each other lovingly."

Lauren seems excited about the exercise, while Tristan is obviously uncomfortable. I'm pretty nervous myself. I don't know if I'm avoiding Zarine's soul or my own.

"Get into a restful position facing your partner," Dave instructs. "When I ring the bell, it begins."

I'm shifting way too much. I feel constricted: in my throat, in my stomach. Zarine touches my hand lightly, as if to say it'll all be okay, and that only makes it worse.

The bell rings.

Zarine and I lock eyes. Her irises are nearly black, and I focus on them, trying to tune out everything else. The voices in my head, the clenching in my body.

Against my will, I'm transported. It's the night of the wrap party, the night of my engagement. I know it's the last time I'll see him, and I'm on the verge of panic. It's the first time I've even allowed for the possibility of true romantic feelings for him. I've been telling myself that even if I were to be attracted to a man again, it wouldn't be this man.

Only it is this man, and I've made a mistake, letting Zarine buy me with a sapphire. Letting her think she owns me. It's possible that he and I were the ones who were meant to reunite. Otherwise, of all the people in L.A., how could we have wound up on this beach together?

Is he saying those words, or am I?

I go to kiss him and he stops me. Once again, he says, "Not this way."

I stare at him in anger and disbelief.

"What I mean is, I've had too much to drink, and I want to be able to remember this clearly. The first time you kiss me and it's not for money."

I start to say something—what would it have been?—but he cuts me off.

"Also, I did something earlier that I'm not proud of. I didn't expect you to come and say this. If I'd known, I wouldn't have...

But it can't be tonight. Soon, okay? When we're back in L.A. and you've ended things with Zarine and I've ended things with Blanche and everyone else."

Everyone else? How many of us are there?

"This isn't just another affair to me." He grazes my face with his fingertips.

"I can't say for sure that Zarine and I are over. All I know is, I want to kiss you."

"You want to kiss me tonight and go home with her tomorrow?"

"We're engaged."

He stares at me, incredulous. "You mean you're still going to choose Zarine, after everything?"

I don't know what to say, so I leave him there, broken. When I first heard he was dead, all I could think was that he'd killed himself. I'd been so full of guilt and remorse. It had almost been a relief to learn it was murder.

But that wasn't the last time I saw him that night. I tried to go back. What did I say? Who did I see?

Tears are streaming down my face and Zarine is holding me. "There, there," she says, like I'm her baby. She thinks the tears are for her.

But they're for Joshua, and for what I'll never have. How different it would have been if I could have loved him when we first met. I'd been a high-end escort and he'd been my youngest client. He was still in college, and I was barely twenty-one. Speaking of high-end, it took a lot of (exceptionally good) work for him to become a Ken doll. His nose, facial sculpting, a chin implant, hair dye, to name a few. That's a big part of why I hadn't recognized him.

I didn't know him long; I could only stand the job for a year. I was drunk or high most of the time, which was the other reason I didn't recognize him. He wasn't just my youngest client; he was my sweetest. He tried to romance me back then, too. Once, we talked all night on the roof of his frat house and never even had sex. He paid me double. I wish I could remember everything about that night. I think I remember this, though, how he believed in my potential. How he told me that same Samuel Beckett quote about trying and failing better.

But I have to get his voice out of my head. He's gone, and Zarine's all I have left. She's changed, and I need to change, too.

Naomi knows that Joshua and I met before the island but I have to hope she doesn't know how we met. My past can't get out. Zarine can't have a former sex worker for a wife.

I have to hope my secret died with Joshua.

FORTY-EIGHT

THE MAJOR

Staring into Naomi's eyes is hell.

I thought it's been hell to share a room with her, but no, this is far worse. It's so much more concentrated. The emotions come one after the other, a succession of waves crashing over me, pulling me out into the undertow, like Joshua's body must have been pulled out, sucked forward, and spit back out, until finally, he's a limp body on the beach. There was nothing left of him. Soon there'll be nothing left of me.

Every day, I've been trying to puzzle it out. How could I have been so wrong about Naomi? When and where and why did the lies begin?

The fact is, I haven't merely loved Naomi; I've admired her. I always thought she was a woman of the highest character and principle but if that were true, then Marla couldn't have acted on her—and on us—like this.

Looking into Naomi's eyes, our lives together are flashing in front of me, all the key moments: meeting her in college, making love for the first time on our wedding night (a physical union as intense as the spiritual), the birth of our daughters, the birth of our gym. All the times she challenged me lovingly, all the occasions when she stood by me, all the ways she's made me stronger. She believed we could strike out on our own and have our own gym; she believed I could inspire people through the boot camps. Through myriad frustrations and difficulties, through the lean years when our debt was mounting, she helped me keep the faith. Naomi has been my motivational speaker for twenty-three years.

My eyes are watering, and so are hers.

All of that was real. That was Naomi. Who she is now, I can't say. How she got from there to here, though, I do know that.

Marla did this, and she's going to pay.

FORTY-NINE
BLANCHE

If I could, I'd be in therapy and exercises and group meals and smoke breaks—especially smoke breaks—morning till night. Because having Tristan nearby confirms something I never believed before: that everything happens for a reason. Joshua's death is going to lead to a new life, and not just for me, but for Lily and Kyle, too. Tristan was not only born to be a dad; he was born to be *their* dad.

I'm getting through this extended absence from my kids by reminding myself that it's an investment in their future. They're trading up from an absentee father, and I'll be trading up in innumerable ways myself. A happy woman is a better mother.

I can scheme and plan and hope and pray but in this second, I can't get any closer to him. It's terrifying, loving like this. Once this sequester is over, I'll lose my access. So I have to make the time count.

My anxiety is rising. I need to confide in someone who knows and loves me. I wish that was my mom, but it's never been that way. So I reach out to Elle. I have to admit that I blamed her a little when I first learned of Marla's editing job. After all, Marla is Elle's friend, which is why I'd trusted so blindly. But Elle probably assumed this season would be like the ones that had come before. And if Elle hadn't introduced me to Marla, I never would have met Tristan, so how mad can I be?

Elle doesn't pick up even though she's the kind of person who's incessantly social. "I'm available for the next hour or two," I tell her voicemail. "Please call me." I systematically work my way through the contacts in my phone, starting with my inner circle and moving outward. I'm getting a bad feeling as I make call after call, send text after text. They all know that I've lost my husband and yet they're icing me out?

I understood why they didn't defend me on social media; no one wants the mob coming for them. But this... I didn't see it coming, and it hurts. Just like I didn't see Joshua's betrayal coming.

I really have no one. No one but Tristan.

If Marla is determined for Lauren and Tristan to leave together, I could be in big trouble. After all, no stunt is too outrageous for this season. Brandon told me the hypnotist is flying in for Tatiana.

I'm running out of time so I'm going to need to go for broke. I don't have a husband and my reputation has been destroyed, online and IRL, too. In the end, the only thing that really matters is love. I've got nothing else to lose.

It's time to make a big move. My gut says Tristan has feelings for me that he's too scared to act on, so I'll need to act for both of us. Social media can say no way, I'm a hag, but they're mistaking reality TV for reality. Why would Tristan choose a woman who needs a camera trained on her in order to be trustworthy when he can have me?

Sam might have lost her taste for blood but Dave sure hasn't. What he lacks in imagination he makes up for in ruthlessness. He and I should definitely have a chat.

Interview between Detective Sonya Mohr and producer Julie Lindstrom, taking place on Glass Island.

Detective: What's bringing you back in today?

Julie: Marla's behind everything.

Detective: Do you have any evidence to support that?

Julie: As a matter of fact, I do. Here.

During the casting process, everyone filled out a 1,200-question personality inventory. They were told that it's for their protection, to make sure they're psychologically fit for the show, but really, it's to learn their weaknesses and vulnerabilities. Then Marla could use their subconscious against them.

Detective: Can you prove that?

Julie: It's common knowledge in the reality TV world. Over the past decade, more than twenty former reality TV stars have killed themselves. Normally, that's a byproduct of the stress but maybe Marla thought it could work in her favor. She'd be an innovator.

She stocked that house with all manner of mental instability: narcissism, sociopathy, paranoia, a superhero complex, a God complex, you name it.

Joshua, for example, had traits of three different personality disorders. He had clear alcoholic tendencies. He was volatile, and Marla knew it. That's why she cast him. He was just as likely to murder as to be murdered.

Read through their test results. It's a wonder the island hasn't blown up yet.

FIFTY

LAUREN

Day Thirteen

It's ominous, to say the least.

Blanche is alone on her loveseat, Tristan is beside me, and then it's The Major and Naomi. No Tatiana, no Zarine. Marla's here, which is never a good sign. There's Dave. No Sam.

"I have some disturbing news," Marla says, and this time, she really does look disturbed. "Tatiana's dead."

Blanche gasps. The rest of us are silent in our shock: eyes widening, mouths dropping open, hands going to lips, or remaining too still, as if paralyzed.

"Her body was found by the pool. While the police haven't said definitively whether she was pushed from her balcony or she jumped, foul play seems likely since all the footage from the entire night has been erased. Efforts are being made to recover it."

"There are no cameras on the balconies," The Major says.

"That's correct," Marla says, "but there should have been footage of someone entering Tatiana's room."

"Unless someone was already in there with Tatiana," Naomi says. "Where is Zarine?"

"Zarine is on suicide watch, given the tendencies she displayed earlier in the shoot." Dave seems eager to get a line in on such a crucial episode.

"And then there were five," Blanche says slowly. "Like the Agatha Christie book Tatiana was talking about at dinner that time."

The Major turns to Marla. "How would footage get erased on your shoot without your knowledge?"

"It's a television show, not a police state."

I reach for Tristan. He reaches back. Finally, he's seeing that he needs me, too. Can he feel how much stronger I've been getting? That we can lean on each other?

"We need more security," Blanche says, her voice shrill.

"I'll look into that," Marla says.

"Well, how long is it going to take? We're the ones in danger." Naomi's getting a little shrill, too. "At the very least, guard your control room so that murderers can't waltz in there and delete their crimes."

It goes on like that for a while, everyone thinking of themselves rather than Tatiana, fear far more acute than sadness. I clutch Tristan tighter. Are we ever going to get off this island?

Therapy is suspended for the day. Dave says he'll make himself available if we need crisis support but basically, we're on our own.

Blanche says we should all stay together, that it's safer that way. Well, she can huddle up with The Major and Naomi. Tristan and I need some alone time. I feel safest when it's just the two of us.

But when I suggest going to our room, he says no, that Blanche is right.

Somehow, we all end up on the beach, which is creepy because that's where Joshua died, but it's better than being out by the pool, where Tatiana died more recently. We're not even in our swimsuits so we're just staring out at the swells coming in. None of us is in the habit of going in the ocean anyway because the first day, we were warned about how many organisms in there could kill us. We used to think the natural world was scarier than the human one.

Blanche keeps swatting at her arms like a lunatic, even though I haven't felt any bugs.

"Maybe we should say a few words about Tatiana," Naomi says.

"She seemed like a lost soul," The Major says.

"*Nice* words," Naomi clarifies.

He shoots her an annoyed look. "It wasn't an insult."

"Whatever I say is going to be misconstrued at home." Blanche swats again. "If I say that I'm sorry she's dead but I didn't like her, then I'm cold. If I say she was a lovely person, I'm inauthentic."

You are both cold and inauthentic. And those are your better qualities.

"Don't worry what anyone at home is going to say," Tristan tells her. "They don't know the real you."

She beams at him, which bugs the shit out of me, no pun intended.

"I really like—liked—Tatiana," I say. "I thought she and Zarine were going to work things out and have a great life together."

"That's one of the saddest parts for me," The Major says. "What's never going to happen. All the things she'll never get to do or be. Her parents are about to get that call, the one we all dread." Naomi goes to hold his hand and he actually lets her. I smile. Sometimes good things can come from tragedy.

Tristan sees my smile and instead of returning it, he looks bothered. It's not like I'm enjoying any of this. Why's he seeing the best in Blanche and the worst in me?

He's probably just scared. Since he's convinced he's the prime suspect in Joshua's murder, he must be thinking he's now the prime suspect in Tatiana's. But I bet there's been a big spike in #ZarineDidIt. She might even edge out #BlancheDidIt, though I hope not. It seems like having a second murder could really shift the investigation. Who has a reason to kill both Joshua and Tatiana?

Blanche still makes the most sense. They should arrest her and get it over with and then the rest of us can return to our lives.

"We can't just stay clustered together twenty-four hours a day," Naomi says. "What are we going to do, have a big slumber party in the great room every night?"

"We wouldn't be safe even if we did," The Major says, "because none of us is the killer. We all know who it is."

Naomi releases his hand.

"Two people are dead! Am I the only one who can see that evil is real?" He stomps off in the general direction of the villa. Naomi jumps to her feet to follow him.

"The Major could be right," I say to Tristan. "About it not being the cast. I mean, you and I have been in that jungle."

"Rainforest," Blanche corrects.

"Whatever." I keep my focus on Tristan, tears filling my eyes. "The forest is dense. Someone could easily be hiding out there. Someone who intends to kill every single one of us."

He moves closer, which is gratifying. "I'm sure the police have accounted for everyone who's flown to the island. It's chartered planes only, remember?"

"What if it's someone who lives here all the time? A savage, or something? Or maybe an angry crew member who stayed behind after the last shoot?" I grip Tristan's arm. "I can't stay here on this beach another minute. Come with me."

"I don't want to be alone either," Blanche says to Tristan. "I'm scared, too."

Tristan looks between Blanche and me. He hasn't had to make such a direct choice before. I see the pleasure she's taking in his hesitation.

"There's a camera trained on her," I say, pointing. "She'll be fine. She's just pretending to be scared."

"You're the manipulator, not me," she shoots back.

"I'm terrified!" I am. I have to get off this island. "Tristan, I'm the mother of your child. I need you."

"If that's not manipulation," Blanche begins, but Tristan cuts her off, saying we should go inside. He looks more resigned than devoted as we make our way to the villa.

In our room, I take off all my clothes, get under the covers, and reach my hand out. "I need you," I say again. I'm thinking of how short life is, but that as long as we're still breathing, forgiveness is possible. It's too late for Joshua and Tatiana, but it's not too late for Tristan and me. That's the silver lining, the lesson for every person at every viewing party. Live each moment like it's your last.

I'm becoming as corny as my mother but I don't care. It's true, no one is guaranteed anything. And you can never give up on the people who matter most.

It feels like an eternity before Tristan accepts my invitation and gets under the covers. He still has all his clothes on and his body is rigid. Yet when I crawl over and burrow against him, when he feels me shivering, he can't help but respond. He wants to take care of me. He always has.

I'm the one who removes all his clothes, piece by piece, each time asking, "Is this okay?" He nods with his eyes closed. It feels kinky somehow, having to elicit his consent at every step, nothing taken for granted. I don't know if the power is in daring to ask or if the power is in his ability to refuse me, but I do know that we're both incredibly turned on. The sex is fast but intense.

Afterward, I want to cuddle and talk but he's distant. "I

need to clear my head," he says. He gets dressed and slips out of the room.

I shrug into a bathrobe and go to the balcony. I wouldn't mind checking on The Major but he's not out there. It's just me and my girl.

"This is progress," I tell her. "Your daddy's finding his way back. He loves us very, very much. I'll always look after both of you."

I'm still crooning to her when I notice that Blanche has remained on the beach, and that Tristan is heading right for her.

FIFTY-ONE

THE MAJOR

Blanche and Tristan are sitting close together in the sand, sharing a cigarette, no camera crew in sight. "Want one?" She proffers the pack.

I shake my head. "I'm glad you're both still here, though."

They laugh, and I'm not sure why. But I don't need to understand these people; we don't have to be friends. What I need are comrades in arms. We can work together to defeat Marla. Good(ish) versus evil. I couldn't convince Naomi of that just now but maybe I can still persuade the rest of the cast.

"Are you feeling better?" Blanche asks me with a solicitude that borders on the offensive.

I wasn't having a psychotic break; I was having a reasonable reaction to unreasonable circumstances. I'm being subjected to the tyranny of a supervillain. People are *dying*. How am I the only one who gets this? "I'm fine."

"I'm not fine," Tristan says. "I'm freaking the fuck out."

"Me, too," Blanche says. "Someone killed my husband, and his girlfriend. I could be next." Is it my imagination or is she watching me closely as she says that? As if Tristan isn't the more likely suspect, with his history.

Okay, so maybe they get it, a little. But they're missing some pretty crucial information.

"We're all wondering who's next," I tell them. "Do you want to sit and wonder or do you want to go after Marla, guns blazing? Look at what she's done to all of us. There's no doubt the woman's evil."

"I get the appeal of blaming Marla," Tristan says, "but do you have evidence?"

"All the footage that could have helped solve Tatiana's murder was erased. On Marla's watch." Do I need to draw a picture in the sand? Would hieroglyphics help?

"Anyone on the crew could have done that," Blanche says. "Or a cast member could have gotten into the control room somehow. If someone's desperate enough—"

"Why are you defending Marla?" I'm trying to stay calm but they're making it tough. I don't know what it's going to take for them to open their eyes and see what's right in front of them.

Blanche looks nervous and Tristan does his protective shtick, putting his arm around her. Has he forgotten his pregnant fiancée? I will never understand these people.

"Just listen to my plan, all right? It's simple," I say. "We have to stay on the island because of the investigation, we don't have a choice about that, but we do have a choice about whether we keep filming."

"The contract doesn't give us a choice," Tristan says.

"You think the contract would be enforceable after two murders? It'd be a PR disaster for the network."

"If we're not filming, then the crew isn't following us anymore," Blanche says. "We lose a layer of security."

"You don't really believe the crew is keeping you safe, do you?"

"Safer."

"They're barely working! Like right now, where are they?"

"I think they went to lunch?" She sounds a little uneasy.

"My theory is that the crew is engaging in some passive resistance. They're not entirely under Marla's control, because they've figured out the truth about her. They know what she's done."

"Why wouldn't they turn her in to the police, then?" Tristan asks.

I shake my head. "Because she has power. Why didn't anyone turn Harvey Weinstein in? Why don't people leave cults?" I can see I'm losing them. "The crew isn't going to keep us safe anyway. Like you said yourself, Blanche, if the killer is desperate, they can still get you. They'll get any of us."

"It's about improving our odds," Tristan says. "Having another set of eyes. Millions of eyes, if you count the people at home. Citizen detectives are working on the case remotely. Who knows what they're seeing through satellite images or by looking frame by frame?"

Interestingly, Blanche seems more perturbed than reassured.

"Why are you both so determined to stay here and do Marla's bidding?" I want to knock their heads together. "Has Marla got something on you?"

"No," Tristan says. Blanche doesn't answer.

With the way Tristan's acting, money's likely to be involved. He's a starving actor/bartender with a child on the way.

"If I'm the only one who refuses to film, I'm probably going to get sued," I say. Solo, Marla could just laugh me off. But if I take everyone with me, she's got no show; I'm hitting her where she lives. Maybe she'd do something crazy herself and then we've got her where we want her. "If we all walk out together, we take our power back, collectively."

They pause like they might actually be considering. Then Blanche says, "We walk out and go where? Where do we sleep, and what do we eat?"

"We'll figure all that out."

But I can see that I've lost them. They don't want to risk any additional hardship in the name of righteousness.

You can do whatever you want if you're willing to accept the consequences. But no one's willing, not even Naomi.

"I think it's going to be okay," Tristan says. "I mean, we all know the most likely suspect." Blanche and I look at him. "Zarine. She tried to drown herself in the pool and then she was basically institutionalized. After she comes back, she finds out that Joshua and Tatiana had a thing going. First she takes care of him but the problem isn't solved. So then she takes care of Tatiana."

"I like that theory," Blanche says, though you can tell she'd like anything out of Tristan's mouth. "With Zarine locked up again somewhere, we should be safe."

"We're not safe!" I stand up, suddenly furious.

There's nothing left to say. If they insist on being the next victims, I can't stop them.

I storm away—again—and they must assume I'm out of earshot or Blanche doesn't know the difference between a stage whisper and an actual whisper because I can hear her saying, "If it's not Zarine, I can think of another suspect." I slow way down. "He's seeming pretty unhinged and that whole Marla obsession... Maybe it's just supposed to throw everyone off the scent."

"Yeah," Tristan says, and he's not even trying to whisper. "It could definitely be him. Or he's covering for someone."

"#NaomiDidIt."

My stomach thuds. Do they know something I don't? Or do they know something I do?

FIFTY-TWO

BLANCHE

The mounting body count means we've dispensed with social niceties. At dinner, The Major is silent and glowering, while Naomi's speechlessness seems more fear-based. Tristan wants to talk to me, I can tell, but Lauren's draping herself all over him, occasionally whispering in his ear. It's not only tacky but transparent, the way she wants to advertise that she and Tristan have just had sex. But joke's on her, I already knew. More significantly, I know that he thought it was a mistake. A moment of weakness, he called it.

He probably would have shared more if The Major hadn't interrupted us to urge a walkout for the hundredth time. But as it is, Tristan's said enough. He's confirmed that whatever I have to do will be for his good as well as mine. He's ready to get sprung.

Lauren might think her behavior is going to make me back off. Actually, I'm emboldened. People who are secure in their relationships don't pee all over their partners. Her little display tells me I'm on track, and I'm getting closer.

When I come out of the bathroom, she accosts me, and she's brought a camera crew.

"You're not acting like you're supposed to and everyone at home can see it," she says. "Your husband died, and you're all over my fiancé."

Oh, right. Because the viewers at home know how you're supposed to act when your husband's been murdered and you're being filmed while on lockdown with a serial killer on the loose. "Just keep playing to the cameras, Lauren. Marla's going to love this." Mentioning a producer ensures that a moment will never air. You can't go breaking the fourth wall.

"I'm genuine, and that's what my fans and followers appreciate."

I laugh, saying nothing.

Her cheeks pinken. "When your kids get older, they'll hate you just like everyone else does."

I wouldn't have thought she had the guts for a remark like that. But it goes to show how far under her skin I've gotten. Speaking of which, her skin is luminous. Sequester agrees with her, or maybe it's the pregnancy. The second trimester was my favorite.

While I do have legitimate fears about how my children are going to cope with their father's death and how it would affect them to read all the vitriol being directed my way, I realize that the news cycle is short and they're still little. I have plenty of time to reverse our family's fortunes, and I know that not everyone hates me. In fact, I have the fan that I want most. Now I just have to lock him down.

"You can have ten million followers, and you're still going to lose Tristan," I say. "Because he's over your damsel-in-distress shit. He couldn't beat it out of your room fast enough today, could he?"

"You're a horrible person," she says, her voice quavering.

"Right back at you."

She steps closer. "I bet you've been relieved knowing the earlier episodes were taken down. But I've got an army of people with those episodes saved to their DVR. They're having re-viewing parties right now, finding moments that show how guilty you are, moments that Detective Mohr might have missed. You think you can compete with that?"

She's scored a direct hit. It's not about my ego because by now, I know America will never like me. But could they hurt me? I'm all that my kids have. I had the same reaction earlier when Tristan talked about the citizen detective brigades.

Lauren's the one who started this tonight but I can't be the one to finish it. Not yet. Slink away, live to fight another day.

Walking upstairs, my head is spinning. If Detective Mohr stops trusting me, if I lose her sympathy, if she digs much deeper...

There are things I've left out. Like my first confrontation with Joshua on the beach that night. And my second confrontation after I'd had even more to drink, had absorbed more of the social media aggression being directed at me alone, and was feeling more incensed that he'd put me in that position.

He'd been down in the sand, couldn't have stood up if he'd tried, and I was hovering above him.

"Back home," I said, "I thought you might have a little problem with drinking, but I never—"

"Is it time for true confessions? Are you finally ready for us to talk? Finally ready to listen?" He didn't wait for my answer. He got to his feet and got in my face. "My father was keeping my business afloat the whole time. Last year, he said he wouldn't do it anymore, so for the first time in my whole life, it was really all on me, and I lost it. I drank before meetings and I bombed them. Or I missed them to be with other women, women who made me feel better about myself for a little while, but then I felt worse. So I drank more, and failed more, and lied more. And you didn't even notice. You never came to help me." He started crying. Noisy, little kid tears. "Why didn't you come to help me?"

Because he's not a kid. I never got to be a kid, why should he get to be one at thirty-four? "Fuck you and your self-pity."

He never came to help me when I was overwhelmed with family and social obligations, with making everyone in our community think we were the perfect couple. It was a lot of work to look perfect, with a husband like Joshua. He never made it easy.

But you do what you have to do, unless you're Joshua, in which case you're subsidized by Daddy, financially and emotionally.

"You really are a bitch." He said it with something like wonder. "Just like everyone says. A coldhearted bitch."

"And you really are a useless piece of shit. There. We've traded insults. Marla will be so disappointed to have missed this."

He looked oddly afraid. "What do you know about Marla? What's she told you?" But then he rushed forward. "I'm in love with another woman."

"I could not care less. The fact is, I've seen you self-destructing in slow motion for years. The only reason I might have intervened was to make it happen faster."

We stared each other down, full of unvarnished, satisfying, mutual hate.

"I'll tell everyone the truth about the scars, Blanche," he said. "Then I can watch you self-destruct."

FIFTY-THREE

LAUREN

Day Fourteen

"It's just us in here?" I ask. "No cameras?"

"You know I wouldn't lie to you about that." I can see how much this is wearing on Julie. She's normally the most fresh-faced and dewy of anyone but under her eyes are purple crescents. My skin's the clearest it's ever been even though the esthetician caught the last flight off the island. It must be the radiance of popularity.

"What did you want to talk about?" I'm hoping she'll cut to the chase. The cleaning closet is pretty stuffy.

"I'm concerned about your relationship with Blanche. That confrontation last night, and your posts, and your comments. You've been 'liking' some pretty fucked-up shit. I mean, she is still a widow. Do you think you're going a little too far?"

"She's been after Tristan the whole time! I'm just defending my family. I'm only echoing what everyone else is saying. They all think #BlancheDidIt."

"You know it's different for you to amplify their voices."

"I stand by everything I've ever said. Blanche has been

bullying me since the beginning." Whose side is Julie on, anyway?

"Social media's a fickle world. Fans and followers can turn on you."

"Not mine." They've surely demonstrated their steadfastness by now.

"What about Tristan? He and Blanche are friends. Do you think he's going to like what you're saying about her?"

Well, I didn't like what Blanche had intimated: that Tristan talked to her about our sex, regretfully. "I'm the one who's going to marry him." It comes out much too loud.

"I'm worried you're going to alienate him, that's all. I'm not attacking you."

"It feels like you're more worried about Blanche."

"I've been looking out for you since day one."

With a few notable lapses but still, Julie's definitely proven herself. "I'm sorry. I'm just under a lot of stress, that's all."

"I get it. My job is to make sure you play it smart, and I don't feel like you are right now, going after Blanche in such an aggressive way. It could make everyone see you differently."

"They're used to seeing me as a victim."

Julie shakes her head. "No, they're used to seeing you as someone relatable. Let Blanche be the one with her claws out."

"I don't want to be managed. I want to be myself."

"Are you hating on the right person?" she asks, a bit tentatively.

"What do you mean?"

"Tristan's the one who keeps going back and forth between you. He's the one who—"

"Do not go there."

She must hear my intensity because she backs down instantly. Good. So Blanche isn't the formidable one anymore; I am. "I just want to help, that's all."

"I appreciate that, but everyone hates Blanche. They have since the beginning."

"Because Marla wanted it that way since the beginning. She storyboarded it. She's put you at each other's throats but that doesn't mean you have to stay there."

I don't know why Julie isn't getting this, why she's worrying about all the wrong things. "It's not about editing. This is who Blanche is."

Her eyes suddenly brim with tears. I have to remember, she's under stress, too. She's trapped on the island with a murderer, too. "I know that you're a good person, Lauren. I know how much you love your baby. But this thing between you and Blanche—it scares me. Marla doesn't care where it ends, even if it's another dead body."

FIFTY-FOUR

THE MAJOR

I'm sitting outside minding my own business when they show up: odd couple of the year Naomi and Dave, plus a camera crew. It's a good-sized balcony with a table for four but it's way too crowded for me. I stand up.

"Naomi thought we could all sit down and talk," Dave says.

Naomi's hair is unbrushed and her face is tear stained. I feel a surge of fear. "What happened? Are the girls all right?"

"They're fine," she says, though she's clearly not.

My heart's pounding but it seems that I'm going to have to wait until we've all taken our seats and the crew's set up. When I look over the edge, I see another crew is filming up at us. What, do they think I'm going to jump? I feel like yelling at them to move along, there's nothing to see here, but maybe they know more than I do.

Finally, Dave kicks it off. "Naomi came to me with some concerns. Naomi, why don't you tell Cain what you were saying earlier?"

Naomi has concerns and she took them to a satanic Dr. Phil?

"I can't do it," Naomi says. "Do you see how he's looking at me?"

"He, meaning me?" I say. "You're talking about me in the third person?" Well, apparently, she has been all morning.

"This isn't the man I married." She has tears running down her face. "We used to be able to talk about anything."

"So talk to me!" I say.

"I can't."

"Because of this show. Turn the cameras off."

"No, I haven't been able to talk to you for the past year, maybe two. I don't know how long it's been. It got worse so gradually that I didn't realize how bad it was. I started to accept it as normal. It was like I'd gotten used to you ranting and then blaming me for not being as angry as you were. Like yesterday, when I followed you in from the beach, and you just turned on me."

Now I'm the one making my case to Dave, and, apparently, all of America. "You want to know why I 'turned on her'? It's because she's always siding with power. Hoping it'll mean she can hang on to her privilege, or get a slightly bigger piece of the pie. Who cares about principles? Who cares about truth, or justice?"

Naomi tells Dave, "He's hell-bent on taking down Marla. It's become a personal crusade, like he thinks he'll make a mark on the world. He was talking about himself like the messiah."

"I would never call myself the messiah!" Why is she doing this? She's always been the one to calm me down but it's like she's trying to rile me up, as if she wants me to look guilty.

She's finally talking right to me. "You don't know what it's been like to live with you these past few years. The girls have felt the change, but I've been covering for you. I've told them there's nothing to worry about because we were coming on this show and getting help."

"Help for our marriage."

"No, help for you. You refused to see a therapist back home no matter how many times I asked."

"I don't trust therapists," I say. "With good reason."

"You've become so obsessed with the ills of the world that you've stopped living. You're full of unproductive rage. All you do is catalogue hate, and it's made you hateful yourself." She's back to crying. "I love you, I always have. I want you to get better."

I feel myself soften, just a little. Then I remember what she's done. "So you came here to show everyone what an awful husband you have and to get yourself a golden parachute out of the marriage?"

"No! I came to get you mental health treatment so you could be yourself again. I wanted you to work on the depression or delusions or whatever it is. You've been saying the world is sick, not you. But I think it's both, Cain. I think it's the world, and it's you." Now she's sobbing. "I tried so hard to connect with you, to love you back to health, but it didn't work. Then we were on the island and I kept on trying. But you've resisted everything from the therapists and from me."

"Did you really think a reality TV show could be the answer?" I ask. "It's the problem!"

"I was desperate," she whispers.

"What Naomi is saying is—" Dave begins.

"I can hear her as well as you can." I turn to Naomi. "I know I've been hard to live with, but what about blindsiding me on Decision Day? What did you think that would do to my mental health?"

"I'm not a saint, Cain. I have my limits. Do you remember our fight in the shower? After that, a part of me was just done. You'd made it clear you didn't want me or our marriage. Yes, I humiliated you on the beach but you've been humiliating me since we arrived. Not to mention the way you've been treating me in front of our friends at home and in the church community."

My head is starting to ache. She seems sincere, but it just doesn't add up. "What about all your tweeting? You started at the wrap party, trying to broadcast your side of the story, making yourself some sort of Christian divorce ambassador."

"Like I said, I was hurt. And yes, I do like having followers. I'm an independent Christian woman who can rise above anything. That's my truth."

"You can rise above me, is that it?"

"Cain." She reaches out to touch my arm, gentle as a kiss. "I'm here, right next to you."

I'm woozy with confusion. I don't know if this is one more betrayal and blindside, bringing Dave here, airing our dirty laundry for all the world to see, or if it truly is an act of love.

I look down at her hand on my arm and my eyes are swimming right along with my mind. This is Naomi. This is my wife. This is my life.

"But how could you do it, Naomi?" I cry. "How could you sleep with Joshua in our bed?"

She stares at me in shock, then retracts her hand as if I've burned her. Which I have but I didn't mean to. For maybe the first time since filming began, I'd forgotten about everything but her.

As angry as I've been, I've kept her secret. I caught Naomi and Joshua together in our bed the night of the wrap party after the cameras were off and I made sure I never spoke about it when they were turned back on. I didn't reveal it during my interrogation with Detective Mohr, though if I'd been asked, I would have lied. I would have done that for Naomi, despite everything.

"I'm sorry," I say. "I didn't mean to say that."

What's Detective Mohr going to think once this airs? Because it will air, there's no question. Marla just struck gold.

No, she didn't strike it. I served it to her on a platter.

Naomi gets clumsily to her feet, and she's never clumsy. She trips over the man holding the boom mic, fleeing our room like it's the scene of yet one more crime.

FIFTY-FIVE

BLANCHE

I'm by the pool, shielding my eyes, looking up at The Major and Naomi's balcony. Alexei is close to the building with his phone out, filming.

Up on the balcony, Naomi is making a hasty exit and The Major is in hot pursuit. "I guess you're not going to get a jumper today," I tell Alexei.

Given how recently Tatiana died, that was probably in poor taste but it's also in poor taste that I'm by the pool at all. There just aren't many places to go outdoors if you rule out crime scenes, and I can't bear to be in the room I shared with Joshua. This island is more claustrophobic by the day.

I'm trying to avoid Lauren, who seems to have unleashed her fan base on me. They're scrutinizing everything I do, so my best option is to lay low. Play dead, basically. Okay, that was in poor taste, too. But I'm going stir crazy, and I'm losing precious time with Tristan.

Alexei comes and sits on the lounger next to me. "You're way prettier than you look on TV," he says.

"Nice neg."

"What's a neg?"

"It's when you flirt by throwing little insults. People feel worse about themselves and they're easier to take advantage of."

The crew that had been filming the balcony is shutting down. They look over and see us, consult briefly, and then instead of approaching, they head inside.

"If you were hoping to make it into tomorrow night's episode by talking to me, your hopes have been dashed," I say.

"That's not what I was hoping for." He moves his chair closer. I spray myself liberally with DEET and he pushes back again, gagging.

"But you are in need of a new storyline since Lauren shot you down."

"The truth is"—he leans in like he's going to tell me a secret and now I'm the one gagging on his cologne, which is frankly worse than the DEET—"I used to think Lauren was sweet but I either had her pegged wrong or she's really changed."

I smile at him with newfound warmth. The enemy of my enemy is my friend, isn't that the saying?

Dave had liked my idea about a forgiveness exercise that would bring Tristan, Lauren, and Alexei face to face (which I knew would give Tristan more flashbacks of Lauren and Alexei together and could make him realize once and for all that forgiveness was impossible). But apparently, Marla told him no, the viewers have already gotten their fill of Alexei.

Now that I've met him, I can see why. Yet he could turn out to have some utility after all. Off camera, he may still be able to drive the plot.

FIFTY-SIX
THE MAJOR

Day Fifteen

At first, after seeing Naomi with Joshua, I thought hell was having to sleep in the same room with her. Then I thought it was staring into her eyes for full minutes. But no, hell is knowing that I've put her in the line of fire. The online trolls are coming for her, with #NaomiDidIt finally unseating #Blanche-DidIt. They've ascribed Naomi all kinds of baseless motives: that after Joshua had her, he threw her away, so she was a woman scorned; that Joshua had made a secret video of them and was going to distribute it; that Naomi was really in love with him and found out about his feelings for Tatiana, hence, she later murdered Tatiana... On and on they go, building on each other's theories, creating a dogpile that could destroy a woman's life.

What she said yesterday was all true. I have been insuffer-able. I was so mired in my own pain that I couldn't see hers. Yet despite my selfishness, she'd been hoping to come to this island and save me and our relationship. I'm finally seeing it all clearly.

I'm not condoning what she did with Joshua but the footage

shows him working her like a pro. He'd groomed her, saying all the things I'd stopped saying. She felt desired for the first time in I don't know how long. And the night of the wrap party, she caved. She was, technically, single, having publicly ended our relationship hours before. But really, I'd been telling her it was over for much longer than that.

I get it now. My eyes are open. But Naomi's door is closed.

She's moved into Tatiana's former room—that's how bad she wanted to get away from me after what I did—and now she's the one who won't speak to me. I've been saying it's about actions, not words. So I have to show her that I'm not just going to rant and rave, I'm going to bring some justice to this world. When I do, it'll take the heat off Naomi. No one will be talking about her at all.

Before I signed on to the show, I read every article and profile on Sam, Dave, and Marla. I learned that Sam and Marla have been friends since college. Hopefully I'm remembering right about Sam and Dave always staying in a white mini-mansion trimmed in blue, with an ocean-facing pool, surrounded by the same dense rainforest that brackets the villa. I also have to hope that I might be able to enlist Sam's help. After all, she'd done a walkout of her own.

If I start walking along the sand at the crack of dawn, it's likely no one will see me since production seems to be sleeping in later and later. Even Marla can't motivate her workforce under these conditions. She has limitations, too. Which means she can be defeated.

The sun is just peeking over the horizon. I pick a direction, praying that I won't have to double back. After following the shoreline for what feels like an eternity but is probably only a couple of miles, I see it. There are no gates and no evident security. I pass the pool and approach the house. Cupping my hands, I peer inside. The layout is similar to that of the villa, though this great room has a large white leather sectional and a grand piano. And there's Sam, lying down in navy satin pajamas.

I tap on the glass lightly, not wanting to disturb Dave if he's upstairs sleeping. But she doesn't stir, so I have to tap harder. Still nothing. Desperate times and all, so I try the door. It's unlocked.

I creep forward, whispering, "Sam?" Then at slightly higher volume, "Sam."

Her eyes fly open and her mouth does, too, in a cartoonish O. But she doesn't scream, thankfully. Her bob is disheveled and unwashed. Her skin is free of makeup and only a little crepey. She's prettier than I remember. Softer, I suppose.

"Well, good morning, sunshine," she says at full volume.

"Shouldn't we talk lower? I don't think Dave—"

"Dave doesn't live here anymore." She indicates the part of the sectional opposite her. "Make yourself comfortable. It's just you? No camera crew?"

"Just me. The crew's easy to ditch these days."

She starts to feel around the large rectangular coffee table like a blind woman and finally locates an open bag of Cheetos. "Want one?" I shake my head. The table is littered with half-eaten microwave meals, junk food, and open cans of diet soda. "Sorry about your marriage."

I don't know what I'd been expecting, but it wasn't this. "Sorry about yours."

"I really did hope you and Naomi would make it. You were supposed to."

"Weren't we all?"

"Marla said we were switching up the formula this season, and I didn't object. She talked about this couple America would love to hate and how she was going to really enjoy watching him humiliate her, and I didn't object then either. Have you heard that parable about how you do nothing and then by the time they come for you, there's no one left to speak up?"

I nod. I'm familiar. But I'm here for clues, and I think Sam's already provided one. Marla knew that Joshua was going to humiliate Blanche? Was his behavior scripted?

"It's just your basic karma. My marriage is over, my career is over. Dave will probably make our divorce messy and public, and I can't go back to seeing clients privately because who'd want a therapist who was involved in this debacle? The only way to keep working is to keep working in this industry, be a psychological consultant or something vile like that."

"Listen, I came here because I need to ask you something."

She's munching another Cheeto, and when she speaks her tongue is partially coated in Day-Glo orange. "Yes, your wife loves you, Cain. I was bummed out when she said no on the beach. Just between you and me, you were the couple I most wanted to help. You made it tough, though. I couldn't seem to break through your shell."

"I'm not here to talk about my marriage. You've known Marla for a long time. Do you think she's capable of murder?"

"I think everyone is capable of murder, with enough provocation. So that's a general yes. More specifically, would Marla kill Joshua and Tatiana?" Sam closes her eyes in deep contemplation. "That I can't see. Though she's also capable of surprising me. For example, that stunt with Zarine..." She makes the cuckoo sign with one hand.

"What stunt?"

"You mean you haven't figured that out yet? With everyone playing the DidIt game at home, I was sure they would have been recognized from an insurance commercial or something by now."

What is she talking about?

"I'll spell it out for you. Those weren't Zarine's parents, they were actors. Zarine cooked up that plan and Marla went gaga for it. She even paid for Zarine's acting lessons. 'You can't do this to me!'" Sam delivers the line in a silly high-pitched voice but the accent sounds just like Zarine. Then she eats another Cheeto.

I wait for her to swallow and wash it down with soda.

"It was supposed to be shock therapy for Tatiana. Zarine would get a break from filming for a few days and meanwhile, Zarine assumed Tatiana would fall apart without her there. Then once Tatiana realized how much she needed Zarine, she'd never get out of line again. You know, she wouldn't go on having her own thoughts and feelings. Then Joshua, of all people, figured it out. Maybe not the part about Zarine's parents but about Zarine being pathologically controlling. He tried to do an intervention on his date with Tatiana, which never aired because of Marla's side deal with Zarine. You following?"

I nod. It's so unbelievable that I believe it totally.

"She's a real piece of work, Zarine. Her 'therapy' while she was away consisted of watching video of the rest of you, including the unedited footage of Tatiana and Joshua falling in love. Tatiana was in denial right to the end, poor thing, but that's what was happening. And Zarine watched it on repeat for hours, like she was inoculating herself. It was insane, and I don't use that word lightly." She swigs more soda. "I should have quit when Marla first told me about what she and Zarine were planning."

"Do you think Zarine could have killed Tatiana?"

"Absolutely not. Zarine really did need a suicide watch after Tatiana was found dead."

"Who do you think killed Joshua and Tatiana?" I hold my breath.

"I have no idea. But I can't see it being Marla. I mean, she's turning lemons into lemonade here, getting extra weeks of filming, but this franchise has been destroyed. No one's ever coming back to this island."

"Maybe it's not about this show. Maybe it's about her next."

"She's as likely to be damaged goods as she is to be hot stuff.

I can't see her taking a risk like that. Marla doesn't like coin flips."

Shit. I really wanted to pin this on Marla.

"That said, I don't know anything about her inner workings these days. She hasn't spoken a word to me since I refused to film, though I'm sure I'll hear plenty from her lawyers once we're back home. If we get back home." She exhales heavily. "Here's a tip. You know Tristan and Lauren's producer, Julie?"

"By sight. We haven't really talked."

"I think she's got some avenging angel in her, too, and a hard-on for Marla." She wipes the orange dust from her hands on her satin pajamas. "Good luck. I'll be watching."

Interview between Detective Sonya Mohr and producer Julie Lindstrom, taking place on Glass Island.

Detective: Welcome back. Again.

Julie: You know those psychological profiles I brought you?

Detective: Yes.

Julie: Tristan has a copy of Joshua's.

Detective: How do you know?

Julie: Because I hold on to Tristan's and Lauren's phones for safekeeping.

Detective: You mean you're still reading through their phones after everything?

Julie: I have to, it's part of my job.

Detective: So after knowing you found the Alexei picture on Lauren's phone and used it for the show, Tristan is still storing incriminating material on his phone where you can see it?

Julie: He might have assumed that I'd stopped reading. Or he thought he'd closed out the document so I couldn't see it. People slip up, especially under stress. I mean, you know that.

But I don't think it incriminates him. It incriminates whoever sent it. Why would someone want him to have it? The only people with access to such sensitive material were Sam, Dave, and Marla.

Detective: You had access.

Julie: I didn't get my copy until I started digging around after Joshua's death. Sam gave it to me.

Detective: Why is that?

Julie: I asked for it. I wanted to help your investigation.

Detective: This isn't a game, Julie. If Marla finds out—

Julie: She'll kill me, too?

Detective: I was going to say she might fire you.

Julie: You're right, it's not a game. I need to keep my job so I can look after them the way I should have from the beginning.

Detective: You mean Lauren and Tristan?

Julie: Yes.

Detective: If you're trying to look after Tristan, why did you bring this to me?

Julie: Because I think he's innocent and someone's messing with him. They either sent this document to him after the fact so you'd find out and he'd look guilty, or if it came in before Joshua's murder, then maybe it was meant to set him off so he'd kill Joshua. Did you happen to notice that Tristan's psychological profile said he's only violent as a protective response?

Detective: You've been hanging out with too many conspiracy theorists. Tristan's not an assassin robot, programmed to kill.

Julie: Those profiles are essentially blueprints. Marla knew that Tristan is wired to be violent only when there's a threat to women and children. Tristan is close with Blanche and she's told him all about her kids. Joshua's profile reads like Tristan's father's. It's like it was customized to push all of Tristan's buttons. Putting those two on the island together was a disaster waiting to happen.

Detective: This is awfully speculative, Julie. You have to remember that I deal in facts.

Julie: You deal in logic, right? There must be some logical reason that Tristan was given access to something he never should have seen. If you figure out who sent it and why, you might have your murderer.

FIFTY-SEVEN

LAUREN

Day Sixteen

I've been going about this all wrong. It's not about getting Tristan's protection; it's about bringing out his inner animal. I need to take us back into the wild.

We're in bed, the camera crew isn't here yet. If we don't put on our microphones and stay under the covers, then they'd get limited visuals from the stationary cameras without any sound. In other words, it's the perfect time to poke the bear.

"I heard from Rick Gloucester," I say. "He messaged me on Insta."

"Who's Rick Gloucester?" For a good actor, Tristan is a surprisingly bad liar. But I appreciate that about him. It means he has a conscience.

"He's a top social media agent. He wrote as if I'd already heard of him, which makes sense. Usually when someone says you and your fiancée can make millions, you'd mention it to her."

"I didn't know if he was for real."

"You can see on his website that he represents the biggest

influencers in the business. Why are you hiding things from me?"

"I didn't say anything because I didn't want to upset you."

"What about millions of dollars would upset me?"

His eyes dart around the room. "Because you and I might not make it, okay? And I thought it would bother you even more if you knew about the potential earnings."

I feel like he's slapped me, and not in the good way. I know we're not where we want to be yet but I thought things were improving. I've been trying so hard to make up for what I've done. Where's his effort? It's our family on the line.

"What about the baby?" I ask.

"She's all I think about."

Another slap. Well, he might as well slap me for real then. Let's do this thing. "You didn't want me to know about Rick Gloucester because all along, the baby and I were just pawns in your moneymaking scheme. You talked to Rick as soon as we got the initial offer from Marla, didn't you? That's probably why you brought me here. You're just like all the other guys. You don't care about me. Alexei was using me for sex, you wanted to use me for money. At least he never pretended to love me."

"I wasn't pretending. I did love you."

"And you don't anymore?"

"I don't know how you can doubt my intentions, after everything," he says. "I came here for you. To save our relationship. Nothing else has ever mattered."

I suddenly have the sense that he's just playing a part, trying to portray himself as the good guy who's been done wrong, because he and I both know that he's not speaking the truth. Before we came, he said that it was dual purpose: to work on us, and to gain exposure for his acting career. Both were supposed to benefit the baby.

"Do you still love me or not?" I demand.

"Just—let me have a minute, okay? I need to think." He gets

out of bed and heads for the bathroom but I run around in front of him.

"So okay, you don't love me anymore but what kind of man wouldn't love his daughter? Would make it so she never sees her parents together? What kind of selfish bastard—"

"Stop it, Lauren." It's working. I can sense the rage just beneath the surface. It's been there ever since the DNA test. No, it was there before. It was with us in the jungle, when it had needed to come out.

"No, you stop. Stop holding it in. I deserve it. Say everything you've been holding back. And if you need to, we'll go back into the jungle."

He pales. "I'm never going back there. Not like that."

"But it helped, right? It's part of why you were able to forgive me then." He didn't hit me that hard; he could have done much worse. It had been in the back so he wouldn't have to look at my face and wouldn't endanger the baby. "Let's go."

He seems on the verge of tears, like a frightened little boy. I know that it scared him, how primal it was, but I hadn't been scared at all. I understood, and I trusted him. I knew it was a release. Just a one-time thing. Two times, if I can get him to take me up on it now.

"Please, Tristan," I say. "I love you. So much. I could not be sorrier for everything. Please let it all out, so you can love me, too. There are no cameras in the bathroom." We need to do this for our little girl. "Just love me again."

FIFTY-EIGHT

THE MAJOR

This is all my fault.

I'd seen it coming and I tried my best to do damage control. I went to Detective Mohr to tell her about the stunt Zarine and Marla pulled, but all the detective wanted to talk about was Joshua and Naomi sleeping together. Why hadn't I told her about that during my first interview? Why hadn't Naomi?

I said it's not because Naomi killed anyone; it's because she was ashamed to have done something so out of character.

Detective Mohr looked dubious, and now Naomi could be in real trouble.

I'm alone in the room we once shared, watching her get crucified on social media. The attacks are coming from all sides. There are people who consider themselves "real Christians" who say Naomi's made them look bad through her adulterous (and potentially murderous) behavior. Then there are the people who say Naomi's confirmed what they always thought about "Christian types": that we sit in judgment while all our supposed piety masks a darkness underneath, a darkness that runs deep enough to kill.

I've never had my own social media accounts, just the ones

for the gym that Naomi manages, and because I'm not commenting and feeding the beast, I've become a bit character in the story. I'm the cuckolded husband. But there have been actual death threats made against Naomi, people saying they'll get revenge for Joshua. For more than an hour, our home address was up. Most terrifying was that someone had posted not only our daughters' names and that they're at UCLA but which dorm they live in. We got it deleted but there's a lag and we don't know who saw it in the interim. And what about 4Chan and 8Chan and the rest of the underground sites with no moderators? Anything could be circulating there among the conspiracy theorists, crackpots, and incels. I already knew there was so much hatred and rage and ugliness in the world just waiting for a target. Somehow I never thought my family would become one.

The unflappable Naomi is flapped. I go downstairs to find her drinking coffee over the kitchen sink, her hand shaking as she lifts the cup. Droplets spill all over her white robe and she doesn't seem to notice. She couldn't even manage to get dressed before going downstairs, which would normally have been unthinkable for her.

"I am so sorry, Naomi," I say. "This is all my fault."

"It can't be all your fault. You didn't have sex outside of our marriage." She closes her eyes like she can't bear to see. "Yesterday I had to tell the girls I cheated on their father; today I had to tell them not to go out anywhere alone and to report any suspicious behavior. At best, I've humiliated them. At worst, I've put them in danger." She's on the verge of tears. "But by some miracle, they don't hate me. Why don't they hate me, Cain?"

"Because they love you too much. You're a good mom. Those people online don't know anything."

"We're so far away. What if...?" She can't bring herself to finish the sentence.

"People hide behind their screens. They're scared to go out in daylight," I say, hoping I sound more sure than I feel. "Our calls to the LAPD and campus police went really well, didn't you think? They're taking the threats seriously."

She nods, but her eyes are downcast. She seems defeated.

I have to do something. This is my chance to come through for her. Whatever mistakes she's made, what she has or hasn't done, I'm going to stand by her. I'm certainly not without sin myself.

I go back up to our room and out to the balcony. I say Lauren's name loudly. Three, four times. It's still early enough, she should be in her room. I'm about to find a pebble or a rock or something when she comes out.

"What?" she says, grumpy as I've ever seen her.

"I'm going to need your help but before I ask for it, you're entitled to the whole truth. Naomi and I came to the island with a plan." She perks up, curious in spite of her foul mood. "In hindsight, I can see my hubris. I don't know how I thought I'd get away with it, that I could fool the cameras and Marla and everyone watching at home. I wanted them all to believe that Naomi and I had fallen back in love. The gym was supposed to see a surge in membership. Then some months down the road, we'd sell it and split the proceeds and get a divorce."

"Wow." Lauren is clearly stunned. "So you were actually using the show, not the other way around?"

"That was never Naomi's plan, though. She wanted to save our marriage and get me mental health treatment." That part of the balcony intervention had never aired; they only used the part where I talked about Naomi sleeping with Joshua. "But after the way I treated her on the island, she gave up on us. That's why she turned me down on Decision Day."

"And what does she want now? What do you want?"

"I don't know about her, but I'm not ready to give up."

Lauren can't resist breaking into her America's sweetheart smile.

"Don't get happy just yet. I'm not sure she'll ever forgive me for telling the world about her and Joshua."

"But now you're even. She did it, you told everyone. You were both wrong and you can forgive each other."

"It's not that simple. I've put her in danger. I've put our girls in danger." I take a deep breath. "If you really want to see Naomi and me back together, I'm going to need your help."

Her smile isn't quite as wide now.

"You've become a social media powerhouse. What do you think about using some of that capital to tell people to back off Naomi?"

"It might seem rough right now but she can just wait it out. They'll move on to someone else. Or better yet, back to Blanche. Everyone knows #BlancheDidIt."

"This is serious, Lauren. They're not just speculating about Naomi at viewing parties. They're releasing our address, and information about our kids."

"It's just a game, Major." She waves a hand.

"This has a different flavor, I'm telling you. They're not only saying she's a murderer. They're saying she should be murdered. And some of the people who are saying that are your followers."

"I can't control what everyone—"

"Block them, unfollow them, whatever. You need to talk back and tell them that Naomi's a human being. Yes, she's made mistakes but so have you."

"Only I never claimed to be holier than thou." Her gaze is surprisingly steely.

"How many times can I say that Naomi and I don't cast stones?"

"I'm just saying, if the viewers were picking up on something from you guys, or from Naomi specifically, then that's their opinion. I can't tell people what they can and can't say."

I stare at her in amazement. "This isn't about free speech. It's about hate speech. I'm asking you to take a stand for what's right."

"I never 'like' negative comments about you or Naomi. But I don't want to pick fights either. I'm not sure I can risk alienating people when I've got all this momentum."

I narrow my eyes. "Maybe you 'like' people suspecting Naomi. If she did it, then Tristan didn't, right? Because #TristanDidIt is third in line, after Naomi and Blanche."

She shakes her head. "You know I'm all about #BlancheDidIt."

"Yeah, I've noticed." I move closer to Lauren. She needs to look at me while I repeat, "They posted my address. They posted the girls' dorm."

She averts her eyes. "I want to help, okay? But I need to think it through."

"The way you think through everything you post about Blanche?"

"I have a lot of followers, and they're all pressuring Tristan to forgive me. If I start calling them out and the tides turn, then where will I be?"

"And who'll be left to speak up when they come for you?" She looks confused. But this is hardly the time to explain my conversation with Sam. "Your popularity is a house of cards. It can tumble down at any time."

"Is that a threat?"

"Of course not. I'm just saying, followers aren't friends."

"Tell that to Naomi. She's been racking them up."

"What does that have to do with anything?"

"Naomi signed with Rick Gloucester, though he might have dropped her already. Adultery doesn't fit her brand."

Now I'm the one who's confused. "Who's Rick Gloucester?"

"The agent who reps all the big names from *The Bachelor*. The one who's going to rep Tristan and me. He said that Naomi had signed with him. She was going to monetize being an independent Christian woman." She lowers her voice. "Sorry, I guess she didn't mention that?"

"No, she didn't."

"I like Naomi, you know that. But you shouldn't be so quick to throw stones at me for wanting to protect my family when your wife lives in a glass house."

FIFTY-NINE

BLANCHE

"Detective Mohr, I demand to know the status of the investigation."

She looks up at me with a mixture of bemusement and sympathy. "That's not really how this works."

"Joshua was my husband. I should know how things are proceeding. Who are the main suspects? Are there any new leads? How long will we be here?"

"Sit down, Blanche." She smiles and gestures toward the chair opposite her.

I take a seat, but I'm not happy about it. I'm missing my kids something awful, missing human touch and interaction. I miss feeling loved and giving love. I have so much to give Tristan but I'm pretty sure he's avoiding me. If I'm not around him, then I'm not making any headway and my time apart from my children serves no purpose. I'm starting to think I'd be better off going home and then trying to contact Tristan away from Lauren and the camera's watchful eye. I'm ready to get to safer ground.

"Lauren's followers are trying to frame me," I say. "They're making ridiculous accusations and trying to back them up with clips from the show that are completely out of context. I hope you're not falling for any of it."

"I'm not waiting for Instagram to crack the case, if that's what you're asking." Another smile. "Maybe I should tweet this: 'I'm guided by facts.'"

"Whose facts are you being guided by?"

She pauses and I think for a second that I've offended her but then she says gently, "I can't even imagine how much strain you're under, losing your husband and being forced to live in a house with people you think are plotting against you and reading awful things about yourself online, all while being separated from your children."

I soften. "So you can see why I'd like an update."

She leans back in her chair as if to get a better look at me. "People don't always know why they do the things they do."

"Which people are you talking about?"

"Sometimes they don't know they're lying. There are certain things that are too painful to acknowledge, or maybe admitting those things would threaten our sense of who we are. People might not want to feel like they've been victims. For example, they want to believe they had at least one good parent."

She's been on the island too long. Now everyone thinks they're a therapist? "I have no idea what you're talking about."

"You lied to me, Blanche. You said you were in the car when your father was killed."

"I was in the car. Who said I was lying, my mother? Did she call you?"

"I talk to a lot of people."

"My mother has significant mental health issues. Did she happen to mention her nine suicide attempts?"

"She did. She also mentioned that you suffer from certain delusions related to your father's death."

"She's the one who's delusional. She's a classic narcissist."

"She seems worried about you. She's concerned that Joshua's death might bring back the trauma of losing your father, and your grasp on reality might—"

"That's rich, coming from her."

It's the most visceral memory of my life: My father in the driver's seat screaming, first at me for breaking our pact by telling my mother, and then screaming because of the headlights of the oncoming car; the blare of the horn; him wrenching the steering wheel; my dress flying up with the impact and the breaking glass slicing my exposed thighs, though it feels more like burning than cutting. He's bloody but breathing. My whole life, I've regretted being too small and weak to pull him from the wreckage. I'm not small and weak anymore.

"The records of the accident are indisputable," Detective Mohr says. "Your father drove into a tree. He was alone in the car and he died instantly. It was most likely a suicide."

"I know what happened. I was there." I stand up on trembling legs.

"It's a delusion," she says, quiet yet firm. "It's not a memory."

I yank up my dress to reveal my thighs. "Where did I get these scars, if I wasn't in the car?"

"Your mother says you used to cut yourself. Always in the same place, on your thighs."

"She's got an answer for everything, doesn't she?"

I leave Detective Mohr's lair and step outside into the sunshine. I need the fresh air. I'm breathing in deeply, eyes closed, and when I open them, I notice that Lauren is on her balcony. She's staring down at me murderously. I stare back the same way.

SIXTY

LAUREN

Day Seventeen

"I keep thinking about yesterday," Tristan says, "and about our time in the rainforest, and I'm so ashamed, Lauren. I don't blame you for thinking of me as a violent person."

"I don't blame you for anything you've done, especially not when it comes to me."

"I should never have put my hands on you. I owe you a huge apology." He kneels in front of me, and my heart flutters. Is he going to propose all over again? The third time's a charm? "I am so sorry, Lauren. Can you ever forgive me?"

"Yes. You're forgiven, 100 percent."

"It's that easy for you?"

"Of course it is. I love you."

He looks up at me with eyes full of gratitude. "You are an amazing woman, you know that?"

I think I finally do.

He comes to sit beside me on the bed. "You didn't tell Detective Mohr about what happened in the rainforest, right?"

"I promised you I'd never tell anyone."

"If we're going to make this work, you need to know everything."

If? We *will* make this work. It doesn't matter what he tells me, I'm in this for life.

"I was with Joshua on the beach the night he died. I'm probably the reason there were signs of a struggle. I punched him in the face and then I walked away. I left him there, unconscious." He squeezes his eyes shut. "For all I know, he never woke up. The tide came in and he was swept out to sea. I might be the killer, Lauren."

"That's not possible." Tristan cannot be a murderer. Or a manslaughterer.

"Detective Mohr seems sure I was there even though I denied it. What if the police find proof?"

"Wouldn't they have found it by now? Besides, she can't prove a negative. You didn't kill him. He was alive when you walked away."

"We don't know that for sure."

"Yes, we do." I stroke his face. "Thank you for trusting me with this."

"If I didn't tell someone, I was going to burst." And he chose me for his confession, not Blanche. "I feel guilty and afraid all the time. Maybe that's why I'm not able to love you or the baby."

Wait, he doesn't love the baby? My hand stills on his brow.

"I feel, I don't know, blocked up. Like no love can flow through me right now. That's why we have to figure out what to do next. I need you, Lauren." He kneels again, pressing against me, into the place where my breasts and belly meet.

Trust is actually a much bigger deal than love, I realize. It's harder to come by. He trusted me with his secret and once I get him out of this, he'll love me more than I ever could have dreamed of. He'll love our family.

"Why were you so mad at Joshua that night?" I ask. "Was it because he threatened me or the baby?"

"No." He seems like he doesn't want to say.

"He threatened your career?"

"It was something I read in, like, a report. He was an actual psycho, the kind you don't think you'll ever meet in real life, someone who hurts people just for the fun of it. So I confronted him. I told him he'd better not hurt his wife and kids, or I'd know about it and I'd find him. I was bluffing, I wanted to scare him. He said, 'They're my wife and kids. I'll do whatever the fuck I want to them.' I saw red, Lauren, and I just slammed him."

So Tristan attacked Joshua to protect Blanche and *her* kids?

I don't know what to say, I truly don't.

But Tristan's got a lot to say. He's feeling much better for having told me, and now he's convinced that I'm right and Joshua was alive when he left. "The real killer must still be on this island," he says, "so we should review the other suspects and their motives. Give the detective something to work with."

"There aren't many suspects left," I say. "It's just you, me, Naomi, The Major, and Blanche. I know Blanche is your friend, but she's got the strongest motive. I mean, you said it yourself, she was married to a psycho who'd do whatever he wanted to her and her kids. Maybe she can plead self-defense."

He goes quiet. Whose side is he on?

"You told me that after you were locked up, you never wanted to go back there again, right?" I ask.

"No, I never do."

"So think carefully. Did Blanche tell you anything, anything at all, that made you think for even a second that it could be her?"

I wheedle until I get it out of him. After, he's more exhausted than I've ever seen anyone. I tuck him in and kiss his forehead. Tell him that I love him, and the baby does, too. Then I head downstairs to see Detective Mohr.

"To what do I owe the pleasure, Lauren?"

"You might already know this, it's probably the first thing you check, but Joshua has a multimillion-dollar life insurance policy and Blanche is the beneficiary. Also, Joshua's business was going under and they're at risk of losing the house."

"And how do you know this?"

"Blanche told Tristan, and he told me." She raises an eyebrow. "I'm his fiancée. We don't keep secrets from each other."

She's got a real poker face, and I'm starting to feel a little bit nervous. "Did Tristan send you here to tell me this information?"

"Of course not."

"You're not the first woman on this island to come here pointing fingers away from Tristan. You might want to think about that."

SIXTY-ONE
THE MAJOR

Lauren's come through. She's standing up for Naomi in a big way, posting that she knows for sure that Naomi wouldn't hurt anyone, that she's never seen Naomi behave in a way that's self-righteous or judgmental. She's shutting down the bullies and the trolls and defending everyone's right to make mistakes regardless of religion, asking everyone to practice kindness and forgiveness.

It's not like all the attacks on Naomi have stopped, not by a long shot, but it does feel like the tides are turning. #Naomi-DidIt has dropped back to second in the rankings.

I know that ugliness can surface at any time, we're not out of the woods. We're not even off the island. Still, I feel a surge of optimism that I haven't felt in a long, long time. Like things can turn around for me, and for Naomi, and maybe even for the world.

Then I get the summons. Marla wants to see me in the control room.

I haven't been there since the night of the walkout when Marla and I entered into a negotiation. I'd agreed not to leave in return for a trip to the control room where I watched Marla delete all the footage about Naomi being a lesbian and me being a lesbian hater. I hadn't known about the workouts Naomi was doing with Joshua or I would have tried to get rid of those, too. But Marla probably wouldn't have made that deal. She only gave up one thing because she had something more salacious up her sleeve. She's always maintained her home-court advantage: unequal access to information, unequal power.

There's a security guard by the door to let me in. Marla is sitting in front of a wall of monitors. All the rooms in the villa are featured, but by this point, they're almost all empty. Tristan and Lauren are snuggled up in their bed. Glad to see those two are working it out. Naomi is with Blanche at the dining room table. They're doing their nails together because they're both afraid to be alone. In other rooms, producers and crews are chatting like they're all on break. Even Dave's just lying on a loveseat in the great room, reading a book. I'm not sure how Marla's going to be able to produce her next episode at this rate. But—my stomach drops—she'll probably think of something.

Marla spins around in her chair. "Cain!" She manages to sound surprised and delighted, as if she hadn't called me here.

It's terrifying, being face to face with evil incarnate. But she looks so ordinary. Messy bun, cat's-eye glasses on a chain around her neck, shapeless charcoal gray shift dress.

Does she know I snuck off and met with Sam? I've been looking for Julie but haven't seen her. Maybe that's Marla's doing, too.

"Why am I here?" I ask.

"You've had a lot to say about me, but I've done you the favor of editing it out."

I need to stay cool. "Am I on camera now?"

"Nope, it's just us. Did you like how I edited the episode where Dave and Naomi confronted you on the balcony? You didn't look like a nut; your wife looked like a slut. Hey, that rhymed!" She smiles.

"Why are you playing with our lives?"

"I'm the executive producer. This is my show. Silly."

"It feels a lot more personal than that."

"A feeling isn't a fact. Wait, that sounds like something you'd say." She completes a full 360 in her chair. "So, let's chat. Did you know you and Naomi were Sam's favorite couple?"

"No, I didn't."

"I'm lukewarm on Naomi but I find you fascinating. You're just so full of delicious contradictions. Overflowing with human frailty. One of my biggest disappointments this season is that you haven't caught on at home, that I haven't been able to get your very particular charisma to translate."

I refuse to thank her.

"You have the makings of a tragic hero *and* an underground villain. I think it's why your editing has been so schizophrenic, which might be interfering with the viewers' ability to connect with you. That's my bad. But I also think that people have trouble keeping their eye on the ball. They've been very distracted this season. There have been a lot of bright shiny objects."

"You mean the deaths?"

Another orbit in her chair. "You have the opposite problem. Tunnel vision. You miss what's right in front of you."

"Is this a confession?"

"You've been so fixated on me that you've turned a blind eye to the far more likely suspects." She gestures to the wall of monitors.

"Who?"

"You think you want to know but you really don't. Like with Naomi and Joshua. She had to actually have sex in your bed to get you to see. But I see everything."

"You're saying that you saw Naomi and Joshua that night? That you never turned the cameras off?" In which case Marla really might know who the killer is. Hell, she could have it on tape.

She shakes her head, and am I picking up the barest trace of sadness? "Joshua liked to tell me things. He was honest with me, much more so than with any of his other women."

Was that a slip, saying "his other women"? Could he have been with Marla, too?

"Consider this a friendly warning," she says. "If you keep obsessing on me, you won't see the real killer coming."

SIXTY-TWO

BLANCHE

We're told to report to the great room for our first group therapy in days. It's agony, watching Lauren wrap herself around Tristan, knowing she thinks she's won. Maybe she has, and my relationship with Tristan has been all in my head this whole time.

Then my eyes meet his, and I know the truth. He's trapped. By her pregnancy, by the viewers' insistence that they end up together, by the million dollars being dangled in front of him by that agent. In this very room, on Parents Day, he rescued me. I have to find a way to do the same.

We're going to end up together. I can't have done all of this for nothing.

The topic for today's therapy? "Guilt and regret," Dave says, like it's a savory dish.

But without Sam here, he has a hard time really driving it home. The Major and Naomi are both visibly awash in guilt and regret, yet they're both practically invoking the Fifth Amendment. Dave can't get them to crack no matter what he hurls at them, and he's fast becoming petulant.

Naomi probably should have felt some guilt where I was concerned. After all, Joshua was my husband. But it's not like she and I have been bosom buddies. I wasn't surprised Joshua would have done that to me. I was, however, surprised that he got Naomi to drop her chastity belt.

Dave's not able to get anything out of Tristan and Lauren either. I would have thought Lauren was going to dive headfirst into this assignment, that we'd all drown in her tears, but instead she says, dry-eyed, "We've worked it all out on our own." When Tristan says, "Lauren's apologized enough, and I've forgiven her," my heart sinks.

How did this happen? Will we ever have another smoke break so I can find out? I've been going to the lounger with my pack of cigarettes multiple times a day but he's not showing up. Whatever arguments she's made, I should be entitled to a rebuttal.

Seeing the tears in my eyes, Dave lights up. "Blanche, what would you like to share with the group? Survivor's guilt is quite common after a loved one is murdered."

"I'll share another time," I say. "It's still too raw."

"Your marriage was built on a foundation of deceit and deception." Aren't those pretty much the same thing? "You came here to perpetrate a fraud, pretending that you and Joshua were an ordinary couple with mundane problems. Do you regret that?"

I stare at him. "Are you asking if I regret coming here? When my husband was killed on this island?"

He has the decency to look abashed, reddening slightly. I didn't know his capillaries even worked. After all the things he's said and done, this is his most mortifying?

"There must be something you would change," he says quietly, "that's all."

"Nothing," I say. I'm sure I'm going to get blasted by everyone at home for my opacity, but they'd flay me even more for the truth.

Ever since Joshua died, I've tried to think the worst of him. I haven't wanted to remember the day in the supply closet when he tried to make us go home (for the second time) and I shot him down because I couldn't leave Tristan. Maybe Joshua was trying to be a better man by removing himself from temptation. If I hadn't cut him off, he might have gone on to tell me about Tatiana and/or Naomi; he may have apologized for what I was likely to see on television. By then, he probably hadn't gone too far. It may have been largely fantasy, or just a few drunken soliloquys to Brandon in the confessional.

Maybe Joshua actually had a conscience then. Maybe he still loved me. Maybe I could have loved him again, or at least hated him less. Maybe I could have been a divorcée instead of a widow.

I look around the room; everyone is looking back. How long have I been sitting here crying silently? They weren't the ugly tears Brandon advised; there'd been no calculation. I just hadn't been able to stop myself.

Tristan, The Major, Naomi, and even Dave seem to feel for me. But not Lauren. From the expression on her face, she doesn't care if I live or die but in my gut, I know she'd prefer the latter.

Interview between Detective Sonya Mohr and executive producer and showrunner Marla Regis, taking place on Glass Island.

Marla: So like I was saying, TV is all about adaptability. You have to recognize where the trends are going, you have to be on the leading edge. Give people what they don't even know they want. Challenge them. Dare them to look away. That's what I was trying to do with this season, even before Joshua's death.

Detective: Had you been getting pressure from the network to change your formula this season? To rough up the participants more?

Marla: I wouldn't call it pressure, and my intent was never to rough anyone up. I was aware that the ratings had decreased the tiniest bit from Season One to Season Two, which isn't the preferred direction.

Detective: Was there anything different about this season's casting process?

Marla: Not really. I was aiming for more diversity but beyond that, no.

Detective: I have The Major to thank. Until he stopped by earlier, I hadn't dug deeply enough into prior relationships between you and the participants.

Marla: Is that a question?

Detective: The consensus from the crew was that you were especially passionate about this season, obsessive, even.

Marla: False. I'm always obsessive.

Detective: You insisted that this season there would be a breakup, and it would be Joshua and Blanche. That's because you wanted Joshua for yourself.

Marla: That's absurd.

Detective: You first met Joshua through Elle almost a year before casting. Blanche must have thought Elle was a good friend of hers but she was a much better friend to you, seeing as Elle convinced Blanche that the show was just the thing to save her troubled marriage.

And you convinced your lover Joshua that this was the way to end his marriage, exposing it for a charade, making Blanche look so awful that no one at home would blame him on Decision Day. But instead, he stayed married, stayed drunk, had sex with one castmate, and fell in love with another.

Marla: Again, absurd.

Detective: I'm assuming you didn't know about Joshua's prior association with Tatiana? That it hadn't come up in either of their background checks?

Marla: No, I wasn't aware they knew each other. But I thought it was a great subplot.

Detective: Joshua had a hand in casting the other couples, didn't he? He knew you wanted more diversity and he steered you toward Tatiana and Zarine. Not that they were a hard sell.

Marla: You should watch more *Jeopardy*. Learn to phrase things in the form of a question.

Detective: Joshua helped you cast the show, didn't he?

Marla: No, he did not.

Detective: It must have enraged you. Here you had compromised your integrity completely by bringing him on your show and giving him a way out of his marriage and he hadn't taken it. Worse, you had to watch him fall in love with someone else. Oh, let me phrase it as a question: What did you feel about that?

Marla: I have no feelings about your work of fiction.

Detective: Did I mention Elle is cooperating with the investigation?

LONG SILENCE

Marla: Joshua and I were never serious. That's why it wasn't a conflict of interest for him to come on the show. I happened to be casting for my first villain, and Blanche was perfect for that role.

Detective: And you had no reaction to his blatant pursuit of both Naomi and Tatiana?

Marla: As an EP, I was thrilled about it. When I'm on this island, I'm only an EP.

Detective: So you and Joshua didn't have any liaisons while you were here?

Marla: No, we didn't.

Detective: Your crew hates you, Marla. The cast hates you. When I call them in here one by one and ask one simple question—"Did you ever witness anything unusual between Marla and Joshua?"—can you be sure what the answer's going to be?

Marla: You're saying that someone's going to frame me?

Detective: I'm saying that they'll only be too happy to tell me the truth. So if I were you, I'd beat them to the punch.

Marla: What exactly do you want to know?

Detective: Did you tell The Major directly that you spoke with Joshua during the wrap party?

Marla: I did but—

Detective: You previously told me that you never spoke to Joshua during the wrap party. So where did this conversation take place? Were you on the beach when he admitted to you that he'd had sex with Naomi?

Marla: It's not like you're saying. I was never in love with Joshua. I was doing him a favor. Giving him a way out of his marriage. I thought he and Blanche breaking up would make for great TV. Two birds, one stone.

That was an unfortunate expression.

I didn't kill anyone.

I swear.

SIXTY-THREE

LAUREN

Day Eighteen

"It's the end," Dave says, and even he sounds relieved. He must want to go home, too, though according to The Major, Dave doesn't really have a home anymore. Sam's given him the boot. "You're all free to go because there's been an arrest." Dramatic pause. "It's Marla."

The Major whoops. "I knew it!" He turns to Naomi, who gives him a high five. It's not the most passionate gesture, but it's a start. I really hope those two work it out, that they can be as happy as Tristan and I soon will be.

I hug Tristan tight. "See?" I whisper in his ear. "I told you it would all turn out for the best." I put his hand to my belly. "Can you feel her kicking?" He nods, his eyes filling with tears.

Poor, dried-up Blanche has no one to celebrate with.

"This is your last time all together in this room," Dave says. "Your last chance to express your feelings to one another."

Blanche is looking right at Tristan but she doesn't say a word. She's probably hoping he will. Fat chance. He and I are bonded for life after what he's revealed to me, and what I've done for him.

Finally, The Major speaks up. "I wish you all the best. Sincerely. But I don't think any more expressing is in order."

We all agree, chorusing our well wishes back to him and to each other, with varying degrees of sincerity. The Major and I are in a good place. I'm sure it helped that I did what he asked. It was only right, and I probably gained as many followers as I lost. I've also repaid Naomi's favor, and I don't see that I'll be needing any more. I've got enough friends. I still have an army to deploy against Blanche. But she'll be irrelevant soon.

We all stand up gingerly, like we're waiting for Marla to jump out at us and shout, "Gotcha!"

"When you leave this room, the cameras are off," Dave says. "Your plane leaves first thing tomorrow."

There it is, the "Gotcha." We're not really free of each other until tomorrow. I can't shed Blanche quite yet. But Tristan and I are rebuilding from a place of trust and there's nothing anyone can do to stop it.

"Stay safe out there." Dave casts a surreptitious look beside and behind him with a note of sadness, and I think it's for Sam, his phantom limb, his better half. "That's a wrap."

But we've heard that before.

SIXTY-FOUR

THE MAJOR

So it was Marla. I knew it all along. Now it's time for Naomi and me to put all of this behind us. To start fresh.

She leaves the bathroom with a towel turban around her head to find me down on one knee, holding an empty jewelry box. She bursts out laughing.

"The show took their ring back," I say. "When we didn't recommit on Decision Day. But I want you to know I'm recommitting now. I want to marry you all over again after we're home. Do it the right way. You, me, our kids, close family and friends. We don't need America. What do you say?"

"Stand up, Cain, please."

I feel a pang of anxiety. Maybe she won't choose me again, knowing what she knows.

Her phone pings and she checks the social media alert. "Nothing for us to worry about. #MarlaDidIt."

I can't wait to get back to L.A. and see with my own two eyes that my girls are all right. Show them that their dad has come to his senses.

"You're killing the romance," I tell Naomi.

"That's the thing about being this many years in. Sometimes romance has to take a back seat."

I can't handle the suspense. "Do you want to marry me again, Naomi?"

She sets her phone down. "I need to know something first. Did you ever think I had something to do with Joshua's death?"

"It crossed my mind."

"It crossed my mind, too. About you."

Me, a killer? I'm the biggest pussycat on Glass Island.

"You haven't been yourself for such a long time, Cain. I thought maybe seeing Joshua and me together like that had pushed you over the edge. But then I thought about what kind of man you are, and how you would never do something like that." She pauses. "Are you sure of me?"

"Yes." So what if she never told me about that influencer agent. I don't need every bit of information; what I need is truth. From now on, that's all Naomi and I are going to tell each other. "I know I brought us here for all the wrong reasons. They were misguided and borderline wackadoodle"—I'm glad to hear her laugh again—"because I was just looking for a way out of my life. I wanted it to seem noble rather than cowardly to end our marriage. But now all I want is a way back in."

She hesitates. "Back into your life, or into our marriage?"

"Both. They're the same thing. I'd been telling myself I was doing you a favor, that you'd be better off without me. But what I need is to be better. I'm ready to do the work. On myself, and on us. Ready to get us some real therapists."

She starts to smile. "I never thought I'd hear you say that."

The way she's looking at me, I think I might be able to do it. Make the move. Kiss my wife the way she ought to be kissed.

Then she puts her hand to my chest. Another stop move, like on the beach. Another blindside?

"Joshua was nothing," she says. "Being with him that night was about feeling wanted but it was also about revenge. That's why I was in our bed. But I want you to know that I've never been in love with anyone but you."

"Is that a yes?"

She bursts out laughing. "Can this really be happening? You thought I might have killed the man I cheated with, I thought you might have killed him, and now we're on the cusp of renewing our vows?"

All it took was a cockamamie plan, an evil producer, a blindside, an affair, and two murders.

The Lord works in mysterious ways.

SIXTY-FIVE

BLANCHE

Our final dinner together is a celebration for everyone but me. Oh, and Zarine, who I suspect is somewhere suffering, maybe on this island, maybe back in L.A. But at this table, it's all revelry. The Major, especially, is over the moon, crowing that he's been right all along. But he'll find out soon enough. They all will.

I can barely choke anything down. Tristan notices and looks concerned, though he knows better than to make a display of it in front of Lauren. She's got him where she wants him, but not for long.

"Lauren, can I speak to you privately in the confessional?" I say, after she's eaten every bite of her molten chocolate cake. Enjoy that, Lauren, it's your last supper.

She looks at Tristan and then back at me, gears turning. "Do you mind?" she finally asks him. "It shouldn't take long."

I feel my anger returning. Over the past twenty-four hours, since my time with Alexei, I've been through every emotion imaginable, like an accelerated grief master class. But I've had to hide it from everyone, watching them talk excitedly about getting back to their real lives, toasting to Marla's guilt.

Tristan tells Lauren to go ahead, no rush. He seems more nervous than she is. He probably thinks he's going to be the subject under discussion.

Lauren and I go into the confessional. The camera is still there. "Is this on?" she says. I shake my head. "How can I be sure?"

She needs me to take a drink first to prove it's not poisoned. "I'll show you mine, then you show me yours."

"I don't see why I'd show you anything." She's so smug. She really thinks she's in the driver's seat.

"Have you ever heard that saying, you're only as sick as your secrets?"

"No." She's studiedly casual as she fingers the lens of the camera with one hand, fondles her bump with the other.

"It's from Twelve Step. I actually went to an Al-Anon meeting once. Those meetings are for people who love someone with a drinking problem. I didn't belong."

"Because you didn't believe Joshua had a drinking problem?"

"Because I didn't love him."

"Okay," she says, "I believe you. The camera's off."

"I'm not done." It feels good to confess, even to Lauren. Especially to Lauren because it can't go anywhere. After tonight, whatever she says, no one will believe her. "My mind has kept my father's secret for all of these years. I thought I let him down by not saving him in the car accident, for living when he died. But I wasn't even there."

"What do you mean?"

"I thought I was there. I thought I was the guilty one. Because I didn't want him to be guilty of sexually abusing me. What really happened was that I told my mother and she confronted him and he killed himself." Then I say the words aloud and it feels as good as I could have hoped: "But I was guilty of nothing. I was a little girl."

"Is this true?"

"Why would I lie?"

She's battling with herself. Part of her wants to feel sorry for me, which gives me pause. It doesn't fit the profile. Narcissists don't have empathy.

Still, I won't be deterred when I'm this close.

"You need to see this." I pull out my phone. I've got the video all set up and I stop it after only five seconds, wanting it to seem like I have a lot more footage.

Last night, Alexei came to the villa to pick me up and walk me to his bungalow. I was wary, of course, but curious. A little bit hopeful. After all, he seemed to have an ax to grind with Lauren, too, and he'd texted that he had something to show me. It turned out that he was just eager for company. He wanted someone to appreciate the nature photography he'd taken up during the sequester, all his pictures from the jungle. "Rainforest," I corrected irritably. I thought the night was going to be a wash.

But then it turned around. I noticed on his iPad that he'd taken a ton of photos and videos at the villa, and it was all so completely disorganized that he didn't even know what he had. As in, they weren't even arranged by date. I wasn't interested in his stash of bourbon or his nature photographs; it was another stash I was after. So I oohed and aahed over his poorly composed shots of butterflies and generic shots of the ocean and I refilled his glass again and again. Finally, he said he was too tired to walk me back to the villa, would I mind sleeping on the couch? No, I definitely didn't mind. Just leave the iPad, Alexei.

I didn't even know what I was looking for, and as low an opinion as I had of Lauren, I was still shocked by what I found.

Lauren's shocked, too, as I play it for her. She jumps back like it—or I—might be radioactive. "Where did you get that?"

"Doesn't matter." I take a little pleasure in doing the old "there are more copies where this came from and if anything happens to me, they'll get released" trick from TV shows, and Lauren is now fully freaked out.

How could Alexei—how could anyone—not realize the significance of that video? It was of Lauren and Tatiana talking intently on Tatiana's balcony the night she was killed. Sure, it's for less than ten seconds since Alexei was really just scanning the grounds, but by the morning, he would have heard about Tatiana's murder. No one could be that stupid. Maybe he's actually retained some hint of feeling for Lauren, or maybe he wants it in his back pocket for ammo someday. His plans make no difference to me. Lauren's going to prison for a long, long time.

But first, I'll "induce a confession," as the professionals say. I'm going to succeed where the therapists and Detective Mohr failed.

"That could have been doctored," Lauren says, though her voice is faltering. "By the therapists and Marla and the rest of the producers. Remember how we all said they'd stop at nothing?"

"I think you're the one who'll stop at nothing."

Her face crumples and tears stream down her face. "Please let me explain," she begs. I didn't expect her to roll over so quickly.

"You killed Tatiana," I say, "and you killed Joshua." I don't have proof about Joshua but what are the odds there are two murderers on one island?

She looks like she's about to faint. "Can I sit down, please? Then I'll tell you everything."

I like that she needs to ask me for permission. I nod curtly. She takes one of the velvet chairs and I'm across from her on Brandon's seat.

"I never meant to kill anyone," she says.

"But you did. It wasn't an accident. You killed two people." It's a statement, not a question. She still seems on the verge of passing out as she closes her eyes and does the slightest of nods.

I knew it, but somehow, having it actually confirmed... I feel a little lightheaded myself.

"Tell me everything you did, and why." She should have to say it, though part of me wishes I didn't have to listen to it. Despite everything, Joshua was still my husband.

"I've never been violent before. I've never even had a fist fight."

"Start with the wrap party."

"At the wrap party, I was a total mess," she says, her eyes pleading for understanding. "The whole thing with Alexei and the DNA test had just happened and Tristan really seemed to hate me. Then we were all on our phones and I saw how Joshua had talked about Tristan while he was drunk."

"You killed someone for what they said on a reality TV show?"

She shakes her head, eyes closing again, seeming genuinely pained. "Joshua made a point of coming up to me at the party. He said I was better off without Tristan anyway, and he was boasting about how he's in with Marla, who's in with everyone in Hollywood, and Joshua would see to it that Tristan's acting career never got off the ground. Joshua said, and I quote, 'I'll make sure Tristan's a failure in the eyes of his daughter.'"

Now I'm shaking my head, not because I don't believe her but because she's a total moron. "You killed Joshua because you thought he had the power to ruin Tristan's career?"

"It wasn't, like, a rational decision. I felt so angry at Joshua and so protective of Tristan, who hasn't done anything wrong, ever. He's been loyal to me since the beginning, and this show should have launched his career and now it was going to do the opposite because of me. I felt like I owed it to Tristan, you know?" She doesn't wait for my answer. "Meanwhile Joshua had pretended to be this vanilla guy when he was actually a freak and a liar, playing Tatiana and Naomi right under your nose."

"Please don't pretend to care about my nose."

"He was a horrible person is what I'm saying, and he seemed capable of anything."

"You can't claim the moral high ground here, Lauren. You killed my kids' father."

"Was he a good father, though? Or a good husband?"

I glare at her. Who appointed her executioner of every lame-ass parent and spouse?

"I know how wrong it was, and I never meant to do it. Like I said, I was an emotional wreck over Tristan. I just kept thinking about what he was going through, all I'd screwed up for him, how I'd humiliated him. I was sure he'd never forgive me and he'd be right to never forgive me. And then Joshua had threatened to take away even more from Tristan. It was just so unfair. Tristan shouldn't have to suffer, I should."

Wait, she thinks she should suffer for what she's done?

Narcissistic sociopaths don't walk around worrying about what other people are going through. They're not wracked with guilt. They think everything they do is justifiable, and that they should always be forgiven. My mother's never uttered the words *I'm sorry*.

Narcissistic sociopaths don't love people as deeply as Lauren clearly loves Tristan.

"I went for a walk on the beach and Joshua was passed out drunk," Lauren continues. "There was no one there to see, no cameras, and I didn't even think; I just acted." She's imploring me with her eyes, I'm trying to keep mine steely but I have to admit, she's getting to me. I remind myself this is what she does. "It wasn't easy, dragging him into the ocean. He was really heavy, and I was grunting and sweating, but he never even moved a muscle. So maybe he was dead already, like he'd choked on his own vomit or something. Are you sure you want to hear this? I mean, do you really want all the details?"

It is making me queasy and we still have one murder to go but I need to stay the course. She should have to face what she did.

"I thought of letting go of Joshua, leaving him there on the beach, but that would have been like giving up on Tristan, failing to protect him, and failing to protect the baby's future, so first I pulled by the legs and then I tried under his arms and finally, he was in the water, under the water." She closes her eyes like the memory haunts her. If it's a performance, it's an astonishingly good one. "I felt like I'd done the right thing for my family even though I'd never ever tell them about it. And from what you've said about Joshua, maybe it's good for your family, too. Tristan would say that a kid is better off growing up with no father than a mean drunk."

Kyle and Lily would be best off with Tristan for a father. "Go on, without the editorializing."

"Once Joshua was in the water, I was panting from the exertion and I turned around and I could make out Tatiana coming down the beach. Weaving down the beach, I should say, because she was so drunk. There was nowhere to hide, and Joshua was under the water just a few feet away.

"I walked toward her, trying to seem normal. She asked what I'd been doing out there, I said just looking at the moon, and she sort of squinted at me but I couldn't tell what it meant. She said she was looking for Joshua, had I seen him? I said he was back at the party, and she basically let me lead her there. I thought I was in the clear. Then I heard the hypnotist was coming."

"So the second time it was just cold-blooded murder? You killed Tatiana before she could talk to the hypnotist?"

"No. I went to talk to her the night before she was going to meet with the hypnotist. I wasn't planning on killing her. I just wanted to try to find out what she knew. I liked Tatiana." Her eyes fill with tears. "I never wanted to hurt her or anyone. It probably sounds naïve but I thought if I needed to, I could just explain myself. If I told her why I killed Joshua, she would understand."

"You thought you could just explain away a murder?"

She does a small mirthless laugh. "I know, right? But it really is like a drug, all these people talking about how much they love you and wanting a piece of you. You start to feel, I don't know, omnipotent. Untouchable."

Is she gloating? "Go on."

"I started to think I had this power over people, that they'd always see the good in me. So Tatiana and I were out on her balcony, where there weren't any cameras, and we weren't wearing our microphones. Zarine was sleeping in the room, wearing earplugs but seriously, would I have tried to kill someone with a witness in the room if I'd been thinking straight?"

"I don't know." It's an honest answer. The fact is, I can't know. When The Major said none of us can really walk in anyone else's shoes, he's right. Viewers at home love to say, "I'd never do this," or "I'd never do that," but how can any of us be sure? Have they ever been in a situation even remotely similar to the one Lauren and I have been subjected to for the past weeks? They might argue that we signed up for this, but no one would have signed up for this.

I never meant to flaunt my feelings for Tristan but they were there, for everyone to see. I could have left the island when Joshua asked me to; I could have saved his life then. Or I could have saved it even sooner if I'd done anything about his increasingly outlandish behavior at home. He wanted to get caught.

I didn't murder him, that's true. I can safely say that I've never killed anyone, and that I never would, under any circumstances.

But I can't say it with conviction. Is there anything I wouldn't do to protect those I love, when it comes down to it?

"I told Tatiana I felt bad for what I'd done," Lauren continues, "but that I also felt like Joshua was a genuinely bad guy. I named all the ways but she didn't want to hear them. She was determined to explain away everything he did."

"Because she was in love with him."

"And because she was used to excusing Zarine. I couldn't get through to her. She said that if I didn't turn myself in, she'd go to the detective. Then she sort of half turned away and I didn't think, I just shoved. I couldn't even believe my own strength. She must have been so shocked that she didn't even scream, and she didn't thud very loudly either." Lauren's pupils are darting. It's like she's back there, in the panic and the horror. "I looked over the balcony and I knew she was dead. Her eyes were open, wide open, like she was still surprised. I thought that some camera somewhere must have captured it. I went to the control room and banged on the door and Marla was there. I told her the whole story because it was my only hope, and she deleted the footage. She said she was going to keep me a star."

"But when Detective Mohr accused her, she must have told the truth. She must have tried to save her own skin."

"I guess Detective Mohr didn't believe her. And in a way, she is behind everything. None of this ever would have happened without her."

"That's quite a rationalization." But if Marla's convicted, you can't really say an innocent woman is behind bars. Still, I can't imagine it going that far. You get the justice you can afford, and Marla must be loaded.

"I've had trouble sleeping at night with what I did to Tatiana. But if she'd gone to the police, my daughter would have grown up without me. So really, it came down to Tatiana's life or my baby's. I have to be with my baby, Blanche."

What is she saying? That she'd kill me, too? "Tristan knows where we are."

She looks at me through unfocused eyes. "What?"

So she wasn't threatening me; she was begging me for mercy. One mother to another. "Does Tristan know what you did?"

"No." I expect her to ask me not to tell him but instead she says, "If I have to give him up to keep her, that's what I'll do."

"What does that mean?"

"There's nothing I wouldn't sacrifice for my baby. You've seen how I feel about Tristan. It'll practically kill me to give him up; I want to have a family with him more than almost anything. But let me break up with him. Then I suffer but my baby doesn't have to. She never has to know what I did, and Tristan doesn't either."

She's angling for a plea bargain: She breaks up with Tristan and I don't turn her in. "I'd keep the evidence," I say. "You ever try to get back together with him, and the deal's off."

She nods with eyes full of hope and heartbreak.

"You ever hurt anyone again, and the deal's off."

"Of course."

I can't believe I'm considering, but I am. Because I was wrong about Lauren. She gets what my mother and Joshua never did: that love involves sacrifice. You give to get, and then you give much more. Unlike my own mother and Joshua, Lauren does have the makings of a real parent.

Joshua's dead, but Lauren's child hasn't even been born yet. If we cut a deal, her daughter doesn't have to grow up knowing she has a murderer for a mother, and Tristan won't have to raise a child saddled with that kind of baggage. And looking just a bit further out, I won't have to be a stepmother to a child with that baggage either.

It would be callous to call it win-win, but Lauren did rid me of a philandering deadbeat alcoholic, and I'm going to be two million dollars richer thanks to the insurance policy. Lauren still loses the most, by far, but she doesn't have to lose everything.

For the moment, I don't think justice would be served by sending her to prison. But if it turns out she's lied to me or she steps out of line in any way, I can still take the video to the police. At that point, Tristan would take full custody of their child. But for now, it's kinder to keep this to myself and not burden him.

Lauren should have the chance to be a mother. With one more condition.

SIXTY-SIX

LAUREN

Day Nineteen

I'm in our room, packing. Tristan's suitcases are already lined up by the door. He can't wait to walk out of here, alone. Or maybe he's not alone at all. He could be with Blanche right now. I suppose I can't blame him. He is single.

It sure doesn't feel like it right now, but I keep telling myself it could be for the best. Maybe now my ledger has been settled. I can work on becoming a great mom with no distractions.

I guess I should be grateful that Blanche accepted my deal. She added a term: I had to publicly end my feud with her. Tell the world I'd been wrong about her all along. I'm not the angel they've made me out to be and she's not the devil. We're just two women who came together under unfortunate circumstances, and I'd appreciate if my followers stopped attacking someone who's lost her husband in such a traumatic fashion.

I haven't posted yet about my breakup with Tristan, which was agony.

The worst part was how relieved he'd looked. I don't know if he's been staying in this relationship because of his conscience or the baby or for money or because I know his secrets or because he didn't want to look like the bad guy on TV or because he literally couldn't get away from me on this island. But I do know that when I opened that cage door, he was eager to fly away.

I thought of my mom and that saying of hers about how if you set someone free and they don't come back, they were never really yours to begin with. But I think in this case, Tristan used to be mine, no cages involved, and then I destroyed everything. And I kept right on destroying: Joshua, his kids, Tatiana. Maybe now I can finally stop. Blanche stopped me without putting me in my own cage. She's given me a chance to redeem myself. So I guess you really never do know what someone else is capable of, for good or evil.

Still, I was cursing her in my head when I had to tell Tristan that we needed to end things. I said that I didn't see how we could get past so much, that we probably couldn't ever really trust each other again, and our daughter deserves to see healthy relationships, even if those wind up being with other people instead of each other. I kept hoping he'd try to convince me otherwise, that maybe together we could find some loophole to defeat Blanche, but no, his face told me he was glad for the way out. He said he knew I'd land on my feet with Rick Gloucester's endorsement deals. "With your fan base," he said, "you don't need me to make a killing."

To his credit, he didn't fly away immediately. He and I lay in bed together all night, neither of us sleeping. He held me and we cried together. He said we can be good co-parents. I'd never heard the word before and wondered if Blanche had taught it to him. He said it means we'll model for our daughter how to work together without being romantic partners, how to be loving without being in love. The more he talked, the more I realized all that I've lost.

Even if we're not together, he can still inspire me. He was

violent when he was younger and then he stopped (with Joshua and me as the notable exceptions). If Tristan can change, then I can, too, right?

My thoughts were a jumble all night, and sometimes I was hating Blanche for this straitjacket she'd put me in and sometimes I was thinking I needed it. I recalled what Julie said about the storyboards and how Blanche and I were always meant to hate each other, that Marla had designed it that way. Then I remembered this moment Blanche and I had our second day on the island that never made it into the episode.

I'd been about to go lie out by the pool, and Blanche said that standing water made her nervous for me, what with the pregnancy and Zika, was Zika in this part of the world? Just in case, she insisted on covering me with bug spray. She seemed like a big sister, looking out for me, the two of us giggling as she let loose with this aerosol cloud, and then ten minutes later, when I was in my lounge chair, she raced up to me. "I just double-checked—well, I had my producer double-check since I don't have my phone—and DEET is safe for pregnant women." I thanked her, thinking it was the start of a friendship, but we'd become rivals instead.

I'd edited that scene out of my mind, same as Marla edited out all Blanche's better qualities. Blanche being a decent person didn't fit Marla's storyline, or mine.

Who's the real Blanche? And who's the real Lauren?

In some ways, I have no idea. What I've done on this island —I want to think that's not me. That I've been distorted by the pressure cooker Marla put me in; pregnancy hormones; my need to prove my love to Tristan; the overwhelming desire to protect my family. But I can't edit out what I've done. I'm going to have to spend my life making sure certain parts of me stay contained.

There's a knock at the door, and I hope it's Tristan. I might have to spend the rest of my life wishing he's the knock on the door. But if that's my whole punishment, most people would say I'm getting off easy.

It's Julie. "Almost packed?" she asks.

"Almost." I try to smile and be brave but instead, my tears start flowing again. She wraps me in a hug. I can always be vulnerable with Julie, she's proven that. She'll never, ever judge.

I couldn't have survived this experience if it weren't for her. Her emotional support has been unparalleled. Just having someone know the whole truth and still care for me—well, she might be the best friend I've ever had. Then there's what she brings to the table in terms of the strategic and the tactical. I could never have gotten this far without an insider. We make quite a team.

That's why I told just that one lie last night, saying Marla had been my accomplice instead of Julie.

Julie figured out pretty quickly that I was the one who killed Joshua. It was just an instinct she had and when she confronted me, my guilt must have been written all over my face. But she immediately reassured me. She said, "It's okay, I'm sure you had a good reason," and so I told her what it was. She understood completely, which felt a lot like absolution. I'm not saying it was okay, I did take a human life, but come on. It *was* Joshua.

Julie had already started protecting me, laying the ground-work with Detective Mohr. Like The Major, she saw Marla as an evil mastermind who needed to go down, and in the interro-gation room, Julie was painting a pretty damning picture. "All of it true," she said. She felt that Marla had committed so many crimes against humanity that justice would be served just by taking her out of circulation. "She doesn't deserve to have power over people's lives," was Julie's justification, and the more she told me about what had been happening behind the scenes, the more I believed her.

Then after what happened with Tatiana, I had a little trepidation about calling Julie. I mean, we're talking about two murders. Joshua was a total dick but Tatiana was a different story. Could anyone be that forgiving?

It turned out Julie could. After I called her, she not only cleaned me up and absolved me again (it was practically an accident, just a self-defense impulse gone wrong) but she cleaned up the whole mess. She deleted the footage from the control room while wearing gloves, knowing that Marla's fingerprints would be all over the control room from earlier that night.

To be clear, I never asked Julie to do that, or to cover for me with Detective Mohr. She volunteered. She's that kind of a friend. And like The Major, she has a strong sense of right and wrong. Also like The Major, she believes none of this would have happened if Marla hadn't pushed us all to the brink, and Julie wasn't about to let an innocent baby suffer. How would that help anyone?

Julie believes that in a world gone mad, what's right can be wrong and vice versa. There can be no absolute morality. Everything is relative.

"You're a cat," Julie tells me now, "you'll land on your feet."

She's the only person I've told about the breakup, though I didn't say how it came about; she doesn't know about Blanche and the video. No one can. That was Blanche's final term.

"You don't have to pretend," Julie says. "You're allowed to just be sad today. It's not like you're on camera."

"Thank God for that."

"And I've got something for you to look forward to. I have news. Really good news." She's in the opposite situation as me: trying to hold back her smile. "I've been in touch with the network, pitching my own show, and they gave it the green light!"

"That's awesome! What's it about?"

"You." She's still smiling. "It'll document your life after the island. I originally thought it would be about you and Tristan getting ready for the baby's arrival but now with the breakup, it'll go in a different direction. And get this, I was just back on the phone with the execs and they're even more excited. They love the idea of you navigating the world of single motherhood with your trademark grit and vulnerability. Tristan isn't nearly as popular as you are. The way he's gone back and forth between you and Blanche has made him look pretty weak, not like a leading man at all."

I stare, waiting for her to pick up on my horrified reaction. Waiting for her to realize that this absolutely cannot happen.

But she's too caught up in her pitch. "The show will be your journey to motherhood and beyond. The cameras will follow you as you work through everything with Sam as your individual therapist."

"As I work through... everything?" Is she even hearing herself?

"Not *everything* everything. There will be exercises for you to do and other expectant single mothers for you to meet. They can become your support network, or maybe you'll be their role models. I haven't figured all that out yet, a lot will depend on the casting and on the chemistry. Tristan can make cameos. What I'm sure of is the tone. It's going to be uplifting. We're going to inspire people."

"Did you already tell the network that I was in?"

"Yes, I told them that we're in. I'm going to be on the show with you as your best friend as well as your producer. It's going to be great."

"Have you lost your mind?" I exclaim. "I can't do this!"

"Yes, you will."

Then I get it.

Julie's come to my rescue not because of our friendship, or because it's in line with her ethics (she clearly doesn't have any). And it's not because she thinks I have value to the world the way she's been telling me. She's been building me up, building my brand, for the value I can have for her.

Is she the one who gave Blanche that video of Tatiana and me? Did she really delete the footage from that night or has she saved a copy for herself? It's possible she knows everything. That she's behind everything.

Well, not *everything* everything. I'm the one who killed people.

If she could set Marla up and lie repeatedly to the police, what won't she do to me and to my baby?

It dawns on me that it's not only about what you're capable of doing; it's what you're capable of rationalizing. Julie can commit heinous acts and still think she's one of the good guys.

"This isn't just for me," she says. "It's for both of us. I've always felt like we're sort of kindred spirits. We know our softness can be our strength, and we're not afraid to seize an opportunity when it presents itself. I've learned from the best!"

Does she mean Marla, or is she talking about me?

"We should both benefit from all we've been through on the island," she says. "All we've risked."

I can't say no, which she well knows. I'm at her mercy, unless I can turn the tables somehow.

I rub my belly. It's like I told Blanche. There's nothing I wouldn't do for my baby.

SIXTY-SEVEN

THE MAJOR

I know Lauren and I will be on the same plane out soon enough but I'd still like a private moment to say goodbye. To say thank you. To tell her I'm proud of her for how she's changed her tune on social media, first defending Naomi and now burying the hatchet with Blanche.

I don't know if Lauren and I will see each other in L.A., if this is a relationship that can thrive back in our real lives, but I owe her a debt of gratitude. It's not just about the social media; it's also the way she was always rooting for Naomi and me. She tried to get me to see through Naomi's betrayal to the hurt underneath, and the love. Lauren preached forgiveness, and she was right. She's going to set a good example for her daughter someday. Lauren's a hero in my book.

As I'm approaching her room, I see Julie coming out.

"I've been meaning to talk to you!" I say, with a broad smile. "We've never officially been introduced. I've just been seeing you around these past nineteen days."

"Major!" She dimples at me. "I heard about you and Naomi reconciling. I know Lauren was hoping you'd work it out."

"You and Lauren have become pretty close, huh?"

"The closest."

"I'm on my gratitude tour, just about to thank Lauren, but my understanding is that I should thank you, too."

She cocks her head slightly, an almost suspicious look passing over her face.

"Sam and I had a conversation. She thought you might be working from the inside to bring Marla down, and I just want to shake your hand."

She laughs and we clasp hands. Hers is so cold I get a jolt. And it's not just her hands, I realize. It's something in her eyes. But I'm not going to tell this to Naomi, she'd probably think I'm being paranoid again and start worrying.

"Never let evil triumph," I say, but there's a wobble in my voice.

"Never." She grins at me again and saunters off.

SIXTY-EIGHT

BLANCHE

As I'm packing, I stuff the book from Detective Mohr inside my suitcase. Then I move it to my carry-on. I have nothing to be ashamed of.

Detective Mohr was kind enough to stop by before she left. She wanted me to have a copy of my father's autopsy report along with a book that she said had helped her a lot over the years, personally and professionally. I smiled when I saw the title: *Your Brain is Fucking with You*. It's a user manual for the traumatized mind.

Apparently the brain has all these different ways of taking care of itself after abuse or injury, like blocking out pieces of information or remembering just part of a story or having memories that contain both fact and fiction or becoming involved with dangerous people in the present who are reminiscent of figures from the past. You might need to seem perfect or judge others harshly or numb out. You could become a control freak. It's a long list, and a long book. I'm only halfway through. As well as I thought I knew myself, it seems I have a lot to learn.

A part of me always sensed that I needed to protect myself from Joshua. That's probably why I kept him at arm's length.

But with Tristan, I can let down my guard fully. He came to me this morning and said that he and Lauren had broken up, and that he sees a future with me. But we need to start with a clean slate so he told me everything: that Julie gave him his phone back at the wrap party and it had Joshua's psychological profile on it, how he confronted Joshua because he wanted to make sure my kids and I would be safe, and it had gotten out of hand. Tristan had been looking after me and my kids in a way that no one ever has before, and I'm going to look after him right back. I know some people might think this is too soon given that he's fresh out of another relationship. Sure, he's told a few lies and been violent on rare occasions but only with good reason. Besides, I'm so different from Lauren. I'm entirely trustworthy, and I certainly don't need a protector.

I wish I could fully reassure him that he's not the killer because I can tell his conscience is still bothering him. He thinks Joshua might never have woken up from that one punch, and I laughed at that. He's not the Hulk! If only I could tell him it was doe-eyed Lauren after all.

But Lauren and I made a deal, and regardless of what everyone thinks at home, I'm honorable. Also, it might do more harm than good for Tristan to know the truth about Lauren. She is the mother of his child. The mother of one of his children. I can't wait for him to meet Lily and Kyle.

We haven't even kissed (who knows if the cameras are really turned off, once and for all?) yet Tristan and I know what we've found in each other. How rare it is. He's nothing like Joshua. Tristan would never make me wait months to hear those three perfect words.

He whispered them, just in case the walls have ears. I know he wants to spend the rest of his life with me but he's got his baby on the way and I've got my kids to think of. There are decisions to make, like the smartest way to handle the millions from the insurance policy. Tristan's got ideas and I'll take his opinion into consideration but I'll never let a man control me. I've always been an independent thinker.

And I've never been a hopeless romantic, never believed in fate or kismet or serendipity. I don't even like romantic comedies. But Tristan and I were meant to be. That I know.

Every love story is also an origin story. It's about who we've been and who we're becoming. I do have the tiniest bit of worry that keeping Lauren's secret from Tristan will change our story, that it'll shape what comes after in ways we can't begin to predict. Our love began on Glass Island, so could that mean it's built on sand?

No, it's the opposite. Since we've survived Glass Island, we can survive anything.

Tristan and me, together, with no cameras. Now that'll be paradise.

A LETTER FROM ELLIE

Dear reader,

I want to say a huge thank you for choosing to read *The Marriage Test*. If you did enjoy it, and want to keep up to date with all my latest releases, just sign up at the following link. Your email address will never be shared and you can unsubscribe at any time.

www.bookouture.com/ellie-monago

I hope you loved *The Marriage Test* and if you did, I would be very grateful if you could write a review. I'd love to hear what you think, and it makes such a difference helping new readers to discover one of my books for the first time.

Thanks,

Ellie Monago

ACKNOWLEDGMENTS

In publishing, as in life, sometimes a reboot is required. You need a change in perspective and approach, and if you're lucky, you retain the most devoted members of your old team while simultaneously adding strong new members. With this particular book, I've been exceedingly lucky.

I'm so grateful for everyone at Bookouture. At the helm is Harriet Wade, my editor, and she's truly all a writer could ask for: supportive, enthusiastic, astute, a top-notch collaborator, a great communicator, a lovely person. Not to mention, she's my efficiency twin. I've been in traditional publishing before and can really feel the difference with the Bookouture model. I have every confidence they're going to get me where I want to be, and that I'll have fun doing it. I already am.

A million thanks go to the incomparable Sophie Hannah for pointing me in this direction.

And to my abiding team (which includes Jenny, Tara, Avie, Lisa, my parents, and my husband, Darrend): You've never lost belief or faith, never questioned whether I'm meant for this work, and always shared in my excitement for the next project. Because of all of you, there's always a next project. I couldn't appreciate you more.

Made in United States
Orlando, FL
24 September 2024

51836722R00214